Perseverance:

A Zombie Tale

James Lacey

ISBN
0-9846458-0-2 (10 digit)
978-0-9846458-0-0 (13 digit)

Library of Congress Control Number: 2012949980

First Edition

Printed in the United States of America
Published by 23 House Publishing
SAN 299-8084
www.23house.com

Table of Contents

It is close at hand...

Blow ye the trumpet in Zion, and sound an alarm in my holy
mountain:
let all the inhabitants of the land tremble:
for the day of the LORD cometh, for it is nigh at hand;
A day of darkness and of gloominess, a day of clouds and of
thick darkness,
as the morning spread upon the mountains:
a great people and a strong; there hath not been ever the like,
neither shall be any more after it, even to the years of many
generations.
A fire devoureth before them;
and behind them a flame burneth:
the land is as the garden of Eden before them,
and behind them a desolate wilderness;
yea, and nothing shall escape them.

Joel 2:1-3

Part I: Prologue

When it happened I was excited – at first. I was a fan of the movies, the books, the games…all of it. So when those first reports came on the television and hit the net I was probably the most excited person on the planet. I mean, you always wonder "what if" when you see it in films, but then to have it actually happen, it really gets you going. That is, until they're banging on your front door. Or the door of someone you really, truly care about. Someone you love.

That is when the excitement fades to fear. The fear can turn to horror. But right before that there is a brief moment where human instinct takes over and you choose to either fight or run. You don't think, you just act. That is how I'm still alive. And it is probably why she is dead.

My story is not a happy one. It is not about heroics or unity or the fight to persevere. It is the story of survival. The only thing a person could really do during the crisis. It is the story of trying to protect someone you love and failing. It is a story of love, friendship and ultimately death. I'm not holding back. I am going to tell you everything. For some, this story will be harder to read then it was to write. For others, it won't. Either way, this is my story. This is my account of the zombie apocalypse.

1

Chapter One

I am a teacher. At least, I was before it all happened, before I was forced to survive. I taught social studies at the high school. I was also the coach of the school's successful debate team. It was a cold Saturday in January when I heard the first rumor of trouble at a tournament judge's lounge between a few people.

"I heard there's something big going on in South America," one man said.

"I hadn't heard anything."

"Came up on my BlackBerry. I guess some drug lord poisoned a water supply. Entire village died. Government has the place quarantined."

"Wow. What country?"

"Columbia, I think. I'm sure it'll be all over the news later."

"That's sad. Drugs…hmmm…I suppose I'm not that surprised. You remember when they took all those hostages a few months back…"

I suppose that was how everyone processed those first reports. Casual, nonchalant, just more bad news in already troubling times. I didn't even care to look at the report myself.

My team was performing well. We were two wins away from being a contender in the finals. I was focused on the tournament and did not have time for breaking news. My concern was the tournament topic: the reconstruction of Iran. Not a psycho drug lord in Columbia. And then when my team made it to finals, I completely forgot about the village of dead Columbians.

The bus ride back to the school was exciting at first. We came from behind and won the competition. The team was elated and the air was thick with celebration.

It was a long day and we stopped to eat at a rest area off the turnpike. Everyone in the rest area was huddled around a television mounted on a wall. Others were gathered around people with laptops. It was then that I heard the words "terrorist attack" and my elated feelings became subdued. As some of the team moved toward the televisions, I decided to get out my own laptop and see for myself what all the commotion was about.

"What's going on, Coach?" one of my team captains, Keith, asked.

"I'm not sure yet, but we'll find out in a moment."

"TV said something about a worldwide terror event."

"Fancy words they use when they're not too sure themselves." I didn't want anyone getting ahead of themselves. After 9/11, the economy panic of the early century and the Iranian war you learned to be patient with the news. They never had all the facts right away.

I was trying to be reassuring and bring my students back to the mood they were in before we stopped to eat, which not many were doing. But I knew there was something big going on.

I could hear the words "bioterrorism," "widespread" and "thousands dead." I could hear people talking about countries all over the world. CNN had this gorgeous new anchor,

4

Rebecca Mailey and I had a sort of boyhood crush on her. I was 29 and still entitled to fantasize about celebrities. So when she was the one who sent a chill down my spine, I thought it was sort of ironic and could not help but laugh. I'll never forget the colorless look on her face when she uttered, "We are now getting scattered reports of incidents here in the United States."

I never finished booting up my laptop. My instincts told me to get everyone out of the rest area and back on the bus. It was a quiet on the way home. I told everyone to call their parents and let them know that they were okay and would be home soon. As we boarded the bus two police cruisers went speeding in the opposite direction, sirens blaring. It was unnerving, given what we just heard. The rest of the ride home was dead quiet.

* * * * *

When we returned to the school every parent was waiting, save for one. They ushered their students into vehicles and left without much conversation. It was clear that everyone was scared. I became desperate for more information. I was waiting with Keith inside the empty school building.

"You okay?" I asked him.

"I don't know. I guess I don't know enough about what's going on."

"Most people are that way right now, I figure. I am." I decided to change the subject, "You did well today. I checked the results on the way back. Gross improvement over last week. I think you could finish top-three in your event at the next tournament in two weeks."

"I didn't like this block the one kid ran against me. I'll need help figuring out how to beat his logic pattern."

"We'll work on it this week."

"Coach?"

"Yes?"

"I can't shake this feeling that we won't be competing again."

"Try not to think like that. It could just be the media blowing something way out of proportion. Right now, you're a champion. Enjoy what's left of the night and worry about the world tomorrow."

"Thanks, Coach."

We waited the rest of the time in silence. After twenty minutes, I called his parents. There was no answer at home. I had him try to reach his father's cell phone, even though he was out of town. He got through on the second try.

"Hey, Dad...No, I'm fine...Mom isn't home and I'm still at the school...No, I tried her cell too, no answer...uh-huh...one second. Coach, he'd like to talk to you."

I took the phone from Keith, "Good evening, sir."

"Hi. My son said he can't get through to his mother."

"Yeah, apparently not."

"Any chance he can stay with you until I can get through to her? I don't want to hold you up at the school any longer."

"Of course. If it's late, then she can come by and get him in the morning."

"I really appreciate that. Thank you. I'll call Keith when I get a hold of his mother."

I had known Keith's family for over ten years. I coached his older brother six years earlier when I was just a volunteer and a teacher's aide working toward a degree. Keith's older brother had watched me transform from a goofy college kid to a "responsible adult." His family trusted me. Coaching the debate team was also how I met her.

She was a graduate student now. I met her my first year as the coach for the high school, when she was just starting out as a judge, but I had remembered her from a few years earlier, when she was the former state champion in her division. We got to know each other through debate and eventually started dating. I fell in love, almost instantly. I loved her. I still love her.

I have to laugh now. She was a bit younger than I was. My friends used to pick on me a bit. Isn't it funny how age was one of those things we used to care about as a society before the outbreak? Now, like our great-grandfathers and grandfathers who fought their own wars, age is just a number, or a testimony to how long you've been able to survive.

She was at her mother's house when it all began. She had come home to judge at the tournament, but became ill and had to stay back. I called her once Keith and I got in the car.

"Hello?" she answered on the second ring.

"Hi, Ashley. I hope I didn't wake you. How are you?"

"I'm okay. Watching the news. This is crazy."

"I didn't get a chance to see anything yet."

"Oh, well it's pretty incredible. Are you just getting back?"

"Yep. We won. I'm taking Keith back to my place until he can get a hold of his mother."

"Tell him I said hello. Can you come over later?"

"If it's not too late. If not tonight, then I'll be over first thing in the morning. Are you sure you're okay?"

"I'm alright. Just nervous, I guess. There's a lot going on."

"I'll catch up after a shower. Call you later?"

"Okay. Be safe. Love you."

"Love you, too."

When I got back to my apartment Keith went straight for the sofa and turned on the television. I showed him the refrigerator and invited him to help himself to anything but the beer. Then I gave him my computer and went for a shower. I remember taking a long time in the shower. Part of me just wasn't ready to see another attack in progress.

When the Towers came down I was young, and I had been glued to the television from the moment that the first plane struck. I remember watching the live feed as the second plane hit. And then the Hoover Dam collapse in 2014. I just wasn't ready to see another disaster in progress. It was just too soon, even after the Iranian War. After I got out of the shower I put on some sweat pants, grabbed a much needed beer and joined Keith in the living room.

"It's happening everywhere."

"What is?"

"This...thing. People are dying. Riots happening everywhere. They said that there are drugs in the water supply that makes you want to hurt others. Then they said it wasn't drugs, but a massive psychological event caused by a solar flare or something. Another guy said it's been happening for a few weeks, but until now the government had it bottled up. And then..."

"Keith." I had to stop him. The talking heads on TV had him all turned around.

"Yeah?"

"Take a breath. Clearly they don't really know what is happening. So the question remains. Now, what do you know for sure? What do they know for certain? Think simple, Keith."

"I don't know. People are killing each other, I guess. They haven't really said why or how, just that it's happening."

That part bothered me. If it were a terrorist event, then someone would be taking credit by now. If it were a disaster, then they would know the cause. Not knowing information...that is when I became hooked. That is when it became...interesting.

"Hand me my computer." Keith passed it to me and I logged into CNN's website. A flurry of breaking news banners greeted me. I clicked through and found Keith was right; no one was reporting on what was really going on. Talking heads never know. I decided to try a local news stations website. Local sites were always able to present information in a more

8

sensible manner. They were not burdened by "experts" whose opinions were "necessary."

As soon as the page loaded I found what I was looking for...a list of affected areas. I clicked on the page and was immediately drawn to the list of Pennsylvania towns affected. That definitely hit home. There were five towns listed: Philadelphia, Pittsburgh...big cities, no surprises there... Meckinsburg...only three miles from the rest stop we stopped at before. Possibly where the police cruisers we saw on the way home were heading. The other two towns I wasn't familiar with. Whatever was going on was big.

There wasn't anything else I could do at the moment. After unsuccessfully getting through to Keith's parents again I decided to turn in. I called Ashley again, but it went right to voicemail. She probably wasn't feeling well and turned her phone off. I crashed as soon as my head hit the pillow.

* * * * *

When I woke up the next morning I felt refreshed. I had slept really well and had almost forgotten that there was an emergency going on. I rolled out of bed, took a shower and made my way to the kitchen for a bowl of cereal. There was a note on the refrigerator from Keith:

Coach, Mom picked me up shortly after you went to bed. Thanks for everything. See you on Monday?

Hmm...silly question. Of course I'd be there Monday. Was he planning on not going? Ah, well...kids are kids.

I looked up at the clock on the microwave. It was almost 10 AM. I really slept in late. I went and checked my cell phone. Seven missed calls? I realized then that I still had the phone on silent from the tournament. One call from Keith's mom. Two from my parents? That was odd. Four from Ashley. Damn...I had promised to go over early this morning. She's probably pissed right now. I went back into the bedroom and turned the TV on as I checked my voicemail.

"Hi, it's Keith's Mom. Sorry I'm home so late. Thanks for watching him."

All over the country people are fighting against...

"It's mom. Calling to see if you're okay. Call me back."

Military response is beginning to organize...

"I need you! Now! Please hurry! Call me back!"

We have confirmed video reports of...

"Why aren't you answering?! Oh good...I hope...call me back..."

Rising from the dead and attacking...

"They're outside! Help me! I need you! I need to hear your voice!"

All over the world people are coming back from the dead and killing others.

"I love you...Mom! Look out!" There's a crash of glass on the phone.

Stay indoors. Lock your doors. Board up your windows. Do not go outside.

No words on the last message...just another crash and the sound of a scream.

I was paralyzed.

The phone fell from my hand.

I stared silently at the television, hardly breathing. For a few minutes I couldn't process anything. Then I started hearing words and making out images on the television. *This was impossible.* The undead were not really rising and attacking people all over the world. All the movies I used to make fun of, all the books I used to read when I was on vacation, all the games I used to play...it was all just stories. None of that nonsense could really happen.

But the images on the screen were tough to deny. Videos were shown of people being shot and barely stumbling. People were viciously attacking each other without any clear reason, like a soccer riot multiplied tenfold. They were walking upright with serious injuries. The video of a car crash victim standing up and attacking a paramedic was quite profound. I couldn't shake the part of me that began thinking this was the coolest thing to ever happen. The other part...

The other part of me remembered Ashley's message. The sound of a crash and then someone, either her or her mom, screaming. I reached down to the floor and grabbed the phone. I hit her number on the speed dial and held my breath. One ring...two rings...three rings...busy tone? That shouldn't happen. I hung up and tried again. Right to voicemail now. I left a message telling her I was okay and to call me.

Whatever was happening she was clearly in trouble. I didn't care if it were terrorists, zombies or evil clowns from outer space. I had to get to her. I put on a pair of jeans and my hiking boots. I threw on some deodorant and then put on a white t-shirt. Funny how I still cared how I smelt that morning, at the time all of my old habits were still intact. I went to check my phone again. Shit! Three more missed calls! The damn thing was still on silent. It was her. That meant she was okay. I tried calling back. One ring...two rings...Ashley picked up, her voice a whisper.

"Hello?"

"Yeah, I'm here. Sorry. The phone was on silent. What's going on, are you okay?" I asked urgently.

"I'm safe. They heard the phone ring. Chased me into the basement. I blocked the door, but they're trying to get in."

"Who is trying to get in?"

"These things...whatever they are...they killed mom. Oh god, they killed mom!"

"Relax, relax. You're safe. Stay hidden, stay quiet. Is there anything you can use as a weapon? Did you call the cops?"

"Damn it! Everyone is calling the cops! Haven't you been watching?! They're everywhere!"

Actually, I hadn't really processed yet that they were just outside. My mind thought they were only in those towns I read last night. *Out of sight, out of mind.*

"Alright, sorry. What about a weapon?"

"There's a few pool sticks here from the table, that's it."

"Can you get out?"

"No and you know that! I'm damn well trapped down here."

"I'll get you out."

"Don't be stupid. You're dead if you go outside!"

"I'm dead if they get to you before I do."

"But if something happens to me..." she started.

"Then I'll kill them all," I finished. "It's not a discussion. I'm coming for you. Stay quiet, calm down."

"The highways are clogged and you'll never make it on foot."

"I've lived here my whole life. I don't need highways. I know every back road in the area. Might take awhile, but I will find you," I promised.

"Please..."

"Stop fighting me. I love you. I'll call you when I'm close."

"I love you, too." She hung up on the other end, still not wanting me to risk my life for her. I had no choice. Call it heroism. Call it stupid. Call it whatever you want. I didn't care. I was just trying to save someone I loved. Like so many others those first weeks. The only difference between those who died and me was luck.

I almost ran right out the door. I stopped when I reached my window and froze when I looked outside. There was a car crashed into my neighbor's front door – his own car. What the hell happened? I opened my door and stepped out onto the balcony.

I lived on the third floor of a house converted into several apartments. Across the way lived Mr. Felder. And it was his own car wrecked into his house. I went down the steps and walked across the street. The door to the car was open and a trail of blood led into the street.

I followed the trail back the way I had come. It led behind my own building. I walked back, slowly, to find the door to the first floor apartment open. A young couple lived in the apartment. They had moved in a little over a month ago. I hadn't really gotten to know them yet. I knocked on the door and waited. No answer. I rang the doorbell. Still nothing.

I don't know why I opened the door. Despite the news report and as much as I wanted to get to her, I just could not stop myself from going into the apartment. There was a smell on the air as soon as I opened the door. Someone had made breakfast. It smelt really good. But there was something else too, a smell I wasn't familiar with.

I walked into the entryway and stopped to call out hello. There was no response, but I could hear movement and a wet squishing sound coming from the back of the apartment. I moved into the next room, a living room and stopped. The body of a young girl lay bleeding on a broken coffee table, blood running from side of her head and down her arm. I bent down to check her pulse. Nothing. She was gone.

I dialed 911 from my cell and was met by a recorded message. All the lines were busy; please hold for the next emergency responder? 911 was the most advanced and largest staffed phone system in the world. This shouldn't be happening.

She told me earlier that the police weren't helping. And there was no one else around that I could see when I made my way to the apartment. Maybe they had all left town, or at least tried too. Or they were just hiding, too afraid to come outside. I decided to walk farther into the apartment toward the strange sound. It was coming from a kitchen. I stopped in the doorway; behind the kitchen table were two people, one hunched over the other's torso. I could make out the twisted face of the young man – Ted, I think his name was. Blood was everywhere. I inched closer and recognized that it was Mr. Felder who was hunched over his stomach.

"Mr. Felder? What's going on?"

I couldn't believe what I saw. Mr. Felder was eating Ted! Ted's chest was ripped open. The insides were a scrambled mess. Blood was everywhere. Bits of tissue were hanging off shattered bone. I couldn't help but freeze in horror. When I did finally react, I wished that I hadn't.

I don't know what it sounded like, the scream that escaped my lungs. I doubt it was fierce. I imagine it a sort of whimper, followed by a blood-curling sound of terror. Either way, it made the...thing...that was Mr. Felder take notice that I was in the room. The head turned to look at me, bits of mangled flesh hanging from its teeth. It got up slowly, staring at me.

The pupils of the eye were black as coal, blacker than they should have been. The iris, which used to be brown, a smoky gray color. Unnatural and disturbing. It let out a sound that was between a moan and a snarl. I had never heard anything like it before. That hideous sound shook me to my core.

Mr. Felder shuffled towards me, slowly and with a look of hunger in his eyes. But it didn't matter how slow he moved because I found myself completely unable to move.

Human beings, like the rest of the animal kingdom, are ingrained with a basic survival instinct of fight or flight. This base reaction is what guides almost everything that we do. But what happens when that instinct doesn't work? What happens when you become so terrified that your brain will not function? The animals on Discovery Channel that you see run from a lion. They are using flight. The criminals in prison who acted on instinct and shot someone. They use fight. The ones who did not react…animal and human…they are all dead.

The thing that was once Mr. Felder moved toward me faster now, arms outstretched. The sound coming from its lips. It grabbed my arms and snarled. Its head moved in toward my neck. I could smell its fetid breath, feel the air from its lungs. It was different than when a normal human breathes…this air was not warm. It was just air.

I tried to shove it back. The instinct had finally kicked in. I pushed its head back but it would not relinquish my arms. Its grip was like iron. I tried to twist away and broke free of one arm. It snarled and tried to recover, but slipped on the linoleum floor. The blood on its shoes ended up essentially saving my life. We both tumbled to the ground, but on the way it smashed its head into the counter top. It was still moving, but its grip was loosened enough for me to roll away. I stood up quickly and turned to run out the kitchen.

Right in front of me was the young girl. I couldn't believe what I was seeing. *She was dead! I know she was! I knew how to check a pulse!* And yet here she was in front of me. Its eyes were the same smoke and coal color. It snarled and lashed out, but this time I reacted quick enough to get away. As I backed toward the other side of the kitchen I felt something grab my leg. Mr. Felder's arm was grabbing my jeans trying to get a grip on my legs. I kicked out at its body, but it just tightened its grip. The girl was moving in to help. I looked around. There was a knife set on the counter. I grabbed the nearest handle and pulled out a long-bladed steak knife.

I slashed down at my attacker on the floor. I was hacking away at the arm as I tried to keep the woman at bay. The arm wouldn't let go no matter how hard I struck. I kicked away the snapping jaws and turned back to the woman. I tried to slash at her throat, but her arm grabbed my wrist. I thought she was trying to get the knife out of my hand, so I tried to pull away. When she instead tried to bite me I just shoved the knife into her mouth. The blade went in at an upward angle, penetrating the roof of her mouth and continuing upward until the handle was in her mouth. She stopped moving and fell backwards, pulling me forward with her until her grasp on my arm was released. I regained my composure long enough to kick away at the other one's head again.

Turning back to the counter I grabbed another handle, this time pulling a butcher knife out. I whipped my arm down with the intent of severing the hand. But, despite what you might see in a movie, it doesn't work like that. The blade tends to get lodged in the bone if it is not sharp enough. When the blade hit the bone of my attacker my hand slipped from the handle and slammed into the cabinet. But I was able to I cut enough muscle and its grip loosened enough for me to get away. I ran out of the apartment and back up to my own.

I closed and locked the door, then went into the bedroom. Sitting on the edge of the bed I put my hands into my face and let out a scream.

"Ahhhhhhhhh!" I screamed into the empty apartment.

What do I do now? How is this happening?

How can I save her?

Chapter Two

I took a deep breath.

I had to get to Ashley. But I also had to keep myself alive. I would be no use to her dead. I had to act quickly, but smart. I went into my closet and pulled out the warmest, but least bulky clothes I had. I donned a vest with several pockets, my leather jacket, a pair of leather driving gloves I received for Christmas a few weeks ago and my favorite Irish wool cap. I also pulled my old gym duffel bag out and threw in my winter jacket, a sweatshirt and a few extra pairs of socks. Out of habit I grabbed my shaving kit. I had to stop and laugh a moment. Here I was packing like it was a weekend getaway. No, what I needed were supplies and some kind of weapon.

Supplies I could scrounge up. I had a case of water and plenty of dry food in the kitchen. Living alone and not being home much meant I didn't spend much money on food that would spoil. A weapon would be a bit of a problem. I didn't own a gun. And I was probably a lousy shot anyway. The last time I shot anything was in high school at the rifle range I used to live near. There was a replica sword in my bedroom, but the damn thing was so flimsy it would never actually hold up in a fight.

I went into the hall closet and looked around. There was an aluminum baseball bat propped in the corner. Better than nothing. I took what I had so far and loaded the stuff in my car. I dropped the backseat of my coupe to make room, and then went back up for more stuff.

I grabbed my work briefcase and dumped the contents on the kitchen table. Definitely would not need my grade book or the biography of Friedrich Nietzsche for awhile. Seeing the items on the table made me thing of Keith. I hoped he made it somewhere safe and wasn't dead...or worse. I hoped all of my students were safe. They were a great bunch of kids and I hated the thought of them out there in this madness.

I went around the apartment grabbing anything that might be useful. Flashlights, batteries, a few knives, anything I thought I could use. Lastly, I opened the door by the closet where I kept some tools. I grabbed a hammer, a few screwdrivers, a roll of duct tape and another flashlight. I also had a spaded shovel that I bought to dig out a tree stump last year. I took it and locked up my apartment before I left.

Before I got into my car I looked around with fleeting hope that I would be back soon, the same hope that made me lock my apartment door. Then I looked at the blood trail on the ground and knew this place would never be the same, even if I did make it back.

* * * * *

Getting out of my neighborhood was relatively easy. It was a quiet town and had a very low population. There were a few signs of trouble, but nothing in the way. When I got to the end of the road I turned right. Normally, I would go left to the highway, but if the news reports were correct, then I would never reach her unless I took the back roads. Living in the same town all my life had given me the advantage of not needing the highway. On a good day, the route I was planning would take forty minutes or better. I had the distinct feeling that it would take much longer today.

The road out of town was quiet. I passed two other cars before I turned off of the main road. Both were traveling too fast for their own good. Stupid. Getting into a wreck would be an idiotic way to die at a time like this. When I turned onto the next road I stopped a moment to think.

Along this road, toward the end, was a military installation. It employed civilians to repair and build electronic components for military use. It was secure, but certainly not fortified. The base had only a handful of regular soldiers at a given time. Nonetheless, I could not help but wonder if people had fled there as a safe haven. If they did, then when I reached the end of the road I would be either stuck, surrounded or ushered in myself. It was not a risk that I was willing to take.

There was another option. Parallel to the highway was a stretch of road running through state game lands. However, the road wasn't plowed in the winter and was bound to be covered in nearly a foot of snow and ice. And it was gated. My little coupe could probably smash the gate, but there was no way I would be able to get through all that snow. I needed a different vehicle, preferably a truck with a plow if I could find one. I decided to head back to town to begin my search.

I drove slower this time as I looked up and down streets and into driveways for something useful. There were a lot of trucks, but the more I thought about it, the more I really wanted a plow on the front. And around these parts it was only a matter of time before you found one. You couldn't rely on the state to get you out of a snowstorm when you lived in the middle of the woods.

Still, I was growing impatient and about to give up when lady luck smiled at me and I found exactly what I wanted. It was a white pick-up with a regular size cab and a big yellow plow on the front. Then my phone rang. It was Ashley.

"Hi, hon." I said.

"Hey." She was scared. That much was immediately obvious.

"What's wrong?"

"Well, there's a bunch of things banging at my door. And my mom is dead. And you're not here."

"...zombies."

"What?" she asked uncertainly.

"They are zombies," I repeated. There was no response. "I'm on the way. Getting a truck right now."

"What truck?" She asked.

"I'm borrowing a truck. I can't take the highway and I need a plow."

"Whose truck?"

"Doesn't matter anymore," I said. And that was certainly true.

"Be careful."

"I will. Are you okay? Can they get in?" I asked.

"No, I blocked the door well enough. But that means I can't escape while they're out there either."

"I'll deal with that later. Just sit tight. Another hour if I'm lucky. And I have my lucky boxers on, so I'll be okay."

She laughed at that. It was good to hear her laugh. That meant she still had hope.

"I have to go. I swear to you that I will get you out. Okay?"

"Okay. I love you."

"Love you, too."

I hung up the phone and pulled up next to the truck. The door was open and there were footsteps leading away. Apparently I really was lucky. The keys were in the ignition. I loaded up the truck with the stuff I took from my apartment then climbed into the driver's seat. Inside the cab I found a CB radio, which I wasn't sure how to use, but could probably figure out with some trial and error. I opened the glove box to see about an instruction manual and found another surprise.

On top of several booklets was a small revolver. I hadn't shot a handgun in a long time, but I could make it work. I checked my car one last time to see if I had missed anything. I grabbed my debate travel bag which contained mostly hygiene products (left in the car from yesterday) as an afterthought and then left my keys on the front seat. Maybe my car would save someone else looking for an escape. I guess I would never find out.

* * * * *

I was heading in the direction of the highway. The whole time I prayed that the traffic would let me over the bridge. As I passed a gas station I checked the gauge on the truck. Under half a tank. I decided it would be best to get some fuel. I pulled up to the pump and got out. The station still had power, so the pump was still working. I didn't want to go inside, so I pulled out my credit card and filled up. As I was waiting I heard a noise and turned to find six of the undead heading in my direction. I quickly grabbed my baseball bat out of the back and waited. They were moving slowly, but they were making that awful moaning sound.

I used this opportunity to study the zombies. They were almost exactly as Hollywood had portrayed in so many B movies. They moved a bit quicker than Hollywood, but not by much. They were also visibly wounded. Two of the undead looked like guys I knew from a bar down the road, but I couldn't be completely positive.

The only thing that was completely different than anything I'd ever seen in a movie were the eyes, and they were certainly disturbing. All of them had eyes like Mr. Felder's and the young girl. Coal black pupils with a smoky gray iris. To be completely honest, I wasn't positive that these things could see

21

very well. Still, that didn't stop them from moving toward me now.

I heard another sound on the right. Three more were coming from around the side, and another walking out of the station. I was glad I didn't try to go inside. The first ones I noticed were going to be on me before the pump finished. I walked out a bit to the other side of the truck, and their direction changed. They followed me wherever I turned, just like Hollywood predicted. That was useful to know.

I heard the pump click off. I jumped into the back of the truck and yanked the nozzle out of the tank. I closed the cap and jumped out of the bed of the truck next to the door. One was reaching for me as I was still in the back. Another was standing near the driver's mirror. As I tried to close the door it grabbed on. I started the truck and lurched forward, but the bastard wouldn't let go and was being dragged along with the truck.

I stopped the truck away from the others and got out to dislodge my passenger. Gripping the baseball bat in my gloved hands, I started to wail on it with all my strength. It wouldn't let go and was even trying to stand up against my blows. I then knocked it in the head twice, hearing bone smash and feeling the shock through my gloves. The creature let go and fell to the ground. My hands were sore from my efforts with the bat, but the creatures were still staying true to Hollywood mythology.

Note to self: aim for the head.

I climbed back into the truck and turned for the bridge. There were a few cars stopped along it, but I would be able to get through. One of the cars I recognized from earlier, smashed into a guard rail. Stupid. I drove past quickly, not giving my guilt from not stopping to check on the wrecked vehicle a chance to catch up to me. I put the truck in gear and headed across. Below the bridge the highway was a disaster. Cars were wrecked all over. Those things could be seen walking around and banging on windows. Probably someone alive trapped inside. The plow of the truck scraped against another car and I turned my focus back to the road I was on. I couldn't let myself get distracted, as horrible as the scene was below. I needed to get to Ashley.

I made it to the other side of the bridge and turned onto the game lands road. The gate was still intact, which meant no one else had gone this way. That was a good as long as no one was coming the other way on the single lane access road. I found the switch dropping the plow and slammed on the gas. The impact shook my teeth, but the gate came free. I backed up and took a deep breath. So far, so good.

* * * * *

Driving down the unused road was almost serene. The ice and snow on the trees was beautiful in the way it reflected the afternoon sunlight. It made me remember what things were like only yesterday. But my peaceful thoughts became interrupted by the scent of smoke from the nearby highway. Soon, I would make it to the end of the road and I would be right back into the thick of it.

I thought about how stereotypical the undead were turning out to be. How could Hollywood have gotten something no one had ever seen before so accurate? The way they moved, sounded, acted and even died were disturbingly true. Maybe the reason the movies were so accurate were because someone had seen it before. It was an unsettling thought. It meant we could have been prepared for this eventuality, but instead were acting exactly as the movie directors and writers had predicted: scared, unorganized and chaotic.

Part of me wanted to stay where I was, surrounded by the calm of the snow. The purity of the untouched and unspoiled white. That part of me even imagined hearing birds chirping. But whenever I thought of peace I had to think of Ashley, and I knew that I would keep going on no matter what. She meant more to me than anything. Without her there could be no peace. Even if the undead were put back into their damn graves.

Chapter Three

I made it the rest of the way to her house without any problems. There were some slight obstructions and I had to take a few detours once I got off of the access road and back on the regular roads, but I made it. I parked the truck just down the road and looked down toward her house. It was completely surrounded. True to the stereotype, the zombies gathered where the living hid.

I dialed Ashley's phone. She picked up instantly.

"Where are you?" she asked.

"Just outside. The house is surrounded. I'm going to try and draw them away."

"Please, be careful."

"I'll call when I'm on the way in. Keep the door blocked until then. Might get loud, but don't panic, okay?"

"I won't."

"See you soon. I love you."

"Love you, too."

I started the truck back up and leaned on the horn. Coal black eyes began to turn slowly in my direction. I wanted to line them up. My plan was to run over as many as possible with the plow and drive across the street and around the block.

Then, I would walk back to the house and deal with the stragglers.

I kept the horn blowing hard. As the first ones came close, I revved the engine and put the truck in gear. I slammed on the gas and was greeted with the thudding sound of flesh pounding into metal. I circled the house a few times, aiming for anything that moved. Flesh and blood flew around the yard in a scene that looked like a cheap horror film, but was as real as it was going to get.

I stopped the truck outside her house and looked at my handiwork. Bodies littered the ground, some moving, some not. I grabbed my baseball bat and stepped out, fueled with adrenaline and completely abandoning my original plan of parking the truck around the block. I wanted to kill them all. Walking around the back of the truck, I smashed the head of a ghoul crawling on the ground nearby. The sound of the metal and skull crashing together brought a smile to my face and the soreness back to my hands. Sneering with my over-confidence, I grabbed the shovel out of the back and threw the bat into the bed of the truck. I turned toward the house.

Two of them were walking toward me from the direction of the house. I raised my shovel and swung at the first one's head. The spade connected at the jaw line, slicing deep into the skull and connecting with brain tissue. As the creature started to fall I dislodged the shovel and swung it overhead. I let out what I can only describe as a primal roar as I brought the shovel down on top of my second foe's head, splitting the skull over the left eye and felling the ghoul.

Most individuals hear the term "blood rage" in the movies and in games. But only a few really know what it means. With each successful blow against the undead my body pumped more adrenaline into me. I understood now what it meant as a clear, but rage guided purpose overtook me. Kill them. All of them.

I moved toward the house and then inside through a broken window. No point blindly going in a front door when I could see where I was going this way. Part of my brain still couldn't grasp what was happening. I was a history teacher, not a fighter. But I had to get to her. I had to save her.

Climbing through the front window put me in the living room. As I stood up I saw that two more of the undead were moving toward me, arms outstretched, moans in their throats. One came from the kitchen and the other from the direction of her bedroom. The bedroom zombie was closer, so I smashed it at an angle toward its skull and turned back to the other. It had moved closer and I had to roll left to escape its grasp. I dropped my shovel and instinctively kicked at the monster's legs. I connected with its knee, sending it to the floor and slowing it down, but not stopping its advance. I stood up and recovered my weapon. As it crawled toward me I rammed the point of the spade into the back of its neck, severing head from body.

I was startled a moment. The head rolled over, black eyes staring at me in hunger. The jaw was still moving. Of course the fucking head was still alive! I dropped my boot heel into the forehead several times, hearing a crunch and a squish as the last drop ceased that hideous jaw forever. I had to pause and catch my breath. I wasn't an athlete, or even someone who worked out regularly. I knew the only reason I was still going was because of the adrenaline, and I knew it was going to wear off soon. I looked outside and saw more of the zombies coming toward the house. No time to rest. I had to get her out of the basement and out of the house. I pulled out my phone and dialed.

"Hello?" Ashley's voice was unsteady. She must have been shaken by the noises above.

"Start unblocking the door. I'll be down in a moment."

"It sounds like there are a few outside the door."

"I'll take care of it. Hang tight. Only a minute more."

I went down the basement stairs slowly. I reached the bottom and turned the light on. There were three down here. One was banging against a door near the back that led to the room she was hiding in. The other two were already moving toward the fresh prey that entered the room. The one at the door was female and I thought she looked familiar. I had a feeling I knew who it was and the thought unsettled me a moment. As the two moving toward me began to moan I dove between them and under the pool table in the center of the room.

Grabbing a pool stick off the wall, I rolled onto the table. The first one came close and I lunged forward with the stick. I just missed its eye and ended up only pushing it back a few paces. I silently cursed myself. Now was not the time to get fancy. I used the shovel instead and dispatched my two foes easily. Only one more stood between her and I and I had a bad feeling about this one.

"Hey! You undead bastard! Over here!"

It turned. Just as I feared, it was Ashley's mother. But there was something different about her. The eyes were red. Bright red. Like blood in the sunlight. She snarled at me and then charged forward, faster than I could react. I was slammed into the far wall. Shit! I was counting on that slow shuffle and didn't expect this. I shoved her back and rolled as she reached out at me. When I came up I swung the shovel, but she ducked out of the way. It could think! I had a sudden feeling of dread as my confidence began to wane against this new foe.

She charged at me again. I grabbed the pool stick from before and swung at her knees, taking her down enough for me to take another swing with the shovel. This time I lodged the end in her temple, splitting wide her eye sockets and watching her brain matter spew forth from the wound. I dislodged my new favorite weapon and watched the body fall to the ground. As she fell, I tipped my hat to her. At the time I didn't know why. But know that I think about it, I believe it was simply a last sign of respect to the fallen, and someone I respected when they were still human. Her mother was the first zombie I had actually recognized.

I went over to the door and knocked calmly. It opened slowly at first, and then flew open after our eyes met. Ashley's sparkling blue eyes were welling up with tears as she ran into my arms. I dropped the shovel and held her tight, muffling her sobs against my chest.

"Thank you, thank you, thank you." She repeated over and over.

"It's good to see you again," I said.

"I can't believe you made it." She turned her head up to meet my gaze.

"I swore to you that I would. Have I ever made a promise that I couldn't keep? Besides…if something happened to you, then I would have to kill them all. And that seems like it might be a lot of work." I couldn't resist the opportunity for a cheap laugh. Anything to make her smile.

Ashley chuckled a response. I bent down and kissed her softly. I wanted to stay like that forever, but I knew what was coming for us outside. "We have to get out of here. There are more on the way."

"Okay." She broke our embrace but kept my hand locked with hers. Her other hand reached up and clutched a pendant she wore around her neck. It was an anchor-shaped silver charm that her father had given her, and she said she wore it for luck. Over the years I learned that she wore it every time that she was nervous about something.

I picked up the shovel and led her up the stairs and out of the basement quickly. I didn't give her a chance to recognize the body of her mother lying on the floor nearby the pool table. Upstairs I could see outside the large living room windows. The zombies were closing in. We only had a few minutes before we would be under siege again.

"Go into your room and get some clothes. Maybe boots if you have any. When I call you, come back to the living room."

"What are you doing?" she asked.

"I'm going to grab anything that looks useful. Quickly now, hurry!"

We split off and grabbed what we needed. I went to the kitchen first and filled a garbage bag with food. I grabbed a few more knives and headed into the living room. One was at the back sliding door. We had to go. "Hon, now!" I called out.

She came out of the bedroom with a bag of clothes in hand. She had on jeans, boots, a sweatshirt and scarf. She was carrying a small suitcase that looked poorly packed. I took her hand and led her out the front door. As we moved toward the truck one of them came at us from the side of the house, startling us both. I handed the garbage bag to her. "Hold this."

As she took the bag from my hand I brought the shovel up like a baseball bat. I swung at the zombie with the shovel, sending the head flying through the air. I knew that somewhere on the lawn the jaw would still be clacking in ferocious, unending hunger, like they did in the movies.

I led her to the truck and helped her inside. Then I put the stuff in the back, including the shovel and climbed into the driver's seat. Several of the undead were close, but I wasn't concerned with that right now. I started the truck forward and turned toward my love, sitting on the seat beside me.

"I'm sorry," I said.

"You saved my life. Why are you sorry?"

"I had to kill your mother," I was solemn. I liked her mom.

Ashley stared at me a moment before replying. "She wasn't my mother anymore."

"No, she wasn't, I suppose." I was surprised at how swiftly she answered, already separating the living from the undead. For a moment I thought about telling her how her mother was

30

different than the others. It was an unsettling thought, and I decided it was best to keep that from her for now. She had been through enough for one day. And I knew we would still go through more before we could find some semblance of peace.

"What do we do now?" she asked as she stared out the window at the setting sun. It would be setting soon. The thought of fighting at night was not a pleasant one. We needed a place to lay low for the night. I reached across the cab and took her hand. Ashley slid across the truck bench toward me, and I threw my arm over her head and onto her shoulder. I pulled her even closer to me as she rested her head on my chest.

The truck moved down the road, passing wrecked cars and flaming buildings as we went. I had managed to save her, but now I had to figure out how to keep us both alive.

* * * * *

We drove slowly down the road. I didn't know where I was going or what we were going to do. I was overjoyed to have her with me, but now I was terrified of doing something that got us both killed.

As we drove down the back roads of the mountains (I refused to go near heavily trafficked roads), I thought about everything that had happened in the last twenty-four hours. I looked at the blood-stained shovel in the rearview mirror. I thought about the instinctual rage that overtook me back at the house. It was too much at once and I stopped the truck.

"What's wrong?" she asked.

"I just need a minute. It's been a long day." I tried to say it with a smile, but instead I put my head onto the steering wheel and sighed loudly.

"Why did you come back for me?" Ashley asked.

"What?"

31

"You could have gotten away. Found somewhere safe. Why did you risk your life for me?"

I wasn't sure how to respond. "You know why."

"I need to hear it."

"I love you. I need to be with you. If you die, then I have nothing."

"You have your life. You could have stayed safe."

"You act like I shouldn't have come." *Where was she going with this?*

"No, that's not it. I'm really, really glad that you did. I love you more than anything. I just hate you risking your life for me."

"Well, I'll probably be doing more of that for awhile."

"You shouldn't."

I had to laugh. She always told me I did things for her that I didn't need to, or that I shouldn't have done. The fact was that most of those things I did because I wanted too. I did them to see her smile or to hear her laugh. Or just as an opportunity to see her eyes light up. I looked down at her resting against my chest. She was gazing out the window into the passing trees.

"What are you thinking?"

"I'm not really sure," she said as she played with her necklace, the silver charm shaped like an anchor. She had a habit of reaching up and pulling on it when she was lost in thought. It had meant a great deal to her. After a few minutes Ashley turned her gaze back to me, and I knew what was coming. "What about you?"

"I'm glad I got you out of there. Now, what do I do with you? Umm....grrr?" I was again trying to make light of everything. Ashley smiled lightly, at least appreciating the attempt. I shared my rudimentary plan with her, "We need to find somewhere to hide. Preferably somewhere with a TV or radio so we can find out what's going on."

"Doesn't this work?" She reached at to the radio and CB in the truck. I hadn't even thought about using it. I shook my head and smiled at her.

"That's what I keep you around for. I didn't even think about that."

I turned a few knobs on the CB as she scanned through regular radio stations. I wasn't quite sure how the CB radio worked, so I figured I would just keep changing stations until I heard someone's voice. Meanwhile, most of the radio stations seemed to be broadcasting the same emergency message.

...stand-by for more information. This is the emergency broadcast system. This is not a test. Please stay indoors. Close your windows and lock your doors. Do not go outside. Do not attempt to leave your city. Stay away from anyone afflicted by the phenomenon. Do not attempt to rescue friends or family members. Authorities and military assets have been mobilized. Please stand by for more information. This is the emergency...

I snorted in disgust. Phenomenon. Call it what it is. Zombie apocalypse. End of the world. Doomsday. Bureaucracy always had to try and make things sound simpler than they were. Now was not the time to be hiding behind political correct nonsense. People need information about what is going on. Information to survive. If anyone is even left alive.

I was so deep in thought that I almost missed the sound of a voice coming in over the CB radio.

"Hello? Is anyone listening out there?"

We both looked at each other. I grabbed the microphone and pressed the only button that was on it while hoping that I didn't have to press anything else. The number of dials on the CB was a bit intimidating.

"Hi," I started, "Can you hear me?"

"Jesus Christ! Can't believe I figured this thing out. My name is Rico."

"Nice to meet you," I wondered a moment how you introduced yourself over radio? I let the thought pass and continued. "Where are you?"

"I'm in a house off of Marigold Avenue. Where are you?"

"Backwoods somewhere. Where is Marigold Ave?"

"Bryantsville. You have to get here quick and save me, man."

"Are you safe?"

"Yeah, I hid in this place about an hour ago. Found this radio on the second floor."

I could hear noises in the background, like fists pounding on the door. "I thought you said you were safe?"

"There's a bunch of these things outside, but I'll be okay for awhile. You have to help me, man. I don't want to die!" Rico pleaded.

"Hang on a minute. Let me figure this out."

I clicked the radio off and turned to her. She looked at me questioningly, but I think a part of her knew what I would say. Bryantsville was at least an hour drive from where I thought we were at, and that was on a good day.

"We can't help him," I said flatly.

"Are you sure?"

"He's trapped over an hour away, at least. Chances are he won't be alive when we get there."

"Could have made the same argument about me," she countered.

"That's different." I left it at that. I wasn't about to argue with her.

It wasn't that I didn't care about this guy, Rico. Hell, he might even be worth saving. But I wasn't about to risk my neck for strangers. It just would not be practical, running around Pennsylvania trying to save every person that we managed to get on the radio. And I would *not* put her back into danger. If she asked me to help, then I would, but I wouldn't willingly put her back into the thick of it. I clicked the radio back on.

"Rico?"

"Yeah, man. How long until you get here?"

"We're not."

"What?! You've got to be joking, right?" The panic in his voice was disturbing. I felt the icy hand of guilt begin to creep over me. I was causing that panic.

"No. You're too far out. Too risky. I'm sorry."

"Sorry?! Fuck you, man! Get your ass here and help me out you heartless son-of-a-bitch!" His anger poured over the CB.

"Good luck, Rico." I didn't hide it. What I was doing was cold and if I wasn't already going to hell, this would definitely send me there. Unless this was hell…

"Fuck, man! Fuck you! I hope they fucking get you! I hope you fucking…" I turned the radio off, ending his tirade mid-swear. It wouldn't be the last time I would here Rico's voice. His plea for help and angry tirade would plague my nightmares for a few weeks, until I got used to the killing and death.

We sat in silence for a moment. For all intents and purposes, I just sentenced Rico to die a horrible death. A living, breathing human was probably going to die and it would be my doing because I didn't even try to help him. Despite how many ghouls lay dead because of me, this was different. This was someone who was still human. I wanted to break down right then, but I knew I had to go on. I had to keep her safe.

Ashley moved closer to me and buried her head in my shoulder. I put my arm around her and pulled her close again. I kissed the top of her head. As I looked up I could see a figure moving in the woods. Not taking any chances I started the truck and pulled away.

"Where are we going?" she asked.

"I'm not sure. Anywhere we can find that looks safe for now. I don't want to spend the night in this truck though.

Maybe if we can just find a house back here somewhere. It's fairly secluded."

"Looks like a driveway up ahead."

She was right and I turned onto the road. It wasn't plowed and I couldn't make out any tracks in the snow. Definitely a good sign. Down the road a way was a two-story, Victorian style home. There were no lights in the windows. I pulled the truck up as close as possible.

"Stay here. Honk the horn if you see anything," I told her.

"I want to come with you."

"No. If we have to leave in a hurry it'll be easier if you are already here. There's a gun in the glove compartment if you get scared." I wasn't worried about her being able to handle the gun. She had more experience with firearms than I did because of some old camp jobs she used to have.

I got out of the truck and went around the side to retrieve my shovel. I walked up the steps of a wrap-around porch and stopped to look around. It was quiet. The sun was dipping fast behind the trees. I moved over to a window by the door and peeked into the house. Didn't look like anyone had been here for some time. This area was full of people who owned summer homes. That meant if this was one of those, then it probably wouldn't have the utilities turned on, and there wouldn't be any food. But it would be a roof and a locked door for night.

I tried the handle. Locked. Looks like I was going to have to break-in. I tried throwing my weight against the door. It was too sturdy for me to even think about breaking it down. I brought the shovel to bear against the window with a resounding crash.

The high-pitched shrill of the burglar alarm was deafening and scared me out of my wits for a moment. Without knowing the code I probably stood little chance of getting it to stop either. That sound was going to attract attention. Looks like we wouldn't be staying in this house tonight. I ran back to the truck and got inside.

"Guess this place is out," I said.

"Won't it go off on its own after a while?" she asked.

"I don't know. Something is going to hear it though. We'll find someplace else," I started the truck and drove back the way we came. I kept my foot on the gas for about ten minutes before I slowed down to start looking again. I wanted to be sure we were far enough away from anything that would be attracted to the sound of the house alarm going off.

Not willing to break anymore windows and set off anymore alarms our search went slowly. Finally, we found a garage that was unlocked. It was just big enough for the truck after I pushed a lawn mower out of the way. I closed the garage door and then made my way through the house. It was empty. Looked like someone had left in a hurry. I brought Ashley inside and then started bringing in some stuff.

I checked out the house in more detail. There were two doors and a lot of windows on the first floor. Despite the vulnerability, I didn't want to get trapped completely up on the second floor, so I decided we should stick to the first floor and told her to stay in the kitchen, living room or bathroom. Then I moved furniture around to create make-shift barricades. We wouldn't be staying long, so I didn't spend a lot of time with that. As far as I was concerned this place would only be a temporary hideout.

Ashley found some blankets and brought them into the living room. There was a television, but I was unwilling to turn it on and face more death. Lying down on the carpet, I held her in one arm and kept the shovel within reach. I slept then, exhaustion from the day finally overtaking me.

The images from what I had seen on television that morning combined with Mr. Felder, the young girl and the screams of Rico to create one giant, inescapable nightmare.

Chapter Four

I was awake before the sun broke. Glancing at my watch I saw it was nearing six-thirty in the morning. Ashley was fast asleep beside me. I gently edged her aside and rose from our makeshift bed. Light from the early morning was creeping through the windows. I took my shovel and decided to go out onto the deck in back of the house. It had been awhile since I had appreciated a sunrise. I may not have the opportunity tomorrow.

Cold air hit my face as I stepped outside. There was evidence of a fresh snow on the ground. A mountain morning dusting, nothing significant. I closed the door behind me and dusted off a plastic chair on the deck. Sitting myself down, I let out a nice, relaxing yawn. It felt like nothing had happened. I imagined owning this house and doing this same thing every morning, a warm cup of freshly brewed coffee keeping away the morning chill.

Then I looked down at the shovel. Blood covered the spaded end. Instead of a warm cup of coffee my hand grasped a cold, hard piece of wood and metal that I had used to send the undead back to their graves.

How did I get here? I'm a school teacher, for Christ's sakes. By all practical standards I should be dead. I should have died in that apartment, not have killed dozens of these things with a damn shovel. I had no idea how I was able to stay so focused. No idea where I found the strength of body and will. For a few moments I sat staring into the woods just wondering how I did it. I chalked it up to natural instinct and my desire to see Ashley safe as the first rays of the sun found their way over the horizon.

The sky was blood-red. It made me think of my mother. She used to tell me, "Red sky in the morning, sailors warning." I wondered what happened to her and my step-father. I hoped they had made it somewhere safe. My brother and his family had been on vacation. Maybe they were in an area that hadn't been attacked or infected or whatever and were better prepared than the rest of us. I pulled my cell phone out and tried to call my family for the first time, but I was met with nothing but silence. Undoubtedly the network had finally failed, overwhelmed by millions of calls made by millions of people looking for salvation in one form or another.

I turned back to go inside, my mother's voice inside of my head, and stopped as I grabbed the handle. There was a movement in the reflection of the glass. I turned swiftly, bringing the shovel up. Something was in the woods. I could hear snow crunching. Too fast to be a zombie, unless it was more than one. I stepped away from the door, my eyes scanning the area. A low bush shook gently to my left. I moved off the deck and raised my shovel, ready to strike at anything that sprung forth.

It came out slowly. Four legs, black hair with some white patches. Floppy ears and a long mouth. My brain finally recognized it as a dog...border collie, if I remembered the breed correctly. I lowered the shovel and walked down the deck. When I reached the bottom I got down slowly on one knee. The dog looked at me, cautious but curious. It wore a pink collar. I stretched my arm out to it, letting my scent drift in the air.

"Come here, girl."

She cocked her head at me, obviously wary. I noticed red blotches on parts of her white fur, but saw no wound. She had been in a fight. I then wondered if animals could be affected by this zombie thing and tightened my grip on the shovel at my side.

The collie came up to me cautiously and sniffed my hand. She didn't appear to be wounded. Her eyes were a normal brown color. I reached out and ran my hand over the top of her head. She looked me in the eye. It seemed as if we were both checking each other out, each unsure but curious. She bent her head down and sniffed the shovel. I could hear her let out a small growl. The dog knew exactly what was going on, that much was certain.

I released my grip on the shovel and she looked back up at me. She sniffed my face and then started to lick it, her tail beginning to wag. She was convinced that I wouldn't hurt her and she was right. I checked her collar as she kept licking my face. An ID tag indicated that her name was *Alice*.

"You always were pretty good with animals."

I didn't realize that Ashley was standing on the deck. I hadn't even heard the door open up.

Alice moved between the two of us and growled at Ashley, ears pinned back. Apparently, she didn't like being caught off guard either.

"Easy, girl. She's okay," Alice looked back at me and wagged her tail. I was amazed at how smart the dog was and with how fast she seemed to take to me.

"Apparently, I have some competition."

"Nah, she's a good dog. You just startled her. Caught me off guard too," I smiled up at Ashley as I moved toward the deck. Alice followed behind me. I suppose she was planning on

41

sticking around for awhile. I scooped Ashley up in my arms and kissed her hard on the lips.

"Good morning," I smiled at her, staring into her sapphire eyes.

"You could have woken me up. You know I love sunrises."

"I couldn't bring myself to wake you. Who knows what will happen today. You needed to sleep."

"And you didn't?"

"I slept well. Don't worry about me," We walked back inside and I sat down on the couch. It was time to turn the television on and face reality. She came in shortly after, putting a piece of meat down on the ground near Alice. The dog looked up at her warily before eating the food. Maybe she did have some competition. I smiled at both of them.

The TV was static. I flipped through the stations trying to find something. I finally found a station that was broadcasting. The reporter looked haggard as he fumbled through papers on his desk.

"Apparently, no one knows what is going on...Jim, do we have a clip?...alright...hang on folks, we have the latest from Washington coming in now...Damn it, I don't even know if anyone is still listening, Jim...what?...yeah, okay. Here we go, folks."

The screen filled with an image of the Secretary of State, Richard Markin.

"Good morning, Ladies and Gentlemen. At 3:30am this morning the White House was overrun by attackers. Marines quickly moved in and evacuated the President and his family, but rumors suggest an injury in the attack. Contact with Air Force One was lost fifteen minutes ago. Coupled with the death of the Vice President yesterday afternoon, and the disappearance of House Speaker Carlisle Reparry and death of

President of the Senate Rebecca Valentino, I have taken the oath of office. I am acting President until further notice.

"As of this morning we still have no definite answers as to the cause of this incident. Everyone is advised to stay indoors and away from anyone who appears infected. They appear to be attracted to sound and light, so please stay as quiet as possible.

"National Guard units have been activated and our military assets overseas have been immediately recalled. If you remain calm and patient, then help will be there soon. Military leaders have asked that you place a sign in a window indicating non-infected survivors are inside. These will be the first buildings searched by rescuers.

"If you live in the New York City region, then you are being asked to evacuate to established checkpoints as soon as possible. Currently, the military is planning an offensive in the region to stem the attackers currently moving out of the necropolis. Do not stay in your homes if you live in this area, instead, evacuate as soon as possible. The pentagon cannot guarantee that you will be safe from cross-fire if you are in the region.

"Ladies and Gentlemen, in this time of crisis I ask that you have faith in your government. The United States will weather this storm and return to normal as quickly as possible. Good luck, and God Bless America."

I sat in stunned silence, staring at the television. The camera came back to the newscaster, who looked just as stunned as I felt. The station broke to a pre-recorded message just as he started to swear. I turned the television off and turned back to look at Ashley. She was also staring at the television in shock.

"Things won't ever be normal," she said slowly.

"No, they won't be. The government is just as confused as everyone else. I suppose they're doing all they can, but there is probably not much they *can* do."

43

"Are we going to stay here like they said to?" she asked.

"For as long as we can. My guess is those things will find us soon. I have no desire to be here when they show up."

"How long do you think we have?" The worry in her voice was obvious. I steeled my own and tried to be confident.

"At least enough time for breakfast. And maybe a shower." I grinned, raising my eyebrows suggestively at her.

"Is now *really* the best time to think about sex?" she laughed, playfully punching me in the arm.

"I don't see any zombies around," I laughed and kissed her. Anything that took our minds off of what was happening was good, even if it was a joke. Alice looked up and barked at us.

"No, but there is someone else here though. And I get the feeling she is going to be more trouble than the undead."

I couldn't help but laugh, "Let's find something to eat."

We both went into the kitchen and started opening cabinets. We found everything we would need for pancakes. There was bacon and juice in the fridge. It would be refreshing to eat a warm breakfast. Ashley offered to cook while I took the first shower at her insistence that I needed it.

I came out of the shower and was greeted with the scent of breakfast. Once again, I found myself imagining this was my life. There was an older stereo in the living room and I put a CD in it before returning to the kitchen.

"Are you just wearing a towel to tempt me?" Ashley looked at me with a devilish look in her eyes.

"Me? Of course not, I was just hungry and didn't want to waste time putting clothes on," We both laughed and sat down to eat. After breakfast it was her turn to shower. I fought the urge to join her as she danced off to the bathroom. I was glad she was keeping her spirits up. I cleaned up the kitchen and went to get dressed. After I came back to the living room I found myself staring at the shovel I left by the couch. It was a painful reminder of what happened. I decided to clean it.

The blood was dried on the edges. I wasn't sure if it was a good idea to be touching it, but at this point I had come in contact with enough of the stuff to assume it wouldn't kill me, or not kill me. Maybe only direct bites could change someone. I had no idea. After I cleaned the blood off, I decided it might be good idea to sharpen the edges a bit. I remembered seeing a grinding wheel in the garage and went out to use it. I kept the garage doors open while I worked, letting the cool air drift around me.

I wasn't concerned about attracting attention. The grinder would have been loud enough to do that even with the garage doors shut. And I still had no intention of staying another night. Maybe I could rig this thing up to make noise when we left and draw them here instead of chasing us for a bit. I spent a few minutes grinding and then admired my handiwork. The edges were gleaming and sharp. I ran my finger over the edge. It cut but I not enough to draw blood.

I went back in the house. Ashley was in the living room, looking through her bag.

"Hey," I said.

"What was that noise?" she asked.

"I was playing," I held up my newly sharpened weapon.

"Very nice. I should probably find something to use, too."

"Yeah, that's probably a good idea. We'll find something. I think we should take anything we can use before we go."

"I noticed some golf clubs in the other room. I might grab those."

"You hate golf."

"You're not fond of shoveling either." Even now she was as charming as ever.

"You know, my grandfather used to have a cane with a blade built in it. You had to twist the handle to pull it free. I thought it was the coolest thing when I was little. Wouldn't mind having that right now." I reminisced on my grandfather. I was glad he had passed away two years ago and didn't have to see this happening, and I prayed he was not trying to claw himself out of his grave as we spoke

We kept the music on as we scavenged the house. Anything that appeared remotely useful found its way to the back of the truck. Suddenly, Alice started barking from the living room. I went to investigate and looked out the window. Outside, there were two zombies moving up the driveway. I could make out a few more behind them.

"Hon! Time to go!"

Ashley ran downstairs and met me in the kitchen. She had a notebook and a pen in her hand.

"What were you doing?" I asked

"I decided to start a journal."

"Why?"

"I don't know. Just because."

"Well, we have to go. They're outside."

"Alright. I suppose it was nice while it lasted." She looked around the house one last time. I hoped she was thinking the same things I was earlier.

We went into the garage and got in the truck. Alice jumped in the cab without invitation and I smiled. She was a hell of a dog – that was for sure. I started the truck and we pulled away. Along the driveway I had to mow down a few of the blighted bastards with the plow, which I was very glad to have. When we reached the road, I put the pedal down and just started driving. Off again on the road to nowhere, in the land of the undead.

Excerpt from Ashley's Journal

I don't know how I'm alive. I should be dead or at least still trapped in my basement. I can't believe he made it to my house, let alone actually got me out of that nightmare. When he said over the phone he was coming for me, I didn't really believe him. I thought it was an impossible task.

But here we are. Alive.

I should be happy, but I can't shake the feeling that something is...different. Something is different about him. I mean, he's a school teacher for Christ's sake. Yet he saved me. There's a look in his eye I don't recognize and it has me worried. And he's killed dozens of these...things in the process.

I can't bring myself to call them zombies. Not yet. It just seems too easy, too convenient.

Perseverance

Chapter Five

Two weeks and four days. That's how long we drove from house to house. Sometimes we stayed for two nights, but always we ended up driving down another back road. The roads would intersect with highways and these were always the tensest moments. The undead were thickest at these points.

The worst was when we had to stop for gas. Twice we pulled in, only to find that the pumps were not working. We were never sure if the truck would make it to the next station. One stop for gas almost resulted in disaster. The truck was on empty. Zombies were visible all over, but we had no choice.

I remember pulling up to the pump and angling the truck sideways. The idea was that they would only be able to come at me from one side. Ashley stayed in the driver's seat while Alice stayed by my side. If they came too close, then Alice and I would jump in the back of the truck and Ashley would pull away.

Alice ended up saving my life, which bonded us together even more. As the undead moved towards us, I began taking them down one at a time. In two weeks I had become pretty adept at killing the beasts with my shovel, but there was no way I could kill all of them. They would eventually swarm over us. Like locusts, it always began with one, but quickly

49

escalated into much more. That day there was one, then three, then five. I was able to stave all of them off. Then there were six. When they were just outside of my killing circle they stopped moving.

I held my breath. They never stopped before. I've even seen them crawl without legs or arms after their prey. Never resting, never ceasing. Now here they were, staring at me with their coal black eyes and as silent as the graves they were supposed to be in. They weren't moaning, weren't breathing. They were just standing there watching. I slowly looked around. All of them in the area were motionless and silent. This was something new. I tightened my grip on the shovel.

It stood up from behind a nearby car. Slow, careful. Its eyes were red. In life it must have been someone who worked out a lot as tight muscles spread around the exposed portions of its lean body. I braced myself, knowing I was in for a fight. Ashley rolled the window down a bit and called out to me from the cab.

"What the hell is wrong with that one?"

"Remember how I told you about the one that was different from the rest?" I said slowly, not taking my eyes off of the red-eyed fiend.

"Yeah?"

"Well, it looks like we found another one. Roll the window up. We're getting out of here."

Before I could take the nozzle out of the tank, the beast was on me. *Damn it was fast!* It had cleared the distance between us in a matter of seconds. I swung at it with the shovel, but it ducked out of the way and slammed me into a pole next to the pump. I fell to the ground and recognized a clawed hand coming down on me just in time to roll out of the way. I kicked at it, catching it in the rib. It howled in pain and backed away far enough for me to reach out for my shovel.

I grabbed the handle and swung at the monster that was lunging for me again. It deflected the blade, but it bought me enough time to get to my feet. I brought the shovel up defensively and tried to circle back towards the truck. Alice was barking and snarling at the creature. I fought to suppress the urge to call it a zombie. This thing wasn't anything like the others. It was fast, intelligent and stronger, but it also seemed to feel pain. It looked at Alice and snarled as she got too close. Alice instinctively backed up, but kept her teeth barred in anger. I moved closer and feigned a swing, trying to get my opponent to step right, away from the truck.

It was able to recognize what I was doing. It looked at a nearby zombie and let out a guttural sound. The zombie then moved toward the truck. Others joined it as it moved in to continue the assault against Ashley. I couldn't believe what I was seeing. Whatever this thing was it was able to exert some control over the others. A leadership caste of the undead. I didn't have time to process those implications as it attacked me again.

A flurry of activity hit me as I tried deflecting its blows. It caught me in the shoulder, spinning me around but allowing me to fling the shovel around and connect the flat side to its head. The creature fell to the ground and tried to roll, but Alice took the opportunity to lunge at it. She wrapped her jaws around its shoulder and fought with it as it tried to get up. I recovered from my stumble and brought the shovel to bear on its back. Ramming the bladed end into its side, its flesh tore and ribs split apart. It screamed in pain and tried to roll away, but my shovel and Alice kept it from moving. I pulled the shovel up to strike, but before I could bring it to bear again the creature was able to roll and kick my legs out from under me.

Lights exploded in my head as I fell to the hard concrete. I couldn't make out anything at first. I could taste copper in my mouth and knew I was bleeding. I was able to process a screaming sound from the truck. Looking up I saw the blur of the monster kicking at a four-legged creature near the ground that had it by the leg. I saw it coming toward me, arms ready to tear at my throat. I could see its form standing over me, but then I heard a loud bang and saw bits of flesh fly off of its chest as it stumbled backward. More loud bangs and it fell back farther. I heard another scream, then a barking noise. The red eyes of the monster glowed in anger, but rolled backwards as the creature fell.

The rest of the zombies changed their attack in that instant. I remember seeing them turn toward me, an easier prey on the ground than in the cab of the truck. Alice was tugging at my arm, trying to get me to move. Ashley came for me then. Driving the truck as close as she could. Opening the door and bashing zombies aside with a bat. Alice drew some off with her barking as I was pulled me to my feet and toward the truck. I climbed into the cab as best as I could as Ashley pushed me into the driver's side. She climbed in after me and closed the door. She honked the horn and watched Alice jump into the back, landing on one of the many suitcases of supplies we had acquired over two weeks of scavenging. Then she hit the gas and drove away.

She didn't go far. Just a few minutes down the road she stopped the truck.

"Are you okay? Say something!" Ashley cried.

I took a deep breath and felt warm pain at the back of my head where it had connected with the concrete. "I think I might be bleeding." I coughed and red droplets splattered against the window.

She ran her hand through my head and pulled away to find her fingers stained red. "Jesus Christ."

"It's not that bad. Just hurts." *A lot.*

"There's a first aid kit in the back somewhere. Wait here."

"Sure, no problem," I tried to smile, but that hurt too.

As soon as she got out Alice leapt from the back of the truck and into the cab, licking my face.

"Hey, girl. Thanks back there. Couldn't have done it without you."

Alice licked my face again then backed up, like she was wondering how I was feeling. I couldn't help but respond to that inquisitive look.

"Relax, I'm fine. Just banged up a bit."

My love came back into the cab then. Alice moved out of the way as she climbed in. "Turn your head."

I moved too quickly and grimaced in pain.

"Slowly," she added.

"Right, got that. Thanks."

"It doesn't look too bad. Bleeding, but not a lot. You might have a concussion." She was patting me down with cloth trying to clean the wound the best she could.

"Probably. Doubt I'll sleep after that anyway."

Ashley was quiet as she cleaned my wound and bandaged my head. When she finished she gave me some aspirin and water. She also handed me a few granola bars before putting the equipment back in the bed of the truck. By the time she got back into the driver's seat I had already consumed two of them. She started the truck and started driving again. Alice lay on the floor drinking from a cup.

"Aren't you going to eat?" I asked her.

"When we stop. I want to get as far from here as possible."

"What did you do to it?"

"I shot it. Dropped the gun outside in the process," she hit the steering wheel in disgust. "We won't be seeing that again."

"We'll find another one, I'm sure. I'll need a new shovel I guess," I chuckled a bit and instantly regretted it as the pain shot through me.

"How many of them do you think there are?" she seemed frightened now, thinking about what we just came up against.

"The red-eyes?" I asked, my head still pounding.

"Yeah," she said quietly as she turned a corner. Her free hand had gone to the anchor charm around her neck, like it had so many times before in the last two weeks.

"Not sure. Only the second one I've seen in two weeks."

"Why are they different? None of this makes sense."

"I have no idea. They're smart. And fast. And they can control the others. I'm afraid to even talk about what that means." But my brain began to turn over the idea of a leadership caste of zombies. If they were smart enough to group up and organize, then whatever was left of mankind would have a really big problem trying to survive. Assuming there were more survivors then just the three of us…

As she drove I flicked on the radio and CB. The same recorded message was playing on the few stations I could get a signal from. With the CB I did what I had done once a day since we left that first house. I would flip to a station; say a few things into the microphone, wait for a response, then switch to the next. Mostly, I came in contact with truck drivers trapped on a nearby highway. I had become used to hearing them swear at me as I told them I could not help. Ashley looked at me as I went through the routine, doubting my success but hoping I could find someone all the same.

"We'll have to find someplace soon. Sun will be setting in a few hours," she said.

"We could go all night if you want. I'll drive when you want to rest," I offered.

"Absolutely not. Number one, with our luck, you'll black out from that bump on the head and we'll drive into a tree. Number two, we just filled the tank and I am not going through that again today."

"I'm sure I'll be okay. Pain is already less hurting."

"You can't form sentences, let alone drive a truck." She smiled at me. A literature major would always find a way to correct you.

"Hi. Is anyone out there? We're looking for a place to stay." I said into the microphone.

"I wonder if anyone is left," she said. We hadn't seen anyone in weeks, so there was reason to begin doubting. It didn't help that we purposely avoided anywhere with a large population, but you had to think we would have seen someone by now.

"There has to be a safe haven somewhere. Maybe out west or up north. Less populated regions would be easier to clear out and defend."

"*Hello? Who's this?*"

It took me a moment to realize that the voice was coming from the radio.

"Hi. Hello. Um…we need a place to hide." *If there was such a place.*

"*Where are you?*"

"Umm…I think the gas station we were at was in…" I couldn't remember. It was all sort of a blur. She reached over and took the microphone from me.

"Sorry. He's injured. We're about ten miles north of Marrington on Route 17."

"*Injured? Injured how?*"

"Not a bite. Nasty bump on the head."

"*You're positive?*"

"I would have killed him myself by now if that were the case." It was interesting to hear her say that. She was always smart.

"*You're about thirty miles west of us. Next intersection you come to stop and call with a landmark and I'll try to guide you in.*"

"Is it safe?" Ashley asked the stranger on the radio.

"*Safe enough. There's only a handful of us and we have some supplies. Hunting cabin deep in the woods. Haven't seen any walkers in about two days.*"

"Sounds good to me. I'll contact you at our next intersection."

"*Good luck.*"

"Thanks." She clicked the radio off and hung the microphone on the hanger. She looked over past me toward the sun sinking slowly down in the west.

"We'll probably make it just before dark," she said.

"If not, then we'll drive through the night."

"No. I'd rather wait until morning. Who knows what we might run in to," she said.

"You're the boss," I smiled at her. It hurt less now. "Did you mean what you said?"

"About what?"

"Killing me."

"Yes." No sign of hesitation in Ashley's voice.

"Good." None in mine. It was something I had been silently wondering about and was glad to hear her say what I wanted her to.

Five minutes down the road we came to an intersection for Route 47. Ashley radioed in and after a few moments got directions to the cabin. She explained to the voice on the other end that if we did not make it before dark then we would get there in the morning.

While she was talking I sat staring out the window at a zombie moving across the road toward us. I just watched and wondered.

What happened? What turned people into this? I thought about all the movies I used to watch. Viruses, magic, meteors, acts of God. None of them seemed rational, but, then again, this was not a rational world anymore. I hoped whatever caused this was not the by-product of an act of mankind. Hopefully, it was something no one could prevent and there was not a government or company or individual with the blood of possibly billions on their hands. For a moment I thought about how I would feel if I had caused this, but that thought ended seeing myself put a gun to my own head. I would take the easy way out, for sure.

"When you get here you'll be walking a few miles through snow. A few of us will meet you where you stop. The walkers have trouble in the deep snow up here and we can't have you ruining that by plowing your way through."

"I understand. We have a lot of supplies. You're welcome to some of them as payment."

"We'll discuss all that when you get here. Just worry about that part for now."

"Alright, Bill. Thanks again. Call you later."

"Good luck. Stay safe."

"We will." She turned to me. "Feel like hiking today?"

"I told you, I'm fine. Bill, is that his name? Seems like a sensible guy."

"Probably why he's still alive."

"Well, that logic doesn't hold for me then, if only sensible people make it through this." I still couldn't stop myself from trying to joke around. I wanted, above anything else and no matter how I was feeling, to see her smile as much as possible.

"You'll make it." She was serious. Taking away the humor I tried to create.

"We both will."

Perseverance

Chapter Six

We made it to our destination with an hour of daylight to spare. We pulled up next to a gated, unplowed road, similar to the one I had smashed weeks ago. There were three men waiting for us, all armed with rifles. Ashley got out and went to greet our new allies.

"Hi. I was told one of you is Jesse?" She asked.

"Yep, that's me. This is Ryan and Chris. Welcome to our hideout."

"My boyfriend has a nasty bump on the head. He's going to need help," She explained.

"We'll take care of him." Jesse waved his hand and Ryan and Chris moved toward the truck. Ryan was the younger of the two, but both men looked to be in their early thirties. They moved comfortably through the snow and with the weapons. I guessed by the way they moved and how comfortable they seemed with their weapons that they were ex-military. As I watched silently, Chris opened the door and Ryan put his rifle to my head.

"What are you doing?!" Ashley screamed and tried to move toward the truck, but Jesse grabbed her. Alice reacted and started snarling, recognizing that we were both in danger. I was somewhat stunned and unable to react as I stared down the barrel at the eyes on the other end. They were cold and prepared to do whatever had to be done.

"Let go of me, you prick!" I heard Ashley yell at Jesse.

"Relax. You said he was injured. Bill said to make sure." He explained as he wrestled to keep her still.

"He wasn't bitten!" She was angry, but not fighting. Either she realized there was nothing that she could do, or Jesse was stronger than he looked. I looked at Ryan, and then Chris. Chris spoke before I could say anything.

"Let me warn you. No sudden movements or you die. And tell the dog to back down." Alice was practically in my lap with her teeth barred at Chris. I could see her breath turn to puffs of white clouds in unison with her snarling.

I moved my head slowly forward, partly because of the pain and partly because I did not know how fast was considered a 'sudden movement' (nor was I interested in finding out). Putting my arm around her, I calmed Alice down and pulled her from my lap where she had taken a defensive position. "That's a good girl. Easy, now." She looked at me and backed up a bit toward to the driver side teeth still visible and ears pinned back, ready to strike.

"Now slowly get out of the truck," Ryan ordered.

"Can you take the gun away from my head? Might make it a bit easier," I asked slowly. This time I wasn't trying to be funny. The business end was less than an inch from my eye.

Ryan backed up enough for me to get out of the truck. Chris moved closer and began to look me over.

"Turn around."

I did as ordered and felt the bandages being checked. Chris was careful, but thorough.

"He's not infected."

"You're sure?" Jesse asked as he released his grip on Ashley. She ran over to me.

"His wound is still bleeding. If he were infected it would have stopped by now as the blood coagulated. I'll re-bandage him before we get moving."

"I'll do it." Ashley went toward the back of the truck to get the kit.

"Miss, with all due respect, I'm a doctor. I'll do a better job," Chris said.

Ashley glared at Chris. She was unhappy with what just happened, but couldn't fault his logic. She threw the first aid kit at him and he caught it in the air.

"We can't carry all of this in one trip." Ryan was already poking around in our supplies.

She went around back and started sorting through stuff. "We don't need everything. Half of it is probably useless anyway. There's food in the black garbage bags. These two bags are our makeshift suitcases we use. The rest can wait.

"What's in the suitcases?" Jesse asked.

"Change of clothes. A few knick knacks we've found." She was probably referring to her journal, which she had been writing in constantly but wouldn't even let me glance at. If that was what she needed to deal with what was happening, then I let her be.

"We have room. Go ahead and grab them."

"How many of you are there?" Ashley asked.

"Eleven…thirteen with you." Jesse replied, "Eight guys, three girls. We found this cabin by accident. Worked out pretty well since. It's a decent size. You probably won't get your own room, but you'll have some space. And we were starting to run low on food, so this well help, but not for long."

"Fourteen." Ashley countered, "The dog counts. Thirteen is an unlucky number." Jesse regarded her with skepticism, but I knew she was serious about avoiding thirteen. Her hand was once again near her neck while her fingers danced around the anchor.

It was finally my turn to speak. "It's just nice to find another living human. We've been on the road since the start."

"Well, then you'll be happy to know we're not the only ones alive."

"How do you know?"

"House has a generator. Once we got it running we found out it had an active satellite television. We fire it up one hour a day and watch one of the handful of stations still broadcasting."

"Why only an hour?"

"Generator runs on gas. Not much left."

"A lot of places are out of power, so we consider ourselves lucky." Chris seemed friendly enough. There was an optimistic tone in his voice. I held no hard feelings toward any of them after we spoke for a few minutes. I probably would have done the same thing.

"Do you all know each other?"

"We all do now. But Ryan and I served in Iran together. I was a field medic and he was the unit marksman."

"Useful duo," I commented.

"Been told that a few times since the start of all this. Let's get going. You're patched up well enough for now. It'll be dark before we get back, and Vince is convinced it will snow tonight."

"Who's Vince?"

"Another survivor. Used to teach science at the high school nearby. Found him stuck on the roof of a flower shop on our way here."

"It'll be nice to have something in common with him," I said.

"You were stuck on a roof?"

"History teacher."

"History, huh? Going to have a whole new chapter now, I s'pose." Jesse looked at me and then at Alice walking alongside me. "Beautiful dog you have."

"She's not mine." I said.

"Oh?"

"She's a survivor. Same as the rest of us."

The rest of the hike was mostly quiet as we focused on trudging through the snow. Jesse insisted on taking a different route back to not create a path easier for the undead to walk on. The snow crunching around us was the only sound we made as we moved through the woods. As darkness fell our guides pulled out flashlights. I hoped they knew the area really well. The darkness made everything look the same. Occasionally, we would hear a noise in the dark and everyone would stop and listen. Every time that we stopped I looked at Alice. If there was anything out there then she would be the first to know.

It was eerie walking through those woods at night. Quiet, cold and utterly bleak. I was glad that Ashley and I had not been out in the woods prior to this. The only comfort in the darkness was the rifles held by our gracious escort. I had a good feeling about linking up with these folks. If nothing else, then it would be nice to experience somewhat civilized behavior again.

As we came up a hill I could make out a light in the distance. The pace quickened, so I assumed it was our destination. We moved closer and I could begin to make out some crude barricades around the building. Moving out of the tree-line I stopped to check out the place we would be staying.

It was probably a beautiful country escape house for someone wealthy before the outbreak. It had two floors and an attic. Probably a basement. There was a stone chimney which had smoke coming out of it now. There was a wrap-around porch, but I noticed that the staircase was destroyed. I asked Ryan what had happened.

"Fourth night here we woke up to find two of them walking around the porch. We took care of them and then Elise had the brilliant idea to not make it so easy to reach our front door. Not sure if it works yet, since we decided to sleep in rotations after that too. No more surprises."

We went up the porch and into the building. Inside, the rest of the survivors were waiting to greet us.

"Oh, a doggy!" A little girl's voice called out as Alice entered the room.

"Yes, she's a good dog, Becca. She won't bite." Jesse was speaking to the girl who sat in the arms of a big burly man with a graying beard. The little girl ran over to Alice, who sniffed her before letting the small child pet her. She seemed content as the little hands ran through her fur. The man with the beard got up and walked over to us.

"Welcome! Certainly is nice to put a face to a voice. And, may I say, what a lovely face it is."

Ashley accepted the comment gracefully, which was out of character for her. "Thank you. I take it you are our rescuer, Bill?"

"Rescuer? No. You rescued yourselves. I just read a map into a radio."

"Well, we are grateful for your hospitality. This is my boyfriend." She motioned to me.

"Ah yes, the young man with the head wound." He glanced at Chris, who nodded. "How are you feeling?" He reached out his hand as he inquired about my condition.

I shook it firmly. "Still dizzy, sir."

"He needs to lie down and rest, Bill. He lost a lot of blood. I don't want him sleeping, though. If it's a concussion he could slip into a coma," Chris was concerned about me, a complete stranger, which said a lot about his character.

64

"He can use the master bedroom tonight. They both can. I'm sure they need a rest. We'll even fire the generator up in the morning and you can have a hot shower."

"Don't waste your gas on us. We can deal with a cold one." I didn't want to feel pampered by our guests. Once my head stopped pounding I fully intended to contribute to the group.

"I'd like to clean and redress your bandages before you go to bed later. Until then, why don't you both go upstairs and rest. In the morning we'll have formal introductions and trade stories," Chris directed.

We went upstairs and got settled in. In the interim we ate lightly and chatted about our new friend's hospitality. After about two hours Chris came by to clean up my wound. He left after clearing me to sleep with a look of concern and intrigue on his face. I didn't have the energy to ask what was wrong and instead drifted off into a painful slumber.

* * * * *

I woke up to a scream. It was dark and cold. I felt a pair of hands on me.

"Calm down, calm down. What's wrong!?"

It was then I realized the scream was coming from me. The hands were Ashley's. I forced my mouth closed and took a deep breath. Fire coursed through my veins. My heart was racing. I was in pure pain. It was unlike anything I had ever felt before. She was still calling to me, begging me to tell her what was wrong. I could hear her call out for help then. My body was still writing in agony.

The door flew open and light flooded the room. It only added to the pain and made me twist even more maddeningly. Two sets of arms held me down. I could barely make out the voices. Screaming escaped my lips again, unable to remain contained in the fire.

"Relax, buddy. Everything is okay."

In between each painful breath I thought I managed to utter the word 'pain.'

"I'll get a sedative. Hold him down."

"Is he turning?"

"Oh, God…"

"No, I don't think so. Probably a night terror coupled to the pain."

"How sure are you?"

"Damn it, Jesse! He would have turned by now. You saw what happened to Alexis. Put the damn gun down and help us!"

"Here we go! Hold him."

A pinch on my arm. Barely noticeable above the flame. A few more painful breaths, then everything began to fade.

"Let's move him to the other room. Put a guard on…"

Darkness.

* * * * *

Light. Behind my eyelids. I opened them slowly, blinded by the light flooding from a square shape on the wall. I realized it was a window and that I was lying on a smaller bed then I remember. I sat up on the bed. No pain. That's a good sign. Something jumped on the bed, licking my face…it was Alice. I reached out and pet her as I looked around. This was not the room I was in last.

Ashley wasn't here. I jumped out of the bed, anxious to find her. In my flurry I knocked a clock off of the table next to me. It clattered to the floor and the door burst open. There was another gun pointing at me, and a man I'm not familiar with behind the gun staring at me. I glanced at the floor and found the clock. It was two in the afternoon.

"Apparently I slept in," I said.

The gun lowered. The face smirked at me. "You've been asleep for two days, friend."

"Two days…Where is Ashley?" I asked.

"Your girlfriend? She's downstairs, I think. Come on, we'll get you something to eat."

I followed my guide downstairs with Alice in tow. I was greeted at the bottom of the steps by the bearded man's warm smile. I couldn't remember his name, but his face was familiar.

"Glad you're still with us, son."

"Me too, but I can't quite remember who 'us' is." I looked around the living room at the strange faces. At least one was missing from the gaggle of images I could recall. Ashley came through a doorway then and ran over to me as soon as we locked eyes. I wrapped my arms around her.

"I was so scared."

"I'm okay."

"You were really in pain. I thought you were going to die," she said.

"Kiss me." Her lips shot up and met mine. I held her a moment, feeling her against me and forgetting about the other eleven people and the dog watching us. She parted from my grasp.

"I love you."

"I love you, too."

"Ohhh…aren't they adorable?" The source of the comment made some kissing noises and a female nearby smacked him upside the head. "Ow."

"Stop being rude. Ashley was worried," the female said.

"I think it's cute. You never kiss me like that," the wise guy said.

"I wouldn't if you were the last man on earth."

"Maybe I will be someday," he said.

"God save us all," she replied.

"I think it is high time for some introductions." The bearded man led me to a chair and placed a warm cup of coffee in my hands. I thanked him as I sat down.

"We all know who you are, but you don't know who we are. Come everyone, introduce yourselves to our new friend," he said.

A man holding a rifle sitting near the door went first. "I'm Ryan. We met the other day."

"I'm sorry, the last few days are fuzzy. I remember meeting you, but I cannot recall your name. Or yours." I pointed to the man next to him.

"Jesse. I helped you get back here after you arrived. Oh, and I helped pin you down the other night."

"Sorry about that," I said.

"No worries. Glad we didn't have to shoot you." He was serious. Ashley moved behind me and put her hands on my shoulders, giving them a tight squeeze. Jesse didn't know it, but he spoke for her also.

A young lady, mid-thirties, with blond hair went next. "I'm Elise. This is my daughter, Becca."

"I like your dog, mister." The little girl had striking green eyes, like her mother.

We went around the room with the rest of the introductions. Aside from Bill, there was the bearded man named Charlie, my escort from upstairs earlier. He struck me as the biker type with his burly build and bald head. The comedian from earlier was Wes. He was about my age and seemed laid back. Maybe too much. The girl who hit him was Jenn. She came from Pittsburgh and met up with Charlie trying to get out of town. They ran into Bill, and then found a few of the others before coming here.

Then there was John Craftford. He insisted that I call him "Mr. Craftford." He was older, probably about sixty-five. He reminded me of my own grandfather who was a Vietnam

68

veteran. The look in his eye told me he had seen war before, but nothing like this.

The one missing from the group of faces from the other night was Vince. I found out that he shot himself the night after we arrived. The stress of living in hiding was too much for him. I hoped that he hadn't heard my screaming the night before that. I guessed that it would have been enough to push a man over the edge if he was already on the verge of cracking. Finally, we came to…

"Chris," I said.

"Ah, you do remember something from the other day. Yes, I'm Chris, our group's designated medic, mostly because I'm also the only doctor here." He smiled warmly, but his eyes betrayed an air of caution toward me. I recalled the look he had after treating me the other night. It seemed I would have so speak to him in private.

"Thanks for everything everyone. Really," I said.

"One last gift, my friend, and then we'll put you to work." Bill was smiling at me.

"What's that, Bill?"

"Go take a shower. Your stench is enough to gag the living dead." Everyone laughed and I went back upstairs.

Perseverance

Chapter Seven

After my shower I found a fresh set of clothes waiting for me. I dressed slowly. My nose caught a scent on the air – someone was cooking sausages. Since I had been out for two days, I could guess who that someone was. Ashley took care of me; that was certain. Maybe even better care than I deserved. My stomach growled and I went downstairs and into the kitchen. My love was there with Bill and Elise, busy at the stove. Becca was on the floor playing with Alice. It was nice to see people being able to relax again.

"Sit down. Ashley made you something to eat." Elise pointed to a seat by the window in a small breakfast nook overlooking the woods. Bill was eating already and Ashley moved from the stove to the empty plate across from him to fill it up. I thanked her with a kiss and sat down, and saw sausage and potatoes on my plate. I found myself instantly ravished and didn't wait for an invitation to start eating. My stomach welcomed the warm food.

Only after satisfying my hunger did I notice that Bill was watching me intently. "We were all pretty worried, you know."

"You don't even know me."

"You're human. You've made it this long. You managed to save someone that you love while most of us lost those closest to us. What else is there to know?"

"I suppose."

"You don't trust us?"

"That's not it."

"Then what's wrong?"

"We've been on the run for two weeks. The only human contact we've had is with people over a radio that we either couldn't help or were unwilling to try. Now we meet a group of strangers who have been kind to us, me in particular, and I can't shake the feeling that I don't deserve it," I said.

"You shouldn't burden yourself with guilt. You couldn't have possibly saved them all." He said.

"But I didn't even try, Bill."

"Neither did we, son. You came here. We just told you where to go. You made it here on your own."

I was still battling with demons and the voices of those I couldn't help. The first one, Rico, was loudest of all. Bill was probably right. It was probably foolish for me to be feeling guilty. Times were considerably different now, and I only did what I had to in order to survive.

"I guess the only thing we can do is figure out the next step," I said.

"You're welcome here, of course," he said.

Ashley moved up behind me. "Of course we'll stay. Ignore him, he's just modest."

"Good, I'm glad." Bill smiled. "We could use that truck of yours."

"What did you have in mind?" I asked.

"We need supplies. Still have a few months of winter and what little we have will not last us more than a few days at the most. There's a town about six or seven miles from here called

Canick. Not too big, so if we're careful we should be able to get in and out without too much trouble," he said.

I didn't like the idea of purposely going into a town of full of the undead, but I couldn't deny that Bill was right. I wouldn't argue the matter. Twelve mouths, thirteen with Alice, was a lot to feed. I wondered if Ashley still counted Alice now that it affected the number in a different way.

"We'll go. Not everyone, though," I said.

"Of course not. Let me call everyone together and we'll figure this out," Bill got up and left. While he went to get everyone together I turned to her.

"I don't want you to go," I was being preemptive and adamant, but had a feeling it wouldn't matter.

"I'm not leaving your side, and I know you're going to go. So that means that I'm going," Ashley said.

"You're safe now. Stay here," I pleaded.

"No," she refused.

"Please?"

"You need me. I know these things just as well as you do now," she countered.

"I'm not going to win, am I?" She just smiled at me. Of course I wasn't going to win. Ashley would be going whether I liked it or not. Alice moved up to the table. I gave her a piece of sausage and smiled. Alice would definitely be going too. We went into the living room and a few moments later everyone had arrived.

"What's up, Bill?" asked Charlie.

"They're going to stay with us for the time being and we're going to use the truck to go to Canick." He looked around the room. It was quiet for a moment, until Jesse finally broke the silence.

"Glad you guys decided to stick around. We could use your help." He started, "Not too sure how I feel about Canick, though."

"We need the food, Jess. And it wouldn't hurt to get more gas for the generator." Ryan was looking to Chris, waiting for additional support from his old comrade.

"I would like to get more medical supplies," Chris added. "We're probably okay for bandages, but we have almost no medicine."

"We could use wood to board up these windows and that damn sliding door," Charlie seemed more excited about this then the others.

"The truck isn't that big," I was worried about multiple trips. "We'll need another vehicle when we get there."

"So who's going? We can't all go. That would be stupid," Wes commented.

"Me, Ashley and Alice are definitely going," I said.

Charlie was cracking his knuckles. "Hell, I'm in. Get me some goddamn payback."

"I'm in, and I'm sure I speak for Ryan. Ex-military and all that," Chris was looking at Ryan who simply nodded his head.

"One more should do it. That way we can work in pairs," I looked around at who was left. Something told me not to trust Wes in a fight. Obviously Becca wouldn't be going and I would never separate mother and daughter, so Elise was out. Jenn didn't seem like the type who could handle herself if things got rough. It came down to Bill, Jesse and Mr. Craftford. I didn't even get a chance to think it over.

"I'll go." Mr. Craftford's voice was calm, collected and reserved from his chair.

"The hell you will old man. I'll do it," Wes stood up as he spoke.

"Sit down, son. You don't know what you're doing. I'll go," Bill volunteered. I wasn't too sure about the idea of taking Bill either. He didn't strike me as the type. Almost instantly there was bickering between the two of them, each accusing the other of being foolish, unprepared and not ready to go. Mr. Craftford stood up and his voice cut all conversation.

"Enough." Everyone looked at him. Suddenly he didn't seem so old. "I'm going. We're not discussing it further. Now, let's talk about what we're up against."

"They're dead. They walk. Don't let them bite you." Despite the way he said it, no one laughed at Wes' attempt at humor. Mr. Craftford gave him a hard stare and he sat down.

"It's definitely not that simple." All the attention was now on me. Apparently, I had the most face-to-face experience so far. I turned to the fireplace and took a sip of water.

"Go ahead, tell us what you're talking about," Mr. Craftford prompted.

"Well, I suppose you have your basic...zombie," I still couldn't believe what I was saying, even after all the time that had passed. "Slow, unintelligent and focused solely on getting a hold of you. From what I've seen, only damage to the brain is what stops them. I've found a shovel to be a decent weapon, but I imagine any long blade would do."

"So aim for the head, everyone," Charlie grinned.

"Not that simple. The head is a small point on a moving target. I'd recommend handheld weapons for anyone not trained to shoot," Ryan, being an ex-marksman, knew what he was talking about. Charlie's grin lessened.

"Like a camp saw or a machete. Wal-Mart always has them in the hunting department. That's where I used to get my hunting gear. Cheap too," Jesse interrupted.

"You could get most of what we want from Wal-Mart. Is there one in Canick?" Jenn asked.

"Yep," Bill said. Guess that was where we were heading, then.

"Alright, so how are we going to do this then?" Chris spoke up.

"Wait," I started.

"What?" he asked.

"There's another type..."

"Another type of what?" Mr. Craftford asked, a puzzled expression on his face.

"Zombie." The room was dead silent. I continued, "Twice now we've come across a zombie different than the others. Fast, strong and smart. That's how I got this bump on the head."

"Go on," Ryan's voice was barely audible.

"They're also able to feel pain and, from what I could tell, don't need a headshot to go down," that brought some confident energy back to the room. "You'll know when you found one when you see the eyes. Unlike the others, the eyes are blood-red...almost glowing. Not black."

"Son of a bitch! I knew I wasn't stoned!" cried Wes, "I saw one of the bastards when I was leaving my house. Rob said I was still tripping, but I knew it was real," he began laughing. No one else joined in and soon he stopped.

I found myself debating whether or not to tell them the last part as they processed the information. How were they going to view this plan when the possibility of facing organized zombies became a factor? Mr. Craftford was staring at me. He somehow knew that there was something else was he looked at my eyes. I averted his glare and looked at Ashley.

"Tell them," her eyes said it more than her words, but the words brought the focus back on me.

"They seem to be able to control the others," I said it slowly.

The words had the effect that I expected. Everyone seemed to have stopped breathing.

"What did you just say?" Jesse's face was a mixture of shock and bewilderment.

"The red-eyed ones can control the others," I repeated.

"You're fucking joking, right?" He was hoping I was just making it up at this point.

"When we encountered the last one it made the others stop attacking first. Then it had them all attack Ashley to prevent me from getting back to the truck. While it was there they attacked in a somewhat organized manner. Once it died the others went back to their usual, single-minded focus."

"So if we see one of them, then shit gets crazy," Charlie remarked.

"But if we take it out, then business as usual," Ryan said, "Guess we'll just have to be ready." He cocked the hammer back on his rifle, emphasizing his point.

"Should we get going then?" Charlie was definitely anxious. Maybe too much.

"Damn fool. We need to figure out what we need. Need to come up with a solid plan. You rush into enemy territory without knowing why you're there and your ass isn't coming back," Mr. Craftford moved toward a desk along the wall. He took out paper and a pen, and then went back to his chair. I was fine with him taking charge of this crazy idea and slipped away from the group. I made my way out to onto the porch with just Alice in tow. Ashley was still engaged in the conversation in the living room.

I sat down in a chair on the porch that overlooked the front yard and the forest beyond. Alice paced around a bit, and then sat down nearby. The air was cold and I didn't have my jacket on, but it felt good just to sit there. I sat staring into the woods wondering what was going on with the world. I was glad to be here with these people, relatively safe, but I knew it wouldn't last forever. Even if we weren't about to put ourselves intentionally in danger, snow eventually melts. Zombies would have no problem getting here once that happened. Maybe it would be better to face them head on, but it was still going to be risky.

The door opened and I expected to see Ashley walk out to join me. I was surprised to see Charlie. I suppose I still wasn't used to other people around. Charlie seemed like a good guy, even if he did seem way too excited to head for Canick.

"Friggin' cold out here, bro," he sat down in the seat next to me.

"A bit. I guess I haven't noticed."

"You know, she told us what you did for her. That's some hero shit, man."

"I just wanted to keep her safe." I was no hero. If anything, I was selfish.

"Maybe she shouldn't go on this little adventure, then."

"Tried that argument already. She refuses to stay back. Ashley's stubbornness is one of those things I love about her," I'm sure Charlie could tell I wasn't thrilled with the idea of her going with us.

"Well, at least you'll know where she's at," Charlie grinned at me. Like me, he was definitely the type that could make a joke about anything. For a few moments we just sat there staring off into the woods. I was comfortable with the silence. I really didn't want to get to know him better. He might be dead soon. Charlie looked over at Alice and leaned forward in his chair.

"Come here, girl. That's a good girl. Come here."

Alice looked over at him quizzically, but made no effort to get up. I smiled and turned my palm toward her. She stood up and came right to me, licking my hand before sitting on her hind legs.

"That's incredible. You didn't even say anything."

"She's a smart dog."

"Guess she doesn't like me."

"When I found her she was covered in someone's blood. She was cautious of me at first. We sort of bonded over the last few weeks, literally fighting alongside one another. I think she just trusts me," I ran my hand over her head and across her neck. Charlie sat back in the chair and watched a moment then talked for a few minutes about some special he saw on television about dogs that bonded with humans. I nodded along only half listening. I didn't know why Alice responded so well to me, but I was grateful. That was enough for me.

Charlie finished his story and stood up to stretch. "Well, it's a bit cold out here for me. I'm heading in," For a moment I wondered if he was referring to the air being cold, or my demeanor. I shrugged the thought off, and after a few minutes headed back inside myself.

The living room was empty save for Becca, who was drawing pictures at the coffee table. I could hear voices from the dining room. I caught the words "supplies" and "wood" and figured the strategy meeting had relocated. Jesse came down from upstairs carrying a rifle.

"Hey. They went into the dining room. I'll be outside," he said to me.

"Doing what?" I asked.

"Keeping watch."

"Oh. Right. Guess I'll join them." Instead of going into the dining room I went into the kitchen. Jenn and Elise were there. Jenn turned to me. "Bored already?" she asked.

"Never went in. I'm sure they can handle it. I'm just going to drive and try to keep everyone safe." I was lying. The only person I would ultimately be concerned about was Ashley. I was capable of sacrificing any of these people for her if need be.

Jenn didn't reply. Instead, she turned back to the counter top she had been wiping down. Something was bothering her. Maybe she knew I was lying. I didn't know her well enough to ask, so I quietly backed out of the kitchen and into the living room again. I was making my way for the staircase when I heard Chris call out for me.

"Hey, come here. Need your opinion," he said.

"Sure." I grudgingly went into the dining room. Sprawled on the table were lists of supplies and a crudely drawn map.

"What's up?" I asked as I entered, drawing eyes to me.

Bill pointed to the crudely drawn map on the table. "This is Canick. At least, as much of Canick as I could remember. The Wal-Mart is here," he indicated a block on the map, indistinguishable from the others save for the letter 'W' written on it. "Like Jenn said, can get most of what we need there, except for fuel and wood. Fuel we can get at any gas station that looks hospitable, but we need to get more cans first."

"From Wal-Mart," Ryan interrupted.

"Right. We also know that one truck won't be enough, so when we get into town we'll start checking for one or two more we can use," he continued.

"Sounds feasible," I said.

"When you reach Wal-Mart you'll split into three teams. Each team will have a list. Get as much as you can off the list in fifteen minutes, then get back to the truck," Bill paused a moment, Mr. Craftford picked up.

"The lists are divided by type: food, supplies including medicine, extra clothing and blankets, batteries, that sort of thing, and tools and weapons, which will include anything useful that doesn't run on gasoline or needs power. That way we're not all running around the whole damn store. We're taking Jesse now, who will wait by the truck or whatever and honk the horn if there's trouble. Crude, but with the doors open we should hear it and be able to get back."

"What about zombies in the store?"

"We either kill or avoid. No other way to handle it right now." Mr. Craftford had a look in his eye. This was definitely not the first raid he'd ever planned. I wondered about his military record.

"When do we leave?" I asked.

"Just before dawn tomorrow. Gives us more time to prep." Mr. Craftford said.

"Okay." I said.

"Alright then, everyone rest up. If you're going tomorrow get your watch in early so you can be well rested." Bill ended the planning session and everyone went off on their own. Ashley came over to me and we both went upstairs, Alice not far behind. Chris called up that he wanted to change my bandages again. I told him I'd meet him in a bit and we'd do it.

We went upstairs and into the small bedroom. Ashley closed the door behind us and I went and sat on the edge of the bed. She came over and stood in front of me. I looked up at her, tracing her body with my hands until I finally locked eyes with hers. She was absolutely beautiful, even after three weeks of terror. And now she was about to willingly face it again.

"I still don't want you to go," I told her.

"Don't start," she took my hand in hers. "I'm going and that's it." She kissed my hands. I pulled her down onto the bed with me, making her laugh. I kissed her cheek.

"Doesn't mean I have to like it." I kissed her hard and Ashley pulled me closer. Breaking my embrace she rolled on top of me and ran her finger over my lip in a playful manner.

"No, but you do have to like this." She kissed me again. We spent the next few hours just wrapped up in the bed, our bodies intertwined and almost inseparable. It was the first time in weeks that we had time alone that we didn't have to worry about zombies smashing in a window or breaking through a door. It was the most peaceful few hours I had spent with her in a long time. I loved every moment of it.

* * * * *

A while later I found myself downstairs with Alice getting something to drink. Ashley was asleep upstairs and I didn't want to disturb her. As I was sitting there replaying the last few weeks over in my head Chris came in the room. He had a small bag of bandages and the like in his hand.

"I was just about to check in your room for you," he said.

"Must have read your mind." I smiled at him and pulled a chair out for him to sit in. I sat down on the other chair and he went to work.

"Lean forward."

I complied and felt his hands dance over the bandages, unwrapping my head and putting the used bandages aside. I tried to turn and look at them, but he yelled at me to keep still. So I tried making conversation while he worked. "So you're a doctor, huh? How'd you end up here?"

"Ryan and I were on a skiing trip with some friends on the night it started. I was called by the hospital to get back immediately and we left in the middle of the night. But by the time we made it back to the city, chaos had already taken over."

"You guys have any family?" I asked.

"Nah. Ryan's girlfriend left him a month ago. I never really found time for a social life." He was distant, more focused on examining me then talking. Something was wrong.

"What is it, doc?"

"Hmm...nothing. Nothing at all."

"Don't play with me, Chris. I know something's wrong."

"No, I mean literally nothing. The wound is almost completely healed."

"Oh." I didn't understand his concern. "That's good."

"Does it hurt at all?" He asked.

"It's a bit sore."

"Doesn't make sense..." He continued to poke around the back of my head. Suddenly, I realized the problem. It had only been, what, four days since I cut my head open. It should not have healed that quickly.

"What does it mean?" My voice hid my concern. His did not.

"I have no idea. I've never seen anything like this before."

"Is there a scar?"

"Barely." He took up his materials and walked away. I could see the bandages now. They were clear. Not a single speck of blood. Now I was concerned about what the others would think. Chris was starting to exit the room and I stopped him.

"You have to put the bandages on." I said. "Why? You don't need them."

"I don't want to scare anyone, Chris."

He stood for a moment, thinking about how the others might react to my healing time. After a few minutes of silence he nodded his head in agreement.

"I'm not trying to hurt them, Chris. I just don't want anyone to get scared."

"I know," he said. I hoped he really did understand. "You won't say anything to anyone?" I asked.

"Ryan already knows, I spoke to him the other night. He'll keep his mouth shut, though. You can trust him."

"I do. Thanks, Chris."

"One condition."

"Yeah, sure."

"If I can find supplies, then I want to run a few tests."

"Tests on what?" I asked.

"Your blood. You shouldn't be able to do this."

"What do you think you'll find?" I asked. I was afraid now.

"I don't know," his voice was steady one now. "Maybe some answers. My guess is that something infected you too, but it's different somehow."

"Do you think I'll turn?"

"I have no way of knowing that right now," he said. "What I do know is that you're fine for now. Better than fine, actually. Let's just leave it at that before we jump to any conclusions."

We were both silent for a few minutes while Chris applied the unnecessary bandages. He used the old ones again to save supplies.

"Where'd you go to school?" It was a question I used to ask on a regular basis, back when it mattered, and now helped to break the uncomfortable silence that had settled in the room. "Ohio State for eight years. You?" "Penn State, only five though." We both laughed then. The two schools were bitter football rivals. It was funny to be thinking about that stuff now. "So do I still get my sample in spite of that?" he asked. "Whatever you need. If I have to trust someone from Ohio State, then might as well be you." He laughed again. When he finished I shook his hand, thanking him again and solidifying our agreement. I definitely liked Chris and I knew I could count on him in the days ahead. For now, I filed the ramifications of our conversation on the list of things to worry about later.

A little while later I took my turn at a watch and then turned in for the night. As I lay curled up next to Ashley in the bed, I couldn't help but worry about what we were going to try and pull off tomorrow. And part of me couldn't help but feel responsible for their lives and anything that would probably go wrong. But the other was, as always, focused on Ashley and her safety.

Between what Chris and I talked about and the way I was feeling about the raid, I did not get much sleep. I looked over at Ashley and watched her chest rise and fall slowly. I hoped her dreams were peaceful. I found myself staring blankly at the ceiling, waiting for morning.

Chapter Eight

I was up and dressed before the knock came on the door. I had on my boots, jeans, t-shirt and my leather jacket. I grabbed my gloves as an afterthought. I figured that with the adrenaline of today's events I wouldn't be cold, so I didn't layer up. When the knock came I was just putting on my Irish wool cap. It was Mr. Craftford at the door checking to see who was up. After he left I turned to wake Ashley. Part of me wanted to let her sleep, but the other part knew she would kill me if I left without her. As I leaned down to kiss her I was mildly surprised to see her eyes open. She was already up.

"A test?" I asked.

"Yes."

"What would you have done if I let you sleep?"

"I would have come downstairs and yelled at you," she turned and smiled at me, "Thank you. I really didn't want you to go without me." She reached up and grabbed the back of my head, pulling me down for a deep kiss. When she let go I stood up and gazed down at her. *If only this moment could last forever.*

"I'm going to go help downstairs," I said.

"I'll be down shortly."

Downstairs I found Mr. Craftford, Bill, Wes, Ryan, Chris and Elise. Jenn and Becca were still asleep. Jesse was going to wake Charlie, who was staying in the attic. Everyone was dressed in warm clothes, but nothing too bulky. Ryan was wiping down his rifle, the smell of oil indicating he had just cleaned it. Chris was packing a backpack with some bandages and dry food stuff. Bill and Mr. Craftford were looking over the lists, probably making sure everything was ready. Wes was holding a shotgun and looked tired. He was probably on watch. Elise came over to me, holding out a plate with some toast and steak on it.

"Eat up. No one is leaving until you've all eaten something." She smiled at me. Alice was at my side; her tongue rolled out, as she smelled the food. I tossed her some meat and took two slices of toast for myself. Alice ate up quickly.

"Remind me to pick up some dog food." I was semi-serious, but it brought some laughs to the room.

Ashley came downstairs then. She was dressed in hiking boots and jeans too. She had on a wool jacket and a scarf. As she came downstairs she looked at me and then beckoned me to follow her. I went with her to a hall closet. Inside the closet was a collection of tools, bats and a few guns.

"This is where they're keeping the toys." She smiled as she pulled out a sheathed machete. An arm reached past me a grabbed a shotgun.

"Mine." Charlie grinned as he grabbed a box of shells also.

"Be my guest."

Ashley smiled. "Go on, grab something fun."

I studied the closet for a few more minutes. Most of the items were handheld tools and kitchen utensils. I took a few knives and tucked them into my belt. There was a snow shovel, but that didn't seem practical. Baseball bats didn't appeal to me after the last time I tried to use one. Not finding anything appealing, I grabbed a hammer so I was not completely unarmed and went back to the living room.

"Alright, is everyone ready to go?" Mr. Craftford asked. Several calls of ready and silent head nods were his reply. I had a few knives from our previous adventures, a hammer and the truck keys. I nodded yes.

"No weapon?" Craftford asked, looking at me.

I showed him the hammer. "This will have to do until we get there."

"Suit yourself. Alright everyone, let's head out. Stay quiet through the woods."

During the trek through the pre-dawn forest I checked out my comrades. Ashley was armed with a machete, and was walking beside me. Alice was keeping pace with me and alert. I had the distinct impression she knew what was happening. Ryan and Chris both walked behind Jesse. Ryan and Jesse had rifles; Chris had a pistol and the bag of supplies. Mr. Craftford had a pair of binoculars around his neck. He didn't appear armed at first, but then I noticed a revolver around his waist. From the way he carried himself I was sure that my first impression was correct – that he had an extensive military career before all this happened.

We reached the truck without incident. After clearing the light layer of snow off of it, everyone piled in the back. Alice jumped in the cab with me.

"There's an extra seat here," I called back. Several moments of bickering later, Mr. Craftford opened the door and climbed in. Charlie knocked on the window and reminded me to drive slowly before we pulled away. Canick was seven miles from our location, and it would take awhile to get there without anyone falling out or freezing to death. The road had a fresh layer of snow on it, but not enough to warrant using the plow, which I was grateful for, since it was loud and would attract attention.

87

After a while of driving in silence I decided to try and figure out more about Mr. Craftford.

"You know what you're doing," I commented.

"Is that a question?" he asked.

"No," I replied. "I'm making an observation. My guess is you served in the military, but I would also guess you held a command position."

I took his silence as an affirmation. When he didn't say anything more I pushed a little harder. "Korea?"

"I'm not that old, damn it."

"'Nam then."

"I fought in 'Nam, yes. Also fought in Desert Storm. But I was in command during the first days of the Iraqi conflict. I retired before Iran." He turned his head and looked at our passengers. "I don't like to talk about it."

I understood exactly what he was talking about. "My stepfather was stationed at Al Ramadi in 2004 and 2005. I heard enough about that place." I wasn't going to ask anymore, but now he continued without me.

"I hated that war. It was all political. It would have been quicker, no insurgency or anything, if they just untied our damn hands. Iran was even worse." There was a hint of anger in his voice, directed toward the politicians who ran, or used to run, the country. He was silent for a few minutes, and then added, "Guess it doesn't matter now."

"Sure it does. Without a history we have nothing to live for." I looked over and met his gaze. He had a stern look, but his eyes betrayed his agreement with me. "So how come you don't take charge of this bunch?" He had the ability to do so, that was for certain.

"I'm old and retired. I'll help where I can but I'm in no mood to take charge."

"I suppose Bill is doing a good job."

Mr. Craftford snorted. "Bill is a politician, not a leader. Watch up ahead, there's a car on the right."

I saw the car, but took the comment as an indication that the conversation was at an end. The rest of the drive was quiet save for the occasional warning to avoid an obstacle. It took nearly forty minutes to reach the outskirts of town. One of the first houses we passed had a big SUV parked out front. Charlie knocked on the window, pointed, and gave a thumbs up. Mr. Craftford nodded and I pulled over.

I got out of the cab and looked around. Charlie got out of the back and was mumbling something about the cold when we heard the moan. Everyone stopped and scanned the area. Alice was looking in the direction across the street. I followed her gaze to the second floor of a house across the street. A body hung from the second floor window, a rope noose hung around the neck. I pointed and everyone looked over.

"Son of a bitch," Charlie said.

"Damn shame that is. Look, in the window…two more." Ryan was right. There were two more up there now moaning along with the one on the rope. No one had to say it, we could all figure out what happened.

"Let's hurry up, they will attract more." I started moving to the house while Alice followed closely behind. Charlie started to head for the truck.

"Don't touch it," I warned.

"Isn't that what we're here for?"

"Not without keys."

"Maybe they're inside."

"And maybe it has a car alarm." I looked right at him, almost daring him to take the risk. He backed away and followed us to the house. I looked inside the windows before going any further. There didn't seem to be an alarm. I tried the door handle and it swung open.

"Chris, sweep and clear," Ryan called as he moved past me. The two of them moved through the door, weapons raised, calling out to each other as they moved. Mr. Craftford nodded approvingly at their actions. Jesse went in next, followed by myself and Alice. Ashley stayed near the front with Charlie, watching for approaching trouble.

"Ryan, on the left!" Chris called out.

"Don't shoot it! I got him!" I heard the distinctive sound of a gun butt smashing flesh and something fall to the ground, followed by two more whacks. As I entered the next room I saw a zombie face down on the ground, blood coming from the back of its head. It gave a twitch and Ryan brought the butt of the rifle down again. It stopped moving.

"Bottom floor clear. Moving upstairs." Ryan, Chris and Jesse proceeded to the staircase while the rest of us started looking around downstairs.

"Here are the keys." Mr. Craftford grabbed a set off the hook near the kitchen door. I poked around a few closets, hoping to find a more useful weapon.

"Hey! Jackpot up here!" Ryan called down the steps. We all went upstairs to find a den, complete with deer heads on the wall and a glass gun case against the back. Ryan smashed it open and proceeded to take stock.

"Grab everything." He said as Jesse started to grab a rifle off of the rack. There were four of them, as well as two handguns, a compound bow and a police baton. The baton I found appealing and took it for myself. It wouldn't have the range of a shovel, but I could probably use it well enough.

"Take this," Ryan said as he passed me a hand gun.

"I'm not a very good shot." I said.

"You don't have to be. This is a 9mm Beretta, not a lot of stopping power, but definitely accurate. And this," he pointed to a tube mounted below the muzzle, "is a trigger activated laser sight. Lightly press the trigger, the sight comes on, pull back all the way to fire. Look, our boy even has a shoulder holster and extra clips already loaded."

"How do I reload?" I asked, unfamiliar with the weapons inner workings.

Ryan grinned as he showed me the mechanics of the gun and I slung the holster over my shoulder. He pointed out that most holsters go under jackets, so I went ahead and adjusted my set-up. I felt confident enough with the weapon. If nothing else, then at least I could take down a red-eye with it. No longer limited to knives, I felt a bit more useful.

"This is my new toy." He picked up a menacing looking weapon off the rack. "AR-15."

"Looks pretty."

"You have no idea. Closest thing I'll find to an M-16 out here I guess."

"Hey! Hurry up and grab what you want. There's two coming across the street and a few more down the road," Ashley called from downstairs.

"Put the weapons in the SUV so they don't get wet. Careful with the ammo." Ryan directed. We all grabbed everything we could and in one trip cleared out the gun cabinet. Loading up our new vehicle, we split into two groups. The first group was myself, Mr. Craftford, Charlie and, of course, Ashley and Alice. The second group was Ryan, Chris and Jesse.

"Alright, let's find that Wal-Mart." Mr. Craftford rattled off a series of turns we were supposed to make from some hand written directions Bill gave him as we continued onward.

The town was a wreck. Ghouls were everywhere. Cars were crashed, windows broken, and evidence of fire either from smoke or smoldering ruins littered the view. The woman who killed herself was no longer the most horrific thing after a few minutes of driving. You could not find a quiet scene as we moved further and further into town. Every now and again I would be forced to knock zombies aside with the plow. One got stuck on the front and dragged with the truck. What could

91

only have been the stench of flesh being dragged on concrete added to the perverse smell of flames and rot in the air.

Around the next corner I was forced to stop the truck and take a deep breath. In the street was a small child. It was the first time I saw a child turned into one of them. The child was no more than eight or nine years old. I suppose part of me wanted to believe children were safe…that my students were safe. Seeing the young boy there, clothes tattered, blood stains around the mouth, eyes that haunting gray and black staring at the truck…seeing that boy shattered the last bubble of hope I had built around myself.

I opened the door and got out of the truck. Mr. Craftford was silent, watching me. From the back of the other vehicle I heard calls of "What's going on?" but I ignored them all.

As I approached the child its arms stretched out toward me. The hollow moan escaped its lips. Like so many others, it was focused on a single purpose: feed. I moved toward the child. It was close enough to grab hold of my arm. Its grip was firm, but had no more strength than a normal child. As it tried to bite me I shoved it away. I pulled out my new pistol, placing the sight on its forehead. My vision blurred slightly. I pulled the trigger. The shot rang out. The round found its mark. The body crumbled to the ground. A wetness ran down my face. I said a short prayer, even though I was not convinced any god could let this happen to the world. I then went back to the truck. No one said anything. I got in and started driving, taking care not to run over the body of the dead child.

"Make the next left. Two miles on the right should be our target," Mr. Craftford said quietly as he handed me a cloth.

I took the cloth and wiped away the tears, "Sorry."

"Don't apologize. You did what you had to," he said. He seemed to regard me with more respect.

A few minutes and several obstacles later our destination was in view. The parking lot was a mess. We stopped at the entryway and got out of the truck to look around. Mr. Craftford got onto the bed of the truck, binoculars in hand, trying to see if we had a way in.

"How's it look, sir?" Chris asked as he moved toward us.

"Walkers on the right. Few minutes we have to move," Ryan warned. We all glanced in the direction he indicated. They were lumbering toward us, but we had some time. Out in the parking lot I could see others moving in our direction.

Mr. Craftford lowered the binoculars. "No way we're getting to the front door. Too many are in the way." He brought the binoculars back up, trying to find an approach.

In the small plaza where we were parked there were a few other stores. None of them would have anything useful, though. I was looking at the names of the stores I used to shop when I saw something move out of the corner of my eyes, too swift to be a zombie…at least a normal one.

Instinctively, I raised the baton. Alice stood next to me, low and crouched. She saw it too. I could hear the others behind me, but was unwilling to turn and look, not wanting to miss whatever was out there among the debris and dead.

I saw the shadow again, dodging behind a car. In the same car was a zombie, clawing at the glass. I ignored it and kept watching for the shadow. I took a few steps forward, slow and cautious. It ran between two cars. This time I caught a glimpse of fur. Animal of some sort. I backed away toward the others. Alice held her ground. As I backed up, I called for the others, who now watched with interest and raised weapons, except for Jesse. He kept his eyes on the nearest of the approaching ghouls.

There were two of them, a Labrador and a Sheppard. They came out from behind the cars slowly, ears pinned back, teeth exposed. They were looking at Alice, her own teeth bared in response. These dogs were feral, surviving on instinct these last few weeks. I drew my pistol, getting ready to shoot if they attacked. At the same time, I called to Alice, trying to get her to back up. She moved away slowly.

After a few tense moments, the ferals slunk away into the shadows. Alice and I returned to the group, although she kept glancing in the direction the other dogs went. I guessed she was wondering what happened to them. It was time to move again.

"Alright, everyone. Add it to the list of shit we need to watch out for. Here's what we're going to do." All our attention was back on Mr. Craftford. "On the right hand side there is a tunnel they use to get shopping carts into the entryway. We can drive the trucks over that way, back them right up to the tunnel entrance. We'll push the carts into the store to make an entrance and deal with any zombies there. Then we shop."

I nodded, already moving to the driver's seat. The sooner we got in, the sooner we got out. Everyone else got back into their seats and we were off on the next part of the trip. I followed Mr. Craftford's directions around the lot, knocking aside ghouls and debris with the plow. As soon as I put the truck in park I got out and struck a nearby zombie with the baton. I definitely did not enjoy the lack of range or certainty of a kill. I decided that finding a shovel or something with a sharp blade would be my first priority once we were inside.

Mr. Craftford began giving orders immediately, "Alright, everyone inside, just like we talked about. Fifteen minutes and then we're back out here. Yell if you get in trouble and we'll find you. Jesse, honk if they get too close or if there are too many for you. Ready?" Everyone nodded. "Go!"

Ryan and Chris went under the cart tunnel first with Charlie close behind. Mr. Craftford and Ashley went in next. Alice and I brought up the rear. By the time I stood back up, the carts had been pushed in front of the door and two dead zombies lay on the grated entryway, victims to the butt end of Ryan and Chris' rifles. Mr. Craftford passed out lists, each team grabbed a cart, and we went off to get the items on our lists.

Ashley and I were responsible for the tools and weapons list, so we went straight for sporting goods. We tried to move quickly but had to stop twice at blind corners. There were plenty of zombies in the store and we could hear the moans being echoed throughout the building. The power was still on though, so we didn't have to work in the dark. We made it to sporting goods without a problem and began throwing various pieces of equipment in the cart. Bats, golf clubs, fishing poles...whatever we could grab. Our list was relatively vague as to specific needs.

"Hon, grab those water bottles there." She pointed at a shelf and I started grabbing and tossing. "And watch behind you." I turned and saw a nearby zombie reaching out for me. I swung out with the baton and connected with its shoulder. It stumbled a bit from the force but kept coming. Ashley came from the left and brought her machete to bear, severing the head from the shoulders. The body collapsed and the head rolled to the floor. The ghoul's eyes still searched and the jaw snapped, so I kicked it away in disgust.

"That thing isn't very good." She pointed to the baton.

"No, not really." I threw it to the ground. "Think I'll get me one of those fancy knives." I looked at her machete. It was a good weapon choice. I looked into our cart and grabbed one of the several we had picked up, tearing open the packaging. It had a sheath and a belt clip, so I took a moment to attach it to my left hip. Then we went back to gathering supplies.

"Gun case over there." I pointed to the back wall of sporting goods. We both moved over to the case. Alice barked at a ghoul coming down the adjacent aisle. I drew my new weapon and moved to dispatch it. One swift motion from right to left removed its head. Four more were behind it, moaning with arms outstretched. I heard glass break behind me and spared a glance to see Ashley smashing the case and grabbing boxes of ammo. There were no real guns, just air rifles and pellet shooters, useless to us, but the ammo was real.

In front of me, the next zombie was reaching out. Again, I went to dislodge its head, but its arm got in the way of my swing; the machete became lodged in its shoulder. I spun to dislodge it and kicked out with my opposite leg, freeing my weapon and sending the zombie back a few paces, bumping into the others.

"Hurry!" I called out to Ashley.

"I got most of it. Let's go!" I heard the cart move down the aisle and turned to meet up with her. Alice went ahead, seeking out a path. "We have to get tools!" Ashley shouted at me.

A gun shot rang out from across the store. There was a shout and then more shots. It clearly wasn't a shotgun, so I assumed it was either Ryan or Chris. Over the gunshots, I thought I heard a horn honk, but the noise made it difficult to be certain.

We made it to the hardware department and started grabbing hammers, nails, shovels...anything. The cart was getting heavy and would be difficult to maneuver. As I was about to start heading back for the entrance Alice barked and grabbed my attention just in time. A zombie came from a blind corner and attached itself to my back. I felt its hand grab my arm and waist and felt its mouth enclose around my shoulders. *Shit! It was biting me!*

I slammed my body backward, trying to dislodge its grasp. Alice bit at its pant leg and pulled at it, trying to help. It had a firm grasp on my arm, making it more difficult to break free.

"Stand still!" Ashley yelled at me.

"*Attention shoppers. Time to get the fuck out!*" Jesse's voice came over the intercom. I barely heard it over the snarl at my shoulder, Alice's growling, and Ashley yelling at me to stand still.

Fuck this! I reached into my jacket with my free hand and pulled out the 9mm. I put it right against the zombie's head. The sound was deafening in my ear. The zombie released its grip on me and fell to the floor. Straightening myself up, I looked at my shoulder. There were bite marks in the leather, but it didn't break the skin anywhere. I was lucky.

I felt a tap at my shoulder. I looked at Ashley. She was saying something, but I couldn't tell what. Behind her were two more of the undead, and I raised the pistol and dropped them both with two well-placed rounds. I really enjoyed the laser sight. The ringing in my head from the first shot still overpowered everything, though after a moment, I was able to make out, "Are you okay?"

"I'm alright. Let's get the hell out of here."

We ran back toward the entrance. Jesse, Chris and Ryan were waiting. We could see Charlie and Mr. Craftford making their way from the food aisles.

"Going to be tough getting into the trucks, there's a whole shit load outside now," Jesse said.

"We'll draw them off. Just dump everything in the pick-up and we'll deal with it later." Ryan released the safety on his new rifle and nodded to Chris. They both moved back to the cart entrance and ducked outside. Gunshots soon followed.

Mr. Craftford reached us then. "Let's go, now!"

We all followed, shoving the full carts under the entryway. Charlie joined Ryan and Chris, who were in front of the trucks picking off approaching zombies. Jesse and I picked up the first cart and overturned it into the back of the truck. She went to the cab and started it up while Mr. Craftford stood facing the entryway.

Shots rang out from Ryan's AR-15 and Chris' new hunting rifle. We were dumping the last cart when the bullets stopped.

"Umm…guys…" Charlie called out to us as we were putting the cart down.

97

"What?" Mr. Craftford was rearranging stuff so it would not fly out the back. He stopped and looked around. We all stopped. The zombies were not moving. All around us were hundreds of zombies, just staring at us. No moans, no movement. Just blank, black stares. I knew what was happening.

"Everyone get in the trucks. Now." I held the pistol up, searching the horde. Ashley was in the driver's seat of the truck already and opened the passenger door for Mr. Craftford. Alice jumped in the cab with them.. I jumped in the bed of the truck. Chris made it to the SUV and got in, crawling over to the driver's seat. Charlie and Ryan followed. Jesse was near the front of the plow, edging his way slowly to the back. He reached the side and jumped in next to me. As soon as he was in, Ashley started forward, shoving the undead out of the way with the plow.

The scream was unlike anything I had ever heard. It was loud enough to get her to stop and look left. Standing on the hood of a car about seventy feet away was a red-eye. Flanking it were two more.

"Go! Go! Go!" I cried out. The truck lurched forward and began accelerating faster as the creatures began running toward us. They moved with incredible speed. Jesse stood up and began firing at them. I yelled at him to get down. It was hard enough to stand up with everything piled around and underneath us. At twenty-five feet he pegged one in the leg. I couldn't believe they were closing with the truck. We had to be going at least thirty by now. The one he hit went down, knocking over one of the others. The third was too close. It would reach us.

One of my favorite things to do before the outbreak was to go to the movies. I was an avid fan of cheesy sci-fi movies with great special effects, my favorite being when everything just slowed down and went into slow-motion. Whether it was a guy dodging a bullet, or a pair of swords meeting or even a car wrecking in a crash, it was my favorite effect. I never thought it would actually happen in real life.

The red-eye leapt out of the horde of undead alongside the truck from five feet out. Jesse tried to fire. I tried to get a shot off also, but I was moving too slow. It flew through the air and connected with Jesse, sending both of them tumbling over the side of the truck. As I heard Jesse scream, time sped up again and I could see a mass of undead gather round him. Ashley was about to stop the truck, but didn't; Mr. Craftford kept her focused. He knew as well as I did that Jesse was done. Blood splattered onto the SUV trailing us, confirming what I feared. They were tearing him apart.

I heard another scream. The second red-eye had recovered and was running toward us. It leapt out of the crowd aiming for me. I dodged to the side as it landed in the truck. I felt a sharp pain in my side. I had fallen onto something sharp and it felt like it was deep in my ribs. I tried to ignore the pain as I brought the pistol to bear. Pulling the trigger...once... twice...three times. The red-eye fell off the back of the truck and was run over by the SUV. I didn't move.

A few moments later the truck stopped. The SUV doors opened and Chris came running up to the truck. Ashley was already in the bed of the truck.

"Don't move."

"What? Why?"

"There's a screwdriver in your rib." Chris said.

"Oh. Right." I was still dazed, which was good, because it lessened the pain that shot through me when Chris pulled the tool out of my side.

"You're okay. It hit mostly bone." Chris put a bandage on to stop the bleeding.

"Let's get moving." Mr. Craftford said from up front. He was sliding into the driver's seat. There was a moan on the right. A zombie was near. Ashley and Chris helped me into the back of the SUV, and then we sped off back home.

No one spoke the whole ride back. Mr. Craftford used the CB to contact Bill. They had opened the gate at the bottom of the road while we were gone. We wouldn't have to carry anything back. He never mentioned Jesse. They would find out soon enough.

We got back without much trouble, stopping only once for fuel. We didn't have much energy left, so our plan to load up didn't go through. We filled a few containers, the trucks, and left. We no longer felt the sense of adventure. That had been replaced by a sense of loss.

We reached the end of the road some while later. The gate was open. We stopped and kept the SUV by the gate. Everyone piled into the truck. Still no one spoke. We drove up the driveway. The others were waiting outside for us.

No one said anything. None of the others had to ask what had happened to Jesse. Tears welled up in Elise's eyes. Jenn went back into the house. Bill put his head down and uttered a prayer.

At that moment, the snow began to fall.

$\mathcal{P}$art II

How is it that mankind was able to survive? That is a question that we tend to answer with pride, now that the worst fighting is over. We faced almost insurmountable odds against an enemy that was hard to kill, but we managed to pull ourselves together and defeat the undead. Scholars and historians would give you a number of reasons why we were going to win, be it our intelligence (an invalid argument against red-eyes), or our ability to function in regions and in conditions that they could not.

I can tell you why we survived, and it is not because of any reason you've read about on the net. It was because mankind evolved. Our civilization was flipped upside-down and instead of dying off or succumbing to the change, we adapted our entire existence to survive in the new world.

Of course, when you consider that every single one of us was changed in one way or another, then there is a strong argument that mankind did not survive the zombie apocalypse at all.

Everyone died.

Chapter Nine

The rest of the winter was long and cold. However, in our forest hideaway we managed to scrape together an existence that was borderline civilized. We raided Canick three more times in two months, but we never ventured deep. We limited ourselves to houses on the outskirts and a gas station about a mile outside of town. We never had to fight off more than twenty in a raid, and we only saw one more red-eye who Ryan was able to dispatch from afar.

Our biggest scare came from Becca, who came down with a nasty flu in late February and early March. Chris and Elise spent every minute of every day trying to make her better. She was getting so thin at one point that Mr. Craftford began discussing where she would be buried.

It was always interesting when we all sat around and discussed what we should be doing. Everyone was there, but four people usually dominated the conversation. Bill, who was always trying to balance the discussions; Mr. Craftford, who discussed general ideas and what we needed to do; Elise, who would talk about food and supplies; And, surprisingly, Wes, who had become incredibly useful in designing some of our more elaborate defenses that we had built around the cabin.

The cabin had been transformed from someone's vacation spot into our personal fortress. Every window on the bottom floor was boarded up. The doors were able to be fortified at any moment with a second door nailed over it that we pulled from one of the houses we raided. Outside, the porch railing had been extended to the ceiling, creating an enclosed area that we could still see through. Wes had come up with the idea of building a small ramp to the door of the truck. A person could now get into the truck from the porch with some pretty decent protection. The sliding door out of the back of the living room was sealed completely.

We still kept the SUV by the gate and the keys were in a coffee can on the ground nearby. Again, Wes had the idea that the keys shouldn't be kept at the house. The truck keys we kept in the truck since it was close to the cabin.

I kept myself busy by helping out as much as possible and training with Ryan and Chris. At Mr. Craftford's suggestion, everyone practiced with them to become more proficient with the variety of weapons we had in store. Though we didn't fire many rounds because we needed to conserve ammo, Ryan did teach everyone basic breathing and movement techniques with firearms. They also oversaw our practice with melee weapons. I tried to practice with the machete daily, becoming more comfortable with the feel of the blade. Chris also showed me how to make use of the various knives I liked to carry by learning to throw them. We made a mock target in the yard and eventually a game out of it, and I started to become more accurate each day.

I also started getting up early with Ryan and Chris, who spent the mornings working out in order to stay in shape. In a month I had managed to get in the best shape of my life. Chris was surprised with how quickly my body adapted to the physical stress, but that was among other things he was surprised about.

The wound I had received in our first raid was completely healed in three days. Chris still had no idea why or how I could do that. The scar betrayed how quickly it healed though, now a red and pink mark on my skin. Chris said that could only mean my body was regenerating quicker than it should. His only theory was that I was infected with something, possibly the same thing as the undead. It was a chilling thought. The idea that I had something in common with those mindless aberrations was very disturbing. Whatever was happening to me was not something Chris and I shared with the others. I refused to even tell Ashley about it.

She adapted well to our new existence, probably better than any of us. Ashley was always the one that everyone talked to when they were upset. Something about the way she spoke made others trust her explicitly. Every time I would see her listening to one of the others I felt truly lucky that I was the one who won her heart a long time ago. But at the same time I was also very protective of her, especially after what happened to Jesse. We had argued quite a bit when I adamantly refused to let her go on another raid. She had been angry with me for three days after that first episode.

When she wasn't consoling one of the others Ashley spent most of her free time writing in her journal. I was never certain what it was that she was writing, but whatever it was must have brought her some measure of comfort. There were only a few times over those months that I saw her with her hand grasping the silver charm.

Then there was Alice. Alice and I had bonded in a way that I had only read about before the apocalypse. Pre-zombies, I used to read these stories about how dogs and humans who spent a lot of time together had a connection that was indescribable. The only difference was we had established that connection in a manner of weeks, instead of years. She could read me so clearly that sometimes I felt like I could actually talk to her. And after I took care of her when she was wounded, that bond only strengthened.

* * * * *

It was about two days before the last major snowfall that hit us, sometime around the beginning of March. We needed some more gas for the generator and were planning to hit the gas station about two miles south of Wal-Mart. It was far enough away from the main horde that had now drifted to the East. We figured out that the zombies would move in the direction of known prey until they lost all sign of it. Then they would just drift around until they caught wind of something new to hunt.

The plan was simple enough. A smaller group this time would go in using only the truck. We would find anything we could on the way that would hold gasoline, fill up when we got there, and then get out as quickly as possible. Of course, nothing ever went exactly as planned. We drove into Canick and took the side alleys to the gas station. Most of the ghouls we encountered along the way met the plow on a very personal level. When we reached the gas station, Ryan and Chris cleared the immediate area while Charlie headed for the pumps.

My job was to stand about twenty feet away and draw attention to myself. That was something we came up with on the way. If Ashley found out that I was acting as bait, then I would probably have my knees broken so I couldn't go. I jumped out of the truck, Alice at my side, drew my pistol and shot it in the air. The two dozen or so zombies in the immediate area focused on me and began walking in my direction. Meanwhile, Ryan and Chris took down the ones who took an interest in Charlie using melee weapons to avoid extra attention.

Standing in the parking lot about fifteen feet away from the truck and with Alice at my side, I drew my machete and waited for them to get close. I easily took down the first two, but the next wave brought three in range at the same time. I swung sideways at the first, lodging the blade in the side of its head. The second grasped at my arm as I shoved it away and slashed at its leg. It dropped to its knee while I finished my spin, bringing me around to face the third. Alice grabbed the arm of the one on the ground and prevented it from standing up again while I dealt with the final ghoul. That's when they struck. Seemingly out of nowhere, two feral dogs lunged from the left and knocked Alice away. I only caught a blur in my eye as I was turning back. I drew my pistol again, ready to fire, but the tangle of fur made it impossible to find a target. Two more zombies were on me then, drawing my attention. I rolled between them, closer to where Alice could be seen with her jaws around the throat of one of her attackers.

I called out to the others just as the head of a zombie next to me exploded in a shower of coagulated blood. Ryan had already seen what was happening and had brought his AR-15 to bear on the zombies as he moved closer to us. I could hear Chris urge Charlie to finish up over the clatter of the semi-automatic rifle. He was pointing down the street and I followed his arm to see a mass of the undead coming toward us, attracted by the moans of the ones in the immediate area and the gunshots that now echoed from Ryan's rifle.

Alice threw off one of her attackers and I managed to get a shot off before it could get back into the fray. My shot went wide, but it slowed the dog's advance and brought its attention to me. My second round found its mark in the dog's hip, sending it back a few feet. The third shot struck its side and ended its fight.

Having lost its hunting partner the other one relinquished its grip on Alice and ran off past the legs of the approaching horde. I holstered my weapon and ran over to Alice, who was bleeding from two spots. One wound was on her left leg and the other was near her neck. I reached over to the body of a nearby ghoul and tore the tattered shirt enough to make a crude bandage.

Chris, Ryan and I spent the ride in the bed of the truck trying to help Alice while Charlie drove. Chris bandaged her up the best he could. He even gave her some antibiotics, but wasn't sure if the dose would help a dog. When we got back Chris and I spent a few hours cleaning her wounds the best we could. Chris even stitched up the particularly brutal tear on her leg. After that, all we could do was wait.

* * * * *

Alice still had a slight limp, but for the most part was doing fine. I watched her playing in the front of the cabin with Becca, who was gently tossing a ball around with her. It was warm out for the first time in weeks and the snow was melting, so we took advantage of the weather and went outside. Ryan was with me, showing me how to clean and maintain firearms. Charlie and Mr. Craftford were with Wes, who was placing boards between certain trees. We didn't have enough material to build a wall, but the guys came up with the idea of creating choke points around the house. I didn't know if it would work, but it was worth a shot. And it gave us something to take pride in, which was something we all needed.

Elise and Chris were preparing lunch in the kitchen. They were getting close and something told me not to completely attribute it to being in close-quarters for the last few weeks. I could even see Becca treating Chris as a father-figure. I didn't think Chris would mind the added responsibility. In fact, I had a feeling he would embrace it.

Jenn was probably upstairs. She took Jesse's death the hardest. Although she never said anything, I suspected in the few days they spent together they had built a relationship. They gave each other hope. When he died in Canick she lost that thread of hope that she had been clinging on to and slipped into depression. We all agreed to keep a close eye on her.

Bill was in the backroom on the CB radio. Every day he spent an hour before meals trying to raise someone. A few times he was successful, but the people he made contact with were either unable or unwilling to come here. He would spend the afternoon listening for radio broadcasts and would undoubtedly try the television again later in the evening, like he did every other day. The last of the television stations had gone out a few days ago.

Before it went out all together, the television was our only source of news. From what we saw the entire world was in sorry shape. Across the globe the undead were ravaging everything in their path. There was no identifiable pattern to the epidemic, so no one really knew how it started. Red-eyes were seen on video controlling the others, so we were not unique in our finding. There was one video taken that appeared to show the red-eyes communicating with each other, like they were having a conversation, but the camera man met his end too quickly to confirm what was being seen. When they killed Jesse they were definitely acting in a coordinated manner, but we had rationed that as "animal instinct," not conscious communication.

The red-eyes were definitely the most immediate threat. They were strong, very fast and intelligent. But they did not require a headshot to kill, so that was an advantage for us. They also didn't have anywhere close to the numbers that the others did. One military spokesman put their numbers at 1 in every 1,000, but that figure was impossible to confirm. Although it was apparent that they formed packs and worked in tandem with each other, which made them dangerous. According to that same spokesman, they were responsible for the first attack on the White House.

That had turned out to be the first major psychological blow to the nation as a whole. In the first 72 hours of the outbreak the White House had been attacked. The President's youngest daughter had been bitten, but they escaped via helicopter. A few days later, Air Force One crashed in mid-flight. At the scene of the wreckage the President's former staff, now undead, were seen walking around the wreckage. The marines that responded found the President's body. What little was still intact from the crash had evidence of bite marks. The newscasters never said it, but we could all piece together what happened.

There were quite a few incidents that rocked our nation. It was one thing to know you're in trouble, but it was another to know everyone was in just as much trouble as you were and they probably weren't coming to help. The media made plenty of mistakes in their last days. Survivors did not need to see that the military was being overwhelmed, or the remnants of a once strong military base. We did not need to see the satellite imagery of zombie hordes so large they stretched on for miles. We did not need to see zombies that had survived a nuclear blast after whoever was acting President dropped a warhead on Seattle. Hell, we didn't need to know that what was left of the government was so desperate that they were resorting to nuking our own cities.

So that left us trying to carve out a living in the wilderness. We worked at staying safe, staying comfortable and staying alive until the world could start to sort itself out (if that day ever came). Of all of us, Ashley was the only one who seemed to be okay with being completely cut-off from the world. She spent most of her time picking up our spirits and giving us hope. She also spent a lot of time writing, but she wouldn't let anyone see what she had written. Knowing her, she was documenting everything and felt no need to remind everyone of what had already happened. Between Ashley's journal,

Bill's log of information and our experiences in Canick we really knew a lot about what was happening, but at the same time we still felt helpless, lost and confused.

Ashley came outside as Ryan and I were talking football. We had both been avid fans before the outbreak. We were laughing over how we missed the Super Bowl when she opened the door and stepped onto the porch.

"Hello, boys."

"Hey," Ryan said.

"Hello, love."

"Busy, are we?" Her smile eliminated any chill that was left in the air.

"Showing your boy here how to care for his toys." Ryan chuckled and stuck his thumb in my direction.

"Well, play nice." She turned to me. "When you're done, would you come upstairs a moment?"

"Of course. Everything alright?"

"Fine. Just want to show you something."

"Alright. Be up in a little while."

"Thank you, dear." Ashley went back into the cabin and I heard her climb the steps inside.

Ryan had a devious look on his face. I threw a rag at him, knowing what he was about to say.

"Wish someone would show me something." He laughed, knowing I could take a joke.

"Well, last I heard there were a few ladies in town that would love to have a bite with you."

"Ha! Tempting, but I'm not a fan of teeth."

"We're messed up."

"Whole fuckin' world is, bro." He shook his head.

I put the cleaning brush I was holding back on the deck of the porch and went upstairs. I found Ashley in the room we unintentionally took over. She was inside staring out the window. I walked up behind her and slipped my hands around her waist. She turned her head and kissed my cheek.

111

"Hey." She said.

"Hi." We stood in silence a moment. Both of us looking outside into the forest. Our room had a view out the side of the cabin, perfect for sunrises. The forest was unspoiled before us and seemed to stretch on for miles. It was a touching scene until you remembered the undead are probably out there somewhere waiting to feed on you. She gently spun around and kissed me. I held her loosely in my arms enjoying the peaceful setting.

"What did you want to show me?" I asked, almost regretting instantly that I broke the serenity of the moment.

"Nothing really."

"Oh?"

"I just wanted to spend some time alone with you."

"We haven't had much of that lately." Even at night, between watches and everything else, we really hadn't had a peaceful moment like this since we first arrived. But the look on Ashley's face and the way she was standing betrayed her thoughts. Something was bothering her. I knew better than to ask directly because she would just deny it or dance around the subject, so I decided to dance around a few subjects myself to see if I could stumble upon it.

"How is Jenn?" I asked. Even if it had nothing to do with her current state, I was curious. Ashley would probably know better than anyone else.

"She's...troubled."

"Jesse meant that much to her?"

"No. Well, not exactly. It's complicated."

"I have time." I smiled comically at her as I glanced at my watch. She sighed, smiled and then dove into her explanation as she moved to the bed and sat down.

From what Ashley learned about Jenn she used to have an older brother who was killed by a drunk driver. Jenn claimed that Jesse could have been a long lost brother of the family because of how much they looked alike. When Jesse left for Canick and didn't come back, Jenn experienced similar emotions that she went through when her brother died. I felt bad for Jenn. She had attached herself to a "new" brother who disappeared just like the last one. Still, there was another problem that I knew about I had to discuss with her.

"She'll have to get over it soon," I said.

"She will. She needs time, though."

"It's better if she pulls herself together soon."

Ashley stared at me for a moment. "Why are you being so cold?"

"Craftford is grumbling about her not pulling her weight."

"Crotchety old man..."

"With a point," I cut her off before the rant could get started. "We're in this together and she hasn't done anything. Hell, even little Becca helps out." Elise always had Becca help with the dishes after our group ate. Jenn sometimes never even came downstairs and we had to take food to her.

"And what happens if she doesn't? What do we do? Make her leave?" She was standing again, this time with her hands on her hips, clearly agitated that this was even being discussed.

"I don't know."

"Well, then, there's no reason to be so cold toward her." She turned away from me, facing the door. "I don't like Craftford's influence on you."

"Huh?" I didn't quite get what Ashley meant.

"You and him are always talking in hushed tones or in separate rooms. It makes the others, including me, uncomfortable. Same thing with Chris."

"Chris is usually checking my bandages. I don't know if you remember, but I've been a bit beat up lately." I tried to check my attitude, but Ashley never used to accuse me of anything before, and now I was getting the impression that she didn't trust me. That bothered me.

"Don't be a smart ass. If you're just changing bandages, then why am I never allowed in the room!" she yelled.

She caught me off guard. Now I knew what was bothering her. I could read her face clear as day now. Even her blue eyes, usually a mystery, showed that her concern was solely over me. "That's what's bothering you." The thought escaped as a declaration, not as a question.

"What is wrong? Why are you and Chris always alone?"

I stayed silent for a moment.

"Were you bitten?" Her look was serious, but I couldn't help but chuckle a bit.

"I'm pretty sure you would have known that by now." I already felt guilty for laughing. She was angry with me, but still worried.

"Then what the hell is going on?" The venom in her voice paralyzed my laugh.

I stared at her, wondering what I would say and how I would say it.

"Well..." Ashley prodded. I had to say something. She turned to leave the room.

"I don't know."

She stopped at the door and turned back to face me. "What?"

"I don't know what's wrong." It was not the answer that she wanted, but it was the best I could give her.

"What does that mean?" She asked.

"It means that something happened to me, but neither Chris nor I know what."

Her confusion was understandable. I continued my lame explanation the best I could. "I have been healing fast. Too fast. And Chris said my reactions are quicker than they should be. He also said that I should not have been able to get in shape this quickly."

"Huh?"

114

"See, that's why I didn't tell anyone. Chris and Ryan are the only ones who know. I'm quicker and stronger then I should be." I told her.

"You've been working out with them. You're training with ex-military guys and wondering why you're in better shape? That doesn't make sense."

I sighed. Ashley was missing the point. I started over after another deep breath. "You're not hearing me. My body is doing things it shouldn't be able to do. No one knows why and I don't know what to do about it. So that's..." I trailed off, not really knowing what else to say.

I wonder how she would have received this information if it was happening before the zombie outbreak. Comic books always had super heroes revealing themselves to their beloved right before saving the world. Hell, if this was happening before the outbreak I would have been really excited. But the reality was this all started at the same time the dead started to feast on the living.

The red-eyes showed evidence of superior strength and speed. Chris, Ryan and I had discussed the possibility, which usually ended with the promise from both of them that they would shoot me before I could harm anyone. What if I was just experiencing a slowed exposure to whatever had happened to the world? The thought would have been enough to drive me insane if I didn't have enough to worry about already.

I looked over at Ashley. The anger had vanished from her face and was replaced with a look of deep thought and concern. I walked over to where she was standing and put my arms back around her.

"I'm afraid," I said.

She wrapped her arms around me and pulled me down to sit on the bed. Then she started to cry. It was the first time since this all started that I saw her cry. I held her close and allowed myself to cry also. For a few minutes neither of us said anything. We just held each other and let the tears flow. Weeks of stress, pressure, running, destruction and death all built up to a single moment. Feeling each tear come out was like removing a large weight off my back. It was sad, but lifting at the same time. Holding her, letting emotions flow was strangely liberating. I felt free. And I know Ashley did too.

"I love you."

"I love you, too." I reached down to raise her head and kiss her. I wanted to feel her lips pressed against mine. I wanted to stay like that forever.

The sound of a gunshot shattered everything.

Chapter Ten

We both jumped off the bed as soon as the sound registered. I grabbed my vest off of the door rack and put it on. On the dresser waited the pistol and three clips, always full. I tucked the clips into various pockets, holstered the pistol and went downstairs.

Ashley had gone ahead of me and waited at the bottom of the steps holding my machete. I took it from her and started to strap it on as we went out the front door. I could hear Mr. Craftford coming down the steps behind us.

Outside on the porch Elise held Becca close to her. I couldn't see her face but could hear the muffled sobs. Alice was standing next to them, very protective. Chris was on his knees trying to look Becca over, but she was not cooperating. Bill had a ghostly look on his face. Wes and Charlie came running around the corner of the house trying to find out what was happening. Ryan stood motionless, rifle raised to his eye. I followed the muzzle out to the yard where a body lay in the melting snow, painting it red.

"What happened?" I asked.

"It came out of the bush, crawling. Neither of us heard anything until she screamed." Bill staggered back into the chair.

"Ryan, lower the gun. It's clear," I said.

He stood unmoving.

"Ryan?" I called his name cautiously, not sure if he heard me. He seemed to be in shock.

"It bit her," he whispered.

I stopped breathing. I think everyone did. I walked over to Ryan and put my hand on his shoulder.

"It's not your fault." I moved my other hand to the barrel of the gun and pressed it down slowly. He resisted at first but then lowered the gun and turned toward Elise and Becca. Chris was still on his knee, his hand on Becca's back, trying to coax her to show him the wound. Wes and Charlie stood silently off the porch watching.

Elise's face was the worst. It was completely drained of all color. She had a wild look in her eyes and was clearly holding back tears. She must have been using every muscle in her body to hold them back. It wouldn't last long. I walked over and knelt down on the other side.

Jenn stepped outside just as I put my hand near Becca's. Everyone spared her a fleeting glance, but quickly turned back to the scene on the chair. I could guess what Mr. Craftford was thinking.

"Becca," I whispered to the weeping girl. "It's okay sweetheart. Let's see."

In between sobs I could make out the words, "It hurts."

"Sweetie, Chris needs to see it so we can make it all better."

"Noooo…it will hurt more," she sobbed.

I decided to take a different route.

"Alice is standing here. She's worried about you. Can she see it?"

118

Becca sobbed again but loosened her grip on Elise. Slowly, she turned her body toward Chris and me. It felt like all the air was sucked out of the world as everyone stopped breathing. She turned around and lowered her arm. Blood dripped from the cuff of her shirt. Chris reached out slowly and grabbed her hand, then with his other hand took hold of her sleeve and pulled it up slowly.

My heart stopped.

Everyone's did.

There was a bite mark on her lower arm.

No one said anything for what seemed like an eternity. What are you supposed to say when…

When there is no hope…

When a little girl was going to die…

When…

When you might have to…

…kill her?

"It really hurts," Becca said between sobs.

Chris stood up slowly and backed away. I stayed where I was for a moment looking at Becca with both sorrow and dread. I hoped to God she was too young to read the expression on my face. I still pray every night that she didn't know what I was thinking in her last moments.

I stood up slowly and looked at Elise. Her face was a mass of confusion and sadness. The tears were flowing now, but not accompanied by sobs. I looked her in the eye, so that there would be no misunderstanding. It was cold, but it had to be done.

"I'm sorry, Elise."

She looked at me, confused, and then looked at the others. No one made eye contact with her. Everyone knew what had to be done, but would not face it. I couldn't blame them. This was harder to face than Jesse's death. This might be the hardest thing I'd ever face. I couldn't think of anything that could be worse.

"We have to help her," Elise pleaded.

"We can't. You know that," I whispered.

"No! Not my baby! It's only a small bite! Chris, get some medicine, quick!" She started to panic.

"It's too late, Elise." Chris was barely able to speak.

"No! No! No!" she yelled.

"Elise…" I whispered.

"Damn you! Damn all of you! Help her!" she screamed at no one in particular.

"Mommy, what's going on? It hurts!" Becca's cries only made the scene more unbearable.

"Do something!" Elise screamed.

Ashley walked over to Elise and put her arms around her. Then she whispered into her ear. Whatever she said made Elise cry even more. Ashley turned to me. Her eyes told me she would get everything under control.

"Give us a moment," she said to me.

I nodded and stepped away and off of the porch. Chris, Mr. Craftford and Ryan all gathered around me.

"I didn't see it until it had her," Ryan uttered.

"Don't blame yourself, son." Mr. Craftford put an arm on his shoulder.

"Yeah, we were all out here. None of us saw it," Charlie said quietly, walking over with Wes to join us.

"How are we going to do it?" I asked, not having to say what. Everyone was silent for a few moments. I stared at the corpse on the ground a few feet away from us. I really hated the undead.

"I'll take her into the woods and do it," Mr. Craftford started. "I've seen enough death; it won't add more to my sins."

"No," Wes said. "No one should shoot a child."

"She has to die, Wes," I said.

"Wait for her to turn, then." He said.

"Make her suffer? Make her feel the agony of constant pain while she waits for undeath? No, I already failed her. I won't see her suffer," Ryan said. He was not going to stop blaming himself for a long time.

"There has to be another way," Charlie murmured.

Chris put his hand over his mouth, and then started to speak. "I could inject her with the morphine we have."

"That would take the pain away," Ryan said.

"A high enough dose will stop her heart. Relatively painless compared to anything else," Mr. Craftford said.

"Then we shoot her when she reanimates. It'll be less painful that way," I added. Several nods were all that Chris needed to go inside and get the material. The rest of us shuffled around off the porch while we watched and waited.

I was battling with my emotions in the interim. On one hand, I was disgusted that we were able to have that conversation without a second thought. On the other hand I knew that it was necessary. It felt like the entire conversation robbed us of whatever scrap of humanity we still had left. Even though we were still alive, I felt that our souls were now truly dead.

Up on the porch Ashley was still whispering to Elise, who finally seemed to be listening. Poor Becca was still crying; whatever was coursing through her was causing blinding pain. I was reminded of my first night here, the night that put me into a coma for three days. The similarities were shocking, and I had to wonder if maybe she would turn out okay. Ashley looked down at me and nodded.

Chris came outside. He had a syringe in hand. He walked over to Elise. I couldn't make out what he said to her, but Elise nodded. Then Chris and Ashley both stepped away. Elise held Becca in her arms, sharing one last moment with her. I watched Ashley as she made her way down the steps to my side.

"What did you tell her?" I asked before Elise was near.

"The truth."

"It will be as painless as possible," I said.

"You have no idea how impossible that is for a mother," Ashley said.

"I don't think I want to know."

"Neither do I." She glanced at me and I was surprised to see a look of guilt on her face.

Elise came down the porch steps with Becca in her arms. She walked over, then Chris came and joined us.

"They're going to make you all better, sweetie." Elise struggled with the words that I didn't even know if Becca could hear, let alone understand. She handed Becca to me, although I had made no motion to suggest I would take her. I carefully scooped up Becca in my arms. I suppose I would bear the burden of killing a child.

Elise kissed Becca one last time on the forehead and started to cry. Ashley put her arm around Elise and led her back into the house. Jenn was waiting with a blanket. I turned toward the woods and started walking. The others made efforts to join me, but I silently waved them off. No one else should have to do this. Chris ignored my motion and walked with me.

"You're not going alone," he said.

"I have Alice." I wasn't arguing necessarily, but definitely pointing it out. The dog had assumed a solemn position at my side. Her head was lowered and her tail sat still between her legs. She knew.

"I'm going," Chris said firmly. There was no room for argument.

I nodded and began walking into the forest. Becca was light and easy to carry physically, but I did not know where I was finding the strength emotionally. Not in any whacko sci-fi or fantasy dream could I have ever concocted that I would be able to complete this task.

Chris led the way, rifle out as we walked deep into the forest. I made sure that we couldn't see the house. I was hoping

Elise wouldn't hear the gunshot. We found a gulley with a lot of stone. I stopped there. Becca was shuddering with sobs, but her pleas and cries had stopped. She probably didn't have the strength. I laid her down in the softening snow. Chris looked around, then knelt down and took out the syringe and a bottle.

"We're going to make you all better sweetie," he said to her.

Becca opened her eyes briefly. The edges were dusky. Any hope I had of her not turning into one of those damn monsters was gone.

Chris was about to inject her.

"Stop," I said as I put my hand on his arm holding the needle.

"What?"

"We're too late. Save the morphine." I felt her body go rigid. Her breathing stopped. Chris checked her pulse. Then he stepped back and started a timer on his watch. I looked at him quizzically.

"It would be good to know how long it takes." His voice was distant. Part of him probably felt guilty about using Becca in his way. But he was right; it would definitely be good to know. I stood up and moved a few paces back. Then I drew my pistol and silently waited.

Chris never once looked at this watch while we waited. I never asked. Both of us were silently hoping that she would just die peacefully.

It wasn't like anything like the movies. She didn't sit straight up. Her body convulsed for a few minutes, then she rolled over. Slowly, she pulled herself up, like watching a toddler stand up for the first time. She turned around. Her eyes were black. She raised her arms. I raised my pistol.

* * * * *

We used the loose rocks to cover the body. Chris said a short prayer and we made our way back. The task complete, we walked a bit slower.

"Four minutes, twenty-eight seconds." His voice was still distant. "That's how long it took, give or take a few seconds." I didn't say anything. He kept talking. "Given she is about the third of your average size human and that the bite was relatively small, I can guess the average human reanimates as a zombie in less than ten minutes on average."

"Not a lot of time," I mumbled. I suppose it made him feel better, talking it out methodically. I let him talk. He went on for a few moments about various theories he was putting together. I nodded along, but he knew I wasn't listening. Still, it was calming.

A growl from Alice brought the conversation to a halt. We stopped and looked around. Alice was facing east, left of the direction we were traveling. I couldn't see anything.

"Chris, you see anything?" I asked.

"No, nothing." He was looking down the barrel of the rifle.

I drew my machete slowly, the distinctive sound of the blade leaving its sheath a comfort in the silence. Why was it so quiet? It seemed as though even the wind had stopped blowing. Alice was still looking into the woods, her ears pinned back and her body lowered. Whatever was out there was definitely a threat.

No one made a sound.

Alice growled low.

A breeze blew through the trees. Alice raised her ears and then turned back toward us, seemingly fine. She even wagged her tail. I let out a sigh of relief.

"What the hell was that about?" Chris said, clearly relieved.

"I have no idea," I sheathed the machete, "Probably just caught a scent." Another breeze blew through the trees. Alice didn't react so we kept walking. We were halfway back when we heard the gunshot.

"Shit…" Chris said.

"Do you think?"

"Had to be Elise." He replied. Both of us were thinking she just shot herself.

Suddenly, the forest erupted with the sound of gunfire. It was the sound of Ryan's AR-15. We looked at each other once, and then started running as fast as we could. As we got closer we could hear more gunshots join the sound of Ryan's weapon. The distinctive sound of a shotgun fired off two rounds. We ran as fast as we could. Blood was racing through my veins and my muscles began to feel like they were on fire. I hadn't realized the distance we covered on our walk out into the forest.

The backside of the cabin came into view. We ran around the left side with weapons drawn. As we came around the corner we could see the bodies of several ghouls. I scanned the area. They had come from the only road in. Up on the porch Ryan was in a kneeling position on the steps. Charlie was off the porch, shotgun in hand.

"How many?" I asked.

"I counted seven," Charlie started.

"Nine," Ryan said. "Two are down behind the bush over there. Careful, I think the one is still live."

I started walking in the direction of the bush, stepping over bodies. As I passed the road in I glanced down it. They found us. Hundreds of them. The moans began.

Chapter Eleven

We were trapped.

Hundreds of zombies, maybe even thousands at this point, were outside. Every side of the cabin was swarmed. They were packed in deep, some places ten or twelve thick. We could not even go out on the porch. The broken staircase and makeshift wooden fence only held them off for a few minutes before they flopped onto the deck and hauled themselves up. Now the defenses we built were acting to keep them on the porch rather than off. The rest of our fortifications were barely worth the effort it took to make them.

They were everywhere. They were banging against the doors, every single window and even the walls. The first few hours were the worst. Every weakness in our bottom floor defense was rapidly exposed by the relentless foe. Glass was broken and arms reached through gaps in the wooden planks. Boards that were nailed wrong fell off after only a few minutes of pounding. Our back door proved to be our biggest problem. Three of the bastards actually made it inside. We had the couch wedged in there now.

We didn't have a lot of ammunition left over. We foolishly tried shooting the first waves. The AR-15, the shotgun and Mr. Craftford's revolver were almost out of ammo. I had a clip left in my gun and a few rounds in a second clip in my vest. There was still ammo for some of the rifles in the hall closet, but it wasn't much.

We were far from safe. Our defenses were meager and failed frequently. We would have to hurry to try and get our blockades back into place before they could get in. Another big problem was the red-eyes.

We knew they were out there. We had heard the screams and seen the eyes flashing in the woods and among the others. Ryan spent a lot of time trying to pick them off from the second floor windows, but it was impossible to know if he was successful. I was also certain that the red-eyes could jump or climb up that high if they wanted too. I figured it was only a matter of time before they tried.

Despite everything, the worst threat was purely psychological. Thousands of ghouls were moaning incessantly. No part of the house was safe from the sound. The only person who managed to get any sleep was Wes. I had no clue how he was able to do it. I only slept when I became completely overcome with exhaustion, and only for a few hours at a time. Ashley was in the same boat I was.

After three days of siege, we were still okay, but it wouldn't last long. Either the undead would break in, or we would go insane from the lack of sleep and constant psychological torture. The only good news was that we wouldn't starve to death. Our food would last a few weeks. We had enough to ration it and make it stretch for quite a while.

Two more days passed. Bill became angry because the power had gone out. The generator was out of fuel, and what we had was in the back of the truck beyond anywhere from twenty to fifty zombies. Without power the CB radio was useless and the plumbing didn't work. Ashley made an offhand remark that the radio would have been useless in any case, and she did make a good point. Even if someone picked up our

128

transmission, there was no way they would be able to help us. No, we were stuck. And there was a good chance we were going to die.

Eight days into the siege everyone was on edge. We had resorted to using the rest of the furniture and appliances to barricade weak points. The boards we spent so much time nailing into place just could not handle the constant banging. I was sitting in the living room, machete in hand, Alice lying at my feet when I heard Ashley scream.

I ran upstairs, ready to fight. It had to be a red-eye. When I went into the room I was greeted by Charlie.

"She fuckin' cut herself, man!"

"Who?" I hadn't seen any indication that Ashley was on the brink. I knew this was rough, but I would have seen it…

"Jenn."

I couldn't help but feel relieved. It was wrong of me, but the thought of losing my love was unbearable. If Ashley had killed herself, then I would go insane. I'd probably open the door and…

I had to get a grip. I took a deep breath, momentarily silencing the constant sound of walking death. I went into the room. Jenn's body lay on the bed, blood drenching the sheets. The knife she used was in her hand. I looked at her wrists. They were fine. I double-checked her neck. It was also fine. Then I followed the blood back to her legs. That didn't make sense to me.

Chris came in. Pausing at the door, he shook his head. Then he moved over to inspect Jenn's body.

"Is she dead?" Bill asked, following behind him.

"No, but she will be soon. She cut her femoral artery. I would need a surgical team to stop the bleeding," Chris said solemnly.

That's why she cut her leg. She knew about the artery. She knew how hard it would be to stop her. There would be no chance to save her. Ashley walked over to me then and threw her arms around me. She whispered something that I couldn't quite make out.

"I didn't even hear a scream," she repeated, loud enough for everyone to understand. Tears were beginning to soak through my shirt, so I rushed her out of the room. Elise was coming up the stairs. I paused long enough to tell her not to go in before we went into our room. When we got inside I led Ashley to the bed and we sat along the edge. She kept murmuring the same thing, over and over, "She didn't even scream."

I held her tightly. She did the same to me. I never saw her this disturbed before, even after all we had been through in the past few months.

"How could she..." Ashley choked, "...without...without making a sound?"

"Shh, shh, it's okay. It's alright. It's over now." I didn't know what else to say.

"She just..."

"Listen to me," I said softly.

"How could she?"

"Listen, please."

"I don't, I just don't..."

"Stop it." I was firm and pulled her back by her shoulders so I could see her eyes. "Listen to me, now." Ashley stopped and stared in my eyes, regaining her focus.

"Jenn was messed up from day one. She never had a grip on anything. That's not you! That's not us. We can survive. We can ride this whole thing out. We are not...going...to...die!" I stressed every single word. She was staring at me with wide eyes. I must've had a crazed look on my face. "I love you." I whispered these last words quietly.

"I love you, too," Ashley whispered.

"I'll handle it."

"I know."

I got up from the bed and went back outside the room. We were getting out.

* * * * *

At the top of the landing to the stairs I took a deep breath. I had to be calm. I walked into the room where Jenn's body lay. Chris and Ryan were wrapping the body in sheets. There were fresh blood stains coming from the head. I hadn't heard the shot. Craftford was standing in a corner. I wondered if she had reanimated or it was just a precaution. It didn't matter now.

"Leave her," I said. Chris and Ryan looked up. Mr. Craftford turned his head to face me. "We're not staying." I turned and walked out of the room and went downstairs. The others were in tow. I could hear them talking, asking what the hell I was talking about. I went straight for the weapon closet.

Opening the closet I grabbed the kerosene lamps that were in there and a box of matches. I also grabbed the last rifle and a box of ammo. When I turned back everyone was now in the living room. They were shouting at me to explain myself. What did I have to explain? I could feel the adrenaline coursing through me. There was no stopping this rush. If I didn't act now, then I probably wouldn't act at all.

I went into the kitchen and into the cabinet that held various bottles of liquor. We had been saving it for a special occasion. I grabbed a few bottles and then placed them on the table. Everyone was shouting now. I looked up at Chris and pointed toward a broken and boarded window.

"Grab that curtain. Cut it into strips." I ordered, speaking loud enough so that he could hear me clearly over the pounds and moans of the undead.

"What?"

"Now, damn it!" The look in my eyes was enough. He went over and started cutting the curtain. Ashley came in then, pushing past everyone else. She was carrying two backpacks, our designated "on the run" gear, and tossed one in my direction.

"Can someone tell me what the fuck is going on?" Wes said.

"We're leaving," I said calmly. I had taken the lids off all the bottles and was getting ready to make Molotov cocktails.

"Oh," he said. "Alright then. Umm...how exactly?"

"Make a path. Break for the woods. Get in the SUV." I was barely paying attention to the others. Craftford came forward and snatched a bottle of whiskey from me. Before I could say anything he took a long hard drink and then passed the bottle back.

"Don't waste it," he said.

I took a drink myself. The whiskey burned my throat and added to the fire pulsing in my veins. I poured the rest of the whiskey down the drain. Mr. Craftford nodded and started to help. We refilled the empty bottles with kerosene from the lamps, and then shoved strips of the torn curtain in the tops of the bottles. Crude, but it would be effective. Chris looked at Ryan. They nodded at each other and Ryan went off to the other room.

"No...we'll never make it," Elise murmured.

"You're crazy! Help will come soon!" Bill yelled.

I looked at him, shook my head, and then looked at Wes and Charlie. "If you're coming, then go pack. One bag each. Water, some food and weapons. Spare clothes if you want." Wes left the room. Charlie stood by, looking at Bill.

"Don't do it, son. We're safe here," Bill said to him.

I slammed the bottle down. "We're not safe! If these things don't break in and kill us then the lack of sleep is going to drive us insane! Our best option is to get out now before even more come. At the most they're twenty feet deep right now and that's a lot. But what about tomorrow? What about the next day, Bill?"

"Help will come," he said quietly.

"If you really believe that, then stay here and wait for it. I'm leaving with anyone who wants to go." I picked up two of the Molotov's and went upstairs. Ashley and Alice followed me. Ryan met Chris in living room and handed him a bag and a rifle. They each had their own machetes too. Wes came out of his room, bag in one hand, butcher-knife in the other. I made my way from room-to-room, looking out windows and trying to find the part where the swarm of undead was thinnest. That would be my escape route.

"We're going out through the front door," I said as I made my way back to the master bedroom. "Two Molotov's out the sides, the other out the back. We'll fight our way through the ones out the front."

"Shouldn't we just flame the ones out front?" Wes asked.

"You want to meet a friend on fire?" Ryan said, giving Wes an incredulous look.

"The others are coming with you," Mr. Craftford said as he stepped in the room.

"What did you say to them?" Chris asked.

"That if the zombies didn't break in, then one of them would probably set the place on fire after you chucked those cocktails." He grinned. "That got'em moving."

"You ready to go?" Chris asked. Mr. Craftford didn't respond.

"Sir?" Ryan prodded.

"I'm not leaving," Craftford said calmly.

I turned from the window slowly. I didn't have to say anything. He knew what question was coming.

"I'm too old for this constant running. No, I'll definitely stay here. I always wanted to retire in the country and this is as close as I'm going to get," he explained.

"John...I..." Ashley started to say, the first time I had heard his first name since we arrived.

"Don't bother, I've already decided. I'll trade you a rifle for my revolver and cover you the best I can when you make a break for it."

I looked at the rifle in my left hand. What else could I do? I decided that if was probably not worth arguing and held out my arm. He took the revolver belt off and handed it to me.

"Two rounds left," he said.

"Five in the clip, sixteen in this box." I passed him the ammo.

"Guarantee I kill twenty for you," he said as he stuck out his hand. I grasped it firmly and shook hard. I could guess what the last bullet would be used for. I broke the handshake without a word.

"Everyone ready?" I looked at Ashley when I said it. She nodded and I was on the move again without waiting for more responses.

"Chris, Ryan…Molotov's out the sides and back, then head downstairs. Door will be open by then." They nodded and left. I left the room with everyone else in tow. We went downstairs where Bill, Elise and Charlie were waiting.

"Charlie, grab the crowbar and pry the barricade down." I drew my pistol and checked it was ready and loaded before drawing the machete in my other hand. Wes pulled out his knife. Bill had a rifle and Elise had a baseball bat. I heard explosions around the house and knew the Molotov's were burning now. Charlie got the barricade down. The door underneath was splintered in multiple places. If we weren't about to open it I was sure it would have broke in a manner of minutes. Chris and Ryan came downstairs.

"I'll go first. The rest of you follow me." I clicked the safety off and nodded to Charlie. He opened the door quickly.

The first two ghouls that appeared at the door were down before they could take a step. I followed up on the third set of coal-black eyes, and then the fourth and fifth in rapid succession. Alice darted past me and between the legs of the undead, barking and drawing some of them away with her. I stepped out onto the porch and began slashing at the ghouls below me at the base of the steps. One...two...three...I fell into a rhythm.

Slash out, step forward, slash out, step forward. I spun the blade around the left and fell two more. I kicked out at the ones that were on the opposite side of my blade. Others started falling around me and I heard gunfire coming from several directions. One was about to grab my arm when its head exploded. I silently thanked Mr. Craftford and kept moving forward.

Ashley called out behind me while I was in the middle of a downward slice. I turned to see her fighting one that had grabbed her shoulder. I raised the pistol and dispatched the walking blight, then turned back to the swarm in front of me. My muscles were raging in anger. I had no idea how much time had passed. It seemed like hours but was probably closer to seconds. I slashed out at one, spun and kicked a second, then followed up with a headshot on the third.

There was a scream on my right. I saw Bill being pulled into the crowd. One bit his shoulder as another bit his arm. The undead nearest him all turned to feast on his body. Bits and pieces of him were torn off and strewn about. A shot rang out and Bill's head popped in a cloud of blood and brains. Craftford put him out of his misery. It was a better way to die.

"Nooo! Elise! Don't!" Charlie grabbed Elise as she moved to help Bill. She hadn't seen the headshot and was hoping to pull him from the crowd of the undead. I was forced to tear my eyes from the scene to deal with two more sets of ragged arms that were reaching out for me. By the time I turned back I saw Elise being ripped from Charlie. Charlie brought the shotgun to bear, but an empty click was all that came out. Craftford couldn't get a shot off from his angle and the bodies that were

135

in the way. I hoped they would tear an artery or break her neck so the pain wouldn't last long.

Alice barked furiously and leapt up to grab the arm of a ghoul that was almost on Ashley again. I emptied the rest of my clip into the heads of the undead around me. The swarm was a bit thinner now. Zombies were going into the house and after the freshly killed bodies of Bill and Elise. I holstered the pistol and took Ashley's arm with my free hand, pulling her between two more as I cut down at one in front of me.

Suddenly, I looked forward and there were not nearly as many zombies. We made it to the tree line. I turned around as the zombies behind me fell, Chris, Ryan and Charlie coming behind them. One zombie in the forest moved toward us and was dispatched by Ashley's blade.

"Wes?" I asked, looking back into the crowd.

Ryan turned back and found him. "There. Shit."

Wes was surrounded. Ryan and Mr. Craftford shot at the ones nearest to him, but the space around him was closing fast. We couldn't wait long before the gaps would close. Wes' head disappeared. I waited a moment to hear the scream confirming he was done for. But one never came. We held our ground a few moments waiting for something. I was about to tell everyone to go when a body came flying out from between the legs of the undead nearest to us. It was Wes.

"Holy Shit!" Charlie screamed. "You fuckin' crawled?"

"Yeah. Worked for the dog." He stood up catching his breath. His face said he was clearly amazed that he was still alive.

"Time to go," I ordered. Before I turned to the woods I looked up at the roof. Mr. Craftford was standing there, rifle in hand. He saluted us. I waved back to him. Chris and Ryan returned the salute. He sat down on the roof and gave us a "Why aren't you gone yet?" look. In the window behind him

136

zombies were trying to pull themselves onto the roof. We all turned to the woods.

We moved off into the woods dispatching zombies as they got in our way with our melee weapons. From where we entered the woods it would be a straight shot to the road. I felt that we were being watched, though. I stopped and drew the revolver.

"What is it?" She asked.

"We're being hunted. Red-eyes." I said slowly. I don't know if that was true, but I couldn't ignore the feeling that I had and we all knew they were around somewhere. Every hair on the back of my neck was standing straight up. Even though I couldn't see anything I could feel the eyes of our stalkers watching us from the darkness.

"Move together in a tight circle. No one break. Make sure all sides are being watched. You take point," Chris ordered as he nodded at me.

We moved slower keeping pace with one another. Ashley was on my left, Chris was on the right. Ryan and Charlie brought up the rear. No one was more than an arm's length from each other. Alice led the group slightly ahead of us.

The forest was getting dark and a breeze blew through the trees from behind us. It brought with it the scent of burning wood and flesh. I guessed the cabin had caught fire as we predicted. I hoped that Mr. Craftford had been able to get that last round off without a problem.

We kept walking slowly. Occasionally, we would come upon a group of zombies. We avoided the ones that we could, but then just decided to deal with them so that we did not get too far off course. It was in those instances where I became worried about an ambush. The ambush never came, though.

We exited the woods about a half mile down the road from the entrance to the cabin where the SUV waited. The road was almost smooth with the footprints of the horde that ended up at our cabin. I wondered how they found us. For all I knew they had been tracking us since we raided Wal-Mart.

Chris was about to take a flashlight out when I stopped him. It was dark and I had no intention of drawing further attention to us, even though I knew they were already watching from the darkness. As we walked down the road I kept my eyes on the woods. I wished for a moment that the creatures were more like the ones in the movies, and that those blood-red eyes would let off a phosphorescent glow. But it wasn't a movie anymore. Zombies really did walk the earth.

We came around a bend in the road and could see the SUV parked in the distance. Our pace quickened with the salvation from this nightmare in sight. Between us and the truck were about a dozen of the undead, and they would attract whatever more were left up the cabin road. When we were about six hundred feet away and had a few moments before the next zombie would reach us, Ryan called for a halt.

"What's up?" I asked.

"Doesn't feel right," he said. "Feels like we're walking into a trap."

"Can they do that?" Charlie asked.

"The red-eyes could probably do that," Chris said. "They're intelligent for sure."

"What do we do then?" I asked.

"One person goes for the truck, the others cover him from here. That's the driver's side door, so we have perfect cover," Ryan said.

"Except the keys are in the coffee can by the gate. Can't see that from here," I said.

"Shit. Forgot that part."

"Two of us go," Wes said, "Four cover two, then one covers one at the truck." A few heads turned to regard Wes, including mine. He always seemed to have random, but good ideas when we needed them most.

"We'll go," Ashley said.

"I'll go, but there's no way you are if it's a trap," I said.

"I'm not leaving your side." Her voice was firm.

I sighed. There would be no arguing.

"I'll go," Wes said. "I'm not a good shot anyway."

"I am, so I'll cover you. You want to go, Chris?" Ryan asked

"Thanks for volunteering me. Yeah, I'll go." He looked down at Alice. "You want to come too?"

Alice was looking into the woods. She glanced at Chris, and then went back to staring into the darkness.

"I suppose that's a 'no,'" he said. "How many rounds do you have, Ryan?"

"About thirty for this one," Ryan said as he swung a hunting rifle around from his back.

I took the pistol out and put in the last clip I had, even though it wasn't even half full. Then I spun it around and gave it to Chris. "Only seven rounds left."

He took it from me with thanks. Then he looked at Wes, "You ready?" Wes nodded.

"What do you think Ryan, another hundred feet and we'll split?" Chris asked.

"Sounds about right. I never miss inside five hundred," Ryan said with a smile.

We moved down the road a little farther and then Charlie, Ryan, myself and Ashley stopped. Ryan lay down on the road and sighted the rifle. I stood over him helping to act as a spotter. Charlie and Ashley kept their focus on the sides of the road in case there were red-eyes waiting in ambush. As Chris and Wes moved down the gap the undead moaned and turned after them. A few came out of the woods. I kept my eyes focused on Chris and Wes, watching their every move as best I could.

"Two walkers behind us," Charlie said.

"I got'em," Ashley replied. I heard the machete hack into the moaning sound at our rear but never took my eyes off of Chris and Wes. They quickened their pace and were about fifty feet from the truck when a thunderclap from the hunting rifle Ryan was holding ripped through me like a shockwave. I hadn't expected him to fire. I saw a zombie about two-hundred feet away drop down. Chris and Wes paused at the sound of the gunshot and looked back.

"Sorry," Ryan said as he reloaded. "Bastard was going to block my line of sight."

I couldn't help but chuckle. He was one hell of a shot, even in the dark.

A few heartbeats passed and Chris and Wes reached the SUV. I could barely make out the shape of Chris standing by the door of the truck and drawing the pistol. Wes moved away, presumably toward the keys when a blur of motion headed for Chris.

"Sh…"

I was cut-off by the sound of another thunderclap. Ryan saw it and nailed it in the chest. The beast flew back and away from Chris, and then lay motionless on the ground. A scream ripped through the night and suddenly another blur came out of the trees on our left and leapt for the road. Before I could even take a step it had tackled Charlie, hitting him square in the back.

Another shot rang out as I turned to help Charlie. Ashley stepped past me to cover Chris as I unsheathed my machete. A third shot blasted my senses but this time it was not from the rifle. I was slammed in the side by another of our hunters. I hit the road hard on my right side and instinctively rolled out of the way. Two feet landed where my body would have been a moment before. I kicked at the leg, connecting and sending it on its back. I swung the blade around and cut its leg. It howled in pain, but tried to roll away and recover.

Somehow I was quicker than it was. I was able to pull myself to my knees and lash out at it again. I caught it in the shoulder and heard it scream. It lay thrashing about in the road as I stood up and brought the blade down once, twice, three times. It stopped moving. I turned to see Charlie was wrestling with the other. He was guarding his face as the red devil's fists came down on him one after the other. Ashley went in and tried to cut at it, but it kicked at her, connecting with her stomach and sending her back.

Now my adrenaline was filled with rage. I ran up to the fray and dropped the blade as I grabbed the beast and pulled it off Charlie. The red-eye landed on its back and I found myself on top of it, my own fists pounding into it.

I don't recall what happened after that. My next memory was of screaming in rage while I was being pulled into the back of the SUV. My heart was racing at a mile a minute and then everything went dark.

141

Excerpt from Ashley's Journal

Another impossible escape.

He was terrifying in that ferocious sort of way. Right from the moment the doors opened up and he began fighting past the undead. Never looking back, never hesitating. The only thing that drew his attention away from the fight was me. And he saved us. But at what cost?

He's asleep right now. It looks peaceful enough. Charlie had to hit him pretty hard to get him down, but I doubt he's feeling it. But we're all scared. No one is coming out and saying it, but we're scared what color his eyes are going to be when he wakes up. Black and empty like a zombie, or the color of blood, full of fury and rage, like the red-eyes?

Chris told me about his ability to heal, but I had already guessed at that. The way his body has changed in the past few weeks I knew something was up...he's a terrible liar.

142

Chapter Twelve

I woke up in the truck sometime later. Ashley was looking down at me. My head was in her lap.

"Good morning, sleepy head," she said to me. Her eyes were light and airy. She seemed very peaceful.

"Where am I?"

"On the way to the beach. We've been driving for two days." She laughed at me.

"Huh?" was all I was able to get out. This didn't make any sense.

"One too many drinks last night, bro?" It was the voice of Mark Vistagi. He was an old friend of mine. His girlfriend Samantha laughed in the seat next to him in the front of the SUV.

"He's so hung over," Samantha said as she laughed.

"I would be too if I drank like an Irish-pirate." Mark smiled back at me in the rearview mirror. "Hang in there, bro. Hell of a party last night."

I sat up and looked out the window. Outside, the sun shone brightly on cars and trees and buildings. Everything was in bloom. It was mid-summer. Cars went whizzing past on an

143

interstate that seemed somehow familiar, but I couldn't place it.

"Are you okay?" I asked Ashley as I turned my attention inward.

She stared at me with an incredulous look like it was an unexpected question. "I'm fine…"

"You were kicked. Hard," I said, trying to figure out my own words.

She stared at me without a word.

"When we were attacked," I finished.

"What are you talking about?"

Was I delirious? Was it all a bad dream? "On the road to the SUV. By the red-eyes. This SUV."

Mark slowed down a bit. Samantha stopped laughing.

"This isn't right," I said. "I couldn't have dreamt it all up."

"You're really scaring me," Ashley said as she turned her head away.

I tried figuring out how I could have gotten here. It didn't make any sense at all. Even if the zombie thing was a dream, it should be the middle of winter, not summer. There was no way I would have lost track of six months.

"How did we get here?" I asked.

"We got in at home and drove." Her voice was skeptical. She wouldn't look at me.

"This SUV…it's not ours."

Everyone was silent.

"We took this from a house in Canick the day we raided it. The day Jesse died."

"Just stop," Ashley said.

In the front Mark coughed. His eyes flashed briefly in the rearview mirror. They had become a deep black.

She still wouldn't look at me. I was terrified now. Part of me knew this had to be a nightmare. The other part thought that everything felt all too real. The interior of the SUV, the feel of the vehicle on the road, even Ashley. Maybe because it was. I didn't know.

"Look at me," I demanded.

"No."

"Why not?" I asked.

"You'll die." She didn't hesitate in her response.

"So this isn't real then?"

The SUV stopped. Outside everything stopped. The cars around us stopped. The very clouds in the sky stopped. Mark and Samantha began to moan and tried to turn around, but they were held in place by the straps of the seatbelts.

"You should run," Ashley whispered.

"No. Not from you."

"Please…"

"Never," I said firmly.

She took a deep breath. I steeled myself the best I could. My heartbeat was raging in my ears. She turned her head toward me, her eyelids opened. Her eyes were red.

* * * * *

"NO!" I shouted and began to fight. I felt my arms being pinned down and heard Ashley calling my name. My eyes were closed. I opened them and saw her face. Her eyes were blue, like they should be. Behind her was Charlie's face. His arm was reached over her, grabbing my shirt collar. A rifle was in his other hand pointed at my head. I was still in the SUV, but I was back where I should be.

"Relax. It's okay. Just a dream," Ashley said as she held her hand against my face.

"Why do I always wake up with Charlie pointing a gun at me?" I asked as I gasped for air. I took a few calming breaths and looked around. We were in the SUV. I was in the same seat I was in during the dream…no, the nightmare. Outside the landscape was fields mixed with rolling hills in the early morning sun. I had no idea where we were. "How long was I out?"

"Few hours. How do you feel?" Chris asked from the front passengers' seat.

"Good, considering." I did a mental check of my body. No pain. "Yeah, everything seems to be okay. I have to use the restroom though."

"I'll pull over," Ryan said. He started moving the SUV over and slowed down.

"Good idea. I'll drain the lizard too," Charlie said.

"Christ. Don't make me hate being the only girl here," Ashley said as she rolled her eyes. Ryan laughed up front.

The SUV stopped and Charlie and I got out of the back. Alice was in the very back and asleep. She woke up when the vehicle stopped and Ryan opened the back for her to get out. The dog ran up to me and jumped on me, excited to see me awake. In the back was our small assortment of weapons. I grabbed a machete and started off to the field. There was a small tree that would offer some limited privacy and I headed for there.

When I got back to the SUV Ashley had opened up two jars of peanut butter. She handed one to me and kept the other. I watched her take out a knife and use it to scoop some out and then pass the jar to Ryan and Chris. I followed suit.

"Breakfast of champions," I remarked.

"High protein. It's good for you," Chris said. Charlie came back and I passed the jar of peanut butter to him.

"So, what happened?" I asked between licks. Charlie turned away and Ryan sort of focused elsewhere. "Last thing I remember was tearing the red-eye off of Charlie after it kicked you."

"Yeah," she said, not making eye contact with me.

"Come on. I'm alive. You're all alive. What happened?"

"Wes is gone," Charlie mentioned, sort of off-handedly. I had forgotten about him.

"Shit."

"He's not dead. Just…gone," he said.

I looked at the others.

"We stopped about an hour after we escaped the forest. Wes got out and just walked off. We called him to stop, but he just kept going. Charlie went to talk to him. He said he wanted to find his own way. He wouldn't come back no matter what he did. So we let him go," Ashley explained. "What else could we do?"

I had to trust they did everything they could and let the subject drop. I would miss his random ideas. They generally worked. I looked at my remaining friends, considerably fewer in number than two days ago and met their eyes. There was something else.

I finally locked eyes were her. She spoke before I could ask. "You screamed."

The others turned their gazes toward her. I waited until she continued.

"You screamed…like…" She was choking up and tears were welling up in her eyes. She put her arms around me and began crying into my shoulder. I put my arms around her. I waited a moment for her to compose herself. Between sobs and sharp breaths I heard her whisper. "What's happening to you?"

I looked at Chris hoping he would finish what she started. Whatever it was I needed to know. Chris looked away. If he was afraid to tell me, then it was really bad.

"Don't tell me," I said. Everyone looked at me, caught off guard. Ashley stopped crying enough to pull back and look at me.

"Whatever it is, it has you all terrified. Frankly, knowing isn't going to change anything, since I doubt there is anything I can do about it."

"Yeah, but what if…" Ryan started.

147

"I trust everyone here to do what they must to survive."
My brain was able to put two and two together. There was no
point in the discussion. If I was going to turn, which was
probably what they were afraid of, then there was nothing I
could do anyway. I resolved to keep Ashley safe for as long as
possible and just keep going for as long as I could.

"Where are we?" I asked, changing the topic before
anyone could say anything else about it. She pulled away from
me and dried her eyes with the sleeves of her jacket. I reached
out and took her hand in mine. I brought it to my lips and
kissed it gently. Ashley smiled.

"We crossed into West Virginia about an hour ago. Been
sticking to back roads, so it's possible we went back into
Pennsylvania and didn't have a sign to tell us. We kept
changing directions to stay on the quiet roads." Ryan
explained. "And we're going to need gas at the next place we
come across. We're almost on E."

"Well then let's find a gas station and try and get our
bearings," I said.

Everyone piled into the SUV and we started driving. After
a few tense minutes where we were certain to run out of gas we
finally came to a gas station along the road. It looked old and
dilapidated. Even before the outbreak I would have been
cautious about stopping there. The paint was faded and the
boards were falling apart on the walls.

We climbed out of the truck and checked the area. Aside
from the station and a scattering of old tires, there was not
much around but farm land. Patches of snow still dotted the
landscape, but the air was warm.

"Anyone know what day it is?" I asked. "I lost track."

"April seventeenth," Chris said without a pause.

"Wow! That's a good answer. How sure are you?" Charlie
asked.

Chris held up his arm. The digital watch strapped to his wrist was enough of a reassurance.

"Happy Easter, or at least close to it," Ashley said quietly. We went around the area and made sure that it was secure. Except for a few birds in the tree there was little evidence of anything else, dead or alive. Chris and Ryan went into the station to find a way to turn the pump on while I put the nozzle in the tank. Alice darted away, exploring the area on her own while we were stopped. After a few minutes Ryan and Chris both came outside.

"Problem," Chris said.

"No gas?" I asked.

"No power. Fuse box is a mess. Anyone here an electrician?" he asked, even though he already knew none of us were. I don't even know if my old apartment had a fuse box.

"So what do we do?" Charlie asked.

"Drive as far as we can. Hope we find another car or another station before we run out of gas," I suggested. What other options did we have?

We piled back in the SUV and started driving. Ryan made a comment about being lucky because it was around Easter. Ten minutes later when the engine started to putter, Chris started ragging on him for jinxing the situation more. It was just after noon and we had plenty of daylight left. We got out of the SUV and loaded up with the few supplies we still had left. There was probably a long hike ahead of us.

As we walked, we discussed our situation in more detail. We had enough food to ration for about four days, Alice included. We each had a machete, but Charlie's was bent and mine needed to be sharpened. I still had a bunch of smaller knives tucked away in the pockets of my vest. Mr. Craftford's revolver had two rounds in it, and the other guns were all empty save for the hunting rifle Ryan had. Charlie still had the shotgun in case we found ammo. The AR-15 was slung around Ashley's back, useless until we found ammo for it also. Chris also carried an assortment of bandages and medical supplies. Aside from more ammo, we also would need to find a ready supply of water.

After a few hours of walking we came upon a trailer. The sky was beginning to darken with storm clouds, so we decided it would be a good place to stop for the night. The trailer had clearly been abandoned long before the outbreak. Windows were broken, the door did not close properly and dust covered everything. There was no food and the water did not work. It probably was not even hooked up. Despite the fact that the trailer was a complete wreck, I was grateful to be inside when the first drops of rain began to fall outside.

Chapter Thirteen

I thought the roof of the trailer would cave in with every crack of thunder. The early spring storm had us pinned down inside the cramped space. We set up watches, but it didn't matter. No one could sleep with the shattering blasts coming from the sky every few minutes. Part of the roof was leaking and the air inside became damp and uncomfortable. It was still better than being outside, though.

Outside, the rain was falling in sheets. When the wind blew it would change direction and come in the trailer through broken windows and the door that did not shut properly. I couldn't imagine being out in this storm on a regular day, let alone a day in a post-apocalyptic world where a zombie might grab me at any moment. The storm let up in the early morning and we tried getting some sleep. When the sun broke in the morning we left the trailer and kept moving.

It was a harder walk now. We were damp, cold, hungry and we still had no idea where we were or where we were going. Along the road we came across a zombie crawling through the mud on its side. It looked helpless, but still tried to reach out at us. And the moan was still distinctive. Before we killed it we heard another moan in the distance. It would only be a matter of time before we had to fight again. In our current state, I didn't think that was a fight we could win.

We finally came across a house just before eleven in the morning. After dispatching the undead residents we scavenged it for anything useful. We ate heartily what we couldn't carry, and packed as much of the rest as we could. The previous owners had a few bottles of water in the refrigerator and we gladly helped ourselves to them.

Continuing down the road Ashley made the observation that the number of zombies we were running into was increasing. I theorized that could only mean one thing: we were coming up on a more populated area. That meant we would probably find supplies, but at the same time we risked running into a horde of the undead and possibly more of the red-eyes. Charlie mentioned getting a new vehicle as soon as we could. I agreed with him.

As we made our way solemnly down the road I found myself thinking about what I would be doing if life were still the same as it had been in early January. If the undead had stayed dead, then I would be getting into the study of the Vietnam War about now. The debate team would be competing in the State Championships. Ashley would be preparing for finals in her master's courses.

I would have also been finalizing plans for my yearly vacation in the summer. The previous year I had gone to Alaska. It was a phenomenal experience. This year I had talked about maybe going to Europe and touring Italy and Ireland, my ancestors' homes. That would be impossible now. Even if I ever made the trip all of those places would be just as devastated as the rest of the world.

"What's wrong?" Ashley asked. I hadn't realized she was looking at me as we were walking. The look on my face undoubtedly betrayed my inner thoughts.

"Nothing really. Just thinking." I told a half-truth. I didn't want to have this conversation with the other three around. Thankfully, she knew me well enough to realize that and let the matter drop.

"I have five bucks that says there is a town over the next hill," Chris said.

"Not with our luck. Make it ten," Ryan countered.

"Stupid bet, Ryan. Sign in the ditch back there said something was two miles. Name of the place was hidden though," Charlie called out from the rear.

"Damn it, Charlie! Leave it alone!" Chris yelled.

"Money is no good anyway. Might as well use it to start a fire," He countered.

"You're still sucking away what little fun there is to be had," Chris said angrily.

Sure enough, as soon as we ascended the hill there were several houses. An old-fashioned sign indicated we were entering the town of Larshall, population 61,234. As we walked we saw plenty bodies that had damage to the brains. And many of the houses along the sides of the road had doors wide-open. There were zombies in the area, but there were definitely more corpses on the ground then there were walking around.

"Other survivors?" Ashley asked, bending down to examine a body with a wound to the left temple.

"That would be nice," Ryan started. "Hopefully they have a stronghold somewhere."

"Let's not get our hopes up. They may have been passing through or fighting to escape," I said. The last thing we needed now was a false hope. "Let's try to find some water. And I need some dry socks."

We went into the nearest house and looked around. There were not a lot of supplies, but there was power, which meant there was fresh water. It also meant we might be able to find a news report or radio broadcast that could possibly fill us in as to what was going on in the world.

The house was a wreck. Drawers were emptied onto the floor, cupboards were ransacked. I went upstairs to look around. At the top of the landing I ran into a wall of odor that was thick with decay. It was stronger than the normal scent of rot that usually accompanied the undead. This was the smell of weeks', maybe months worth of rotting. Alice stopped at the top of the landing and shook her head. I heard Ashley coming up the stairs behind me.

"Don't come up here," I said.

"Why?" she asked.

"Smell is really bad. I'll take a look and let you know if it's worth coming up."

"Alright. Hey, can you find something for me?" she asked.

"Sure, what do you need?"

"Another notebook." The look in her eyes bordered on pleading. Her hand was playing with the anchor necklace again.

I nodded and went to search upstairs. While I searched the first bedroom I thought about the look she had. I had never seen Ashley like that before. The look on her face was almost desperate. In months of fighting the undead and scraping a survival together I had not once seen her look even close to helpless. I had to wonder just what she was writing in the notebook that would cause her to be so upset over running out of paper. Now, I was worried again about what Ashley was writing, but I knew she would never let me read any of it.

I was absent-mindedly searching through drawers and cabinets while I thought about the notebook. I hadn't found anything useful in the first room. I went into the bathroom next. Even the medicine cabinet was cleared out. I took a brief look around, found nothing useful and moved on.

The next room had belonged to a child and was now the source of the odor. An adult body lay in the middle of the floor. It had deteriorated into a mass of rot and maggots. The blue carpet beneath it had turned brown with decay from the fluids that it absorbed over weeks. The only thing that was distinguishable were the clothes. Whoever it was used to work for a security company. I did not see a reason to search the room and moved on.

The room across was another bedroom. I managed to locate a clean pair of socks and changed before I turned back to go downstairs, but I stopped at the landing. I hadn't found a notebook yet. There had to be one somewhere. My mind thought back to the kid's room. There was a desk on the right. I braced myself for the smell and went back in. I took care to avoid the body the best I could, but there was no way I could reach the desk without standing directly over it. The closer I came to the corpse the worse the smell became and it took every ounce of strength not to pass out. Thankfully I hadn't eaten much, or the contents of my stomach would definitely have found their way onto the already ruined carpet. Alice stood at the entryway of the room whimpering softly. Even she wouldn't come in.

I opened the drawers of the desk and finally found a notebook. It was relatively new with only a few pages of math notes written in it. I took it and also grabbed a handful of pens and pencils from a cup on top of the desk. There was a picture of a bunch of kids taped to the desk near the cup. The picture reminded me of my old students. I hoped that some of them were alive somewhere. The memory of easier times passed with another inhale of the rot beneath me.

I took the meager supplies and retreated from the room. Then I went back downstairs and found the others in the kitchen.

"Find anything?" Chris asked.

"Just this." I handed the notebook and pens to Ashley. "Body rotting upstairs, too. Wouldn't go up there." She took the notebook and pens from me and mouthed the words, 'Thank You.' She looked very relieved. I turned to the others. "Anything to eat or drink?"

Ryan slid me a glass of water. "Some cans of vegetables. Better than nothing."

"TV works!" Charlie called form the living room. We all went in and sat down.

"Don't get too comfortable. House guests are on the way." I pointed to the long bay window. Walkers were a few minutes out and we would have to move.

Charlie turned the television on and started flicking though channels. Every station was the same. Either static or a message about technical difficulties was on every channel. Chris got up and tried the radio, but he couldn't find a station that was broadcasting. It felt hopeless when I noticed the dust covered laptop in the corner of the room on a lone end table. If nothing else, it would be worth a shot.

I walked over and turned it on. It booted up without a problem and I wiped the screen off with a nearby curtain. Outside, the undead were getting closer and their numbers were increasing. An icon in the corner told me the computer was connected to the local network via hard line, and, more surprisingly, the internet was active. I was impressed. Everyone always said the internet would never die. I guess that turned out to be true. I clicked on the browser. The window opened and I was greeted with the message 'Page cannot be found.' I checked the URL. It was set for a social networking site that wasn't loading.

"Hurry up, man!" Ryan called. Zombies were clawing at the front door. I started punching in URL's I thought might work. All of the major news networks were down, so were the newspapers I could think of. I was about to give up when one more popped into my head. I put in the URL for the White House.

I was greeted with a page that held two words, a picture of the American Flag and the Seal of the President. In large, bold letters were the words: HEAD WEST. At the bottom the page indicated it was last updated March 10th, a little over a month ago. Good enough for me. It was time to go.

We went out the back and began moving across yards and over fences. We occasionally ran into a few zombies and paused to dispatch them. I was surprised with how good we were getting at it. It had become easy to take down a group of five or six without thinking. My heartbeat didn't automatically double when I heard the death rattle of an approaching ghoul. Had we been living in the undead world so long it was now a regular thing? Or was it because we knew there were worse things than mindless walking specters? There were those that *could* think.

"White House website was working," I said when it was finally safe enough to talk.

"What did it say?" Ashley asked.

"Head west."

"That's it?"

"Yep. Big red letters. Updated March tenth."

"Guess we're heading west then," Chris said.

"Going to need more food," I said.

"And a road map," Charlie started. "As well as a vehicle. And preferably an open road without zombies, wrecks or red-eyes."

"Wouldn't hold your breath," Ashley remarked.

Alice barked and we all stopped. The dog was looking at the sky in the direction we needed to head. I peered into the clouds. For a moment I couldn't believe what I saw. There was a plane flying toward us!

"Son of a…" Charlie trailed off.

"We have to signal it!" I yelled.

"How?" Chris started. "He won't see us unless he's looking. Hell, we'll probably be mistaken for zombies."

"Can zombies drive?" I looked at him and took off toward the street. If I could get a car and start driving in the open, then hopefully the pilot would notice. Alice and Ashley tailed after me. I went around another ransacked house and found a car wreck out front. One looked drivable but there was a zombie inside. Not wanting to waste time I went over and opened the door. The undead tried to stand up, but was held in place by a seatbelt. I stabbed its head with the machete, unlatched the belt and pulled the body out. The plane was close and would be overhead in a manner of moments.

I jumped in the driver's seat, closed the door and started the engine. Ashley caught up to me and I held a finger up telling her to wait here. The look on her face told me she didn't like that, but I wasn't going to be gone long. The car started without a problem and I took off down the street. I could hear metal dragging, probably a bumper or the exhaust. I was hoping whatever it was would generate sparks and make me more visible.

The plane was approaching low. Definitely seemed to be looking for something. I took the car and turned it in the same direction that the plane was flying. For several minutes, I drove with the plane in sight, avoiding obstacles. The plane dipped its wings twice in my direction. *YES!* The pilot saw me! I stopped the car and got out.

The plane circled around and moved even lower. I stood on the roof of the car and began waving my arms. Something started falling out of the plane as it headed toward me. It looked like scraps of paper. The pilot slowed down and did another wing dip, then accelerated and left, heading northwest. I stayed on the roof and waited for the paper to reach the ground. A piece drifted near me and I picked it up.

158

Military Evacuation Point: North of Charleston. Last planes leaving in one week. Head west if you cannot reach evacuation point. Safe zones established in regions of Rocky Mountains and Arizona Desert. Good luck!

I held the paper and felt a bit disheartened. It would be tough getting to Charleston, but it would be tougher still to make it all the way to the west coast. Yet, at the same time, seeing the plane and getting news that mankind was not completely destroyed was an encouraging thought. I picked myself up from a crouch and looked around.

I had no idea where I was at. In my haste I didn't pay attention to where I was going and now I was definitely lost. Zombies were closing in on all sides. I drew my machete.

I was stuck in the middle of Larshall. I had no food. No idea where I was. And no clue where the others were.

The worst part though...

I was once again separated from Ashley.

Chapter Fourteen

Two zombies were about to close with me. I slashed across with my blade at the first and kicked the other in the knee, forcing it to buckle down to the ground. The first one stumbled backward as the head came loose, but not completely severed. I swung the blade overhead and brought it down on the second zombie, splitting the skull open. There was a gap between a few more that were approaching me from the opposite direction so I took the opportunity to slip through the line and dove through.

Nothing around me seemed familiar as I dodged between groups of the undead. The key would be to keep moving, and hope that I didn't run into a dead end. Or a red-eye. They were stronger and faster than when I had first encountered the one in Ashley's basement. I wasn't certain I could handle one on my own now.

I moved at a brisk pace, not wanting to wear myself out in case I did run into trouble. A zombie moved to block my path and I dodged left, bringing the blade up diagonally and cutting its arm off at the shoulder. I moved through the gap, feeling the fetid breath of a near bite on my neck as I passed by.

How far had I driven? It had only felt like a few seconds, but it very well could have been a few minutes. And with the metal scraping from the car I probably attracted every single walking blight from here to the next town. I was definitely in a lot of trouble. I thought about calling out to try and find the others, but that didn't seem like a very good idea. I already had enough trouble and I didn't need to attract more.

I turned a corner around a house and ran straight into two zombies that were standing there. The smaller of the two latched on to me and tried to bite my arm, causing me to drop the machete, while the other grabbed my shoulder and started pulling in the opposite direction. I managed to keep the jaws off of me with my struggling. My shoulder started to wrench under the strain from the one pulling on my arm. If I didn't do something I didn't doubt it would tear my arm off.

I took a risk and moved my free hand toward the revolver tucked in my belt. The smaller one started biting my arm. I had to hope that the leather from my jacket would prevent it from breaking through. The revolver came free and I managed to make it level with the second zombie. However, the first one jarred my arm and the shot went wide. I stumbled backward and into the house causing the revolver to fall from my hand.

This is it. This is how I am going to die.

* * * * *

I'm back in the SUV. It's driving down the same stretch of highway as before. Ashley is sitting next to me, staring out the window. Mark and Samantha are in the front. I see Mark's eyes in the mirror. They are as black as night. Ashley turns toward me. Her eyes are red.

"What's going on?" I asked.

"Welcome back," she said to me. Her eyes, despite being blood red, appeared friendly.

"Am I dead?"

"Possibly." She turned away. "Who really knows…" I detected a hint of sadness in her voice.

"What am I doing here?"

"Hallucinating again. Only this time, you know it," she answered.

"So you're not bothering to hide it," I commented.

"No point. Your brain figured that part out before," Mark said from the front driver's seat.

"Alright. Then why are you two here?" I pointed to the front where Mark and Samantha sat. "I haven't seen you since Christmas."

"Not sure," Samantha said. "We might have some significance."

"But it is possible that we don't, and we're just the faces your brain filled in," Mark finished.

"That doesn't help," I said, frustrated. "You're just saying what I'm thinking."

"Yes, that's true," Mark said. For a few minutes there was no conversation. All that could be heard were the tires on the road. I was wondering what I should ask my hallucination next.

"Where are we going?"

"Does it matter?" Ashley asked.

"It might," I said.

"It doesn't," She replied.

"Why haven't you attacked me?" I asked.

"Should I?"

"You did before."

"No, I didn't. I only opened my eyes."

"Which are red," I pointed out.

"Yes," She admitted.

"So you should attack me, then."

"Why?" Ashley asked.

"It's what you do. You eat humans."

"And you're human?"

"Of course." *Wasn't I?*

"How sure are you?" she asked.

I hesitated before I answered. Was the point of this hallucination to tell me that I was no longer human? There was evidence to support that I had been affected. But I still maintained my humanity. I still had thoughts. I didn't have a desire to attack others or eat flesh. Still, I had to admit something had happened to me.

"Something is different," I finally admitted.

"Take a look." Samantha handed me a small make-up mirror from the front. I looked at Ashley, sitting next to me. She looked saddened.

I cautiously took the mirror. I knew what I would see. Still, I opened the mirror and closed my eyes. I brought the mirror up to my face. If it was true, then it would be the first thing I saw when I opened my eyes. I took a deep breath. I opened my eyes.

It wasn't what I expected. They were not blood red, but they were not brown either. The color was somewhere in between.

"I don't understand."

* * * * *

I could see its teeth on the leather, trying to break through to taste the warm flesh beneath. My arm was in excruciating pain from the second still wrenching at my shoulder. No! It can't end like this. I would not die! I needed to know what was happening to me – I needed to keep Ashley safe!

I twisted my body, forcing the zombie on my arm into the wall. It didn't let go, but loosened its grip enough for me to slip my arm through the jacket. I twisted right and dodged into the gap between the two. I used my leg to kick at the knees of the one that was now holding my empty jacket sleeve. It dropped down long enough for me to deal with the ghoul that was still gnawing at the leather. I tried punching it and kicking it, but it never let go.

I could see the leather beginning to tear. I wouldn't let it bite me! I screamed and brought my free hand around to the back of its neck. I started slamming on its neck with my fist at the spine. After the second hit I started to hear bone crack. I brought my fist down again and was rewarded with the sickening crunch of the spinal column snapping. The body went limp, and it was torn off of my jacket by its own falling weight.

The second one was starting to recover. I moved behind it and snapped its neck before it could stand up. Both of the zombies were still alive, but were unable to move. Their jaws clacked angrily at me.

I was dizzy from my efforts. The adrenaline that was rushing through me began to subside and I felt weary. I bent over to catch my breath. I was gasping for air. Every breath began to hurt. The all too familiar fire ripped through my body. I fell over. I found myself lying next to a still biting jaw, my body writhing in agony. No matter what I thought I could not move. The pain was incredible.

My last conscious thought was of how badly I had failed Ashley.

* * * * *

I didn't feel it at first. Hell, I didn't feel anything. There were no hallucinations this time. Just darkness and the feeling of nothingness. So when I finally came to I was surprised that it was pouring rain. The ground beneath me was turning softer by the minute.

I forced my eyes open and saw the same head staring back at me with those black eyes. The mouth was moving, but not in the constant, furious way that it was before I passed out. I started to pick myself off of the ground. My body was in pain, the shoulder that was wrenched by the zombie being worse than everywhere else. I took a moment to stretch out and check myself out. No bites, no major injuries. Just really sore. I was lucky.

It was dark out, save for a nearby streetlamp that still worked. I wondered how I managed to survive being passed out in the open. Was I that lucky? *Or was it maybe because the undead do not attack their own?*

The idea flashed through my mind like the lightning above, leaving an impression I could not immediately shake. I tried to push the thought away, tried to banish it completely, but it was too late.

No, I thought, forcing myself to look at it logically. I was not one of them. I could not be. I had no desire to kill. I had no hunger for the taste of flesh. The only obsession I had was to find Ashley.

And right now she could have been anywhere.

Chapter Fifteen

Finding Ashley was going to be difficult. I was lost in an area I had absolutely no knowledge about. It was dark, rainy and the undead were scattered around everywhere. I had no way of communicating with her and we had no designated meeting place. Yeah...it was going to be damn near impossible to find her quickly.

A crack of thunder startled me. I looked around in the pouring rain and tried to get my bearings. In the direction I had come from there were a few shadows standing motionless in the faint light. I still could not figure out how I was alive. I turned to look in the direction I was originally heading. A flash of lighting and another crack of thunder lit the area well enough for me to see only a scattering of zombies in the vicinity.

I started off in that direction, but then turned back, remembering my machete and gun on the ground. I scolded myself for almost forgetting the weapons. I retrieved the weapon and the revolver. I wiped the machete off before putting it back in its sheath at my side. I still had the Beretta under my jacket, but no ammo for it. I took a deep breath and started walking – I had to find Ashley.

After a few minutes of hiking through the rain I decided it might be a good idea to find a flashlight. I had one in my bag, but I had dropped the bag when I dashed for the car. Either way, it was hard to see out, and I certainly could not rely on lightning bolts and street lamps to light the way. I ducked into a house and out of the rain.

This house had definitely been raided already, but it appeared better off than some of the others. Inside the house, a lone zombie staggered at me after I entered. I dispatched him quickly.

Outside, the rain became heavier. The torrential downpour slamming into the sides of the house made me grateful to be indoors and I hoped it would lighten up before I went back out. No matter what it was doing outside, I would definitely be leaving to continue my search.

I rummaged through the one level home as quickly as the debris would let me. I managed to find a small flashlight in the kitchen. There was also an opened box of cereal. I ate some and drank some water. I took the bag out of the box. Even though it was mostly stale, it was still edible and I didn't want to leave it behind. I put the cereal in a backpack that I found in one room, grabbed some batteries from the TV remote and headed back out into the rain. It hadn't lightened up at all.

After walking for a few blocks through the small residential area I heard a rumble in the direction that I was heading. At first I thought it was thunder. The rain lightened and I could make out the sound better. It wasn't thunder, but the sound of many roaring engines. I also thought I could hear shouts over the weather. I started running now, excited at the prospect of finding help. As I made my way through the rain and past the random zombie, I could hear sporadic gunfire erupt in the direction that I was heading.

The rumbling sound became louder. I could see headlights come around a corner and turn down the road. I ran as fast as I could to the intersection. There were several motorcycles and a jeep tearing away from me. I tried shouting and getting the attention of the driver, but my efforts were lost in the rain and sound of the engines roaring. I stood in the street looking after the riders. I was drenched to the bone and had no hope of catching up to them.

Suddenly, I heard a barking sound. It was Alice! I ran in the direction of the sound, from where the riders had come. As I ran I called out to Alice, and was rewarded with more barking. She appeared at the top of a street that led into a more commercial district of town. She ran up to me and almost knocked me over. I bent down to pet her fur, matted thick with water. Alice looked up at me and then ran off in the direction she had come. I got up and followed her.

We ran past several zombies along the way. They all turned to follow us as we ran past. Up ahead I saw a body against the wall of the building. Alice led me straight to the person. My heart sank as I gazed upon Ryan splayed out on the ground.

"Ryan? Hey, Ryan! Talk to me, man!" I could see his chest rising and falling, so I knew he was alive. Blood was mixing with rain water beneath him. I didn't see any wounds.

"Come on, man! Give me something!" I tried opening his eyes. They were unresponsive. Alice barked and I turned to see several undead closing in, hoping to feast on the helpless human that was lying there. I had to move him somewhere safe.

"Ryan, listen to me! I need to know where you're hurt."

His head bobbed and I heard the word 'right.' I checked him out. He was bleeding from the ribs on his right side. I moved to his left and swung his arm around my shoulder. I supported most of his weight. He seemed to be coming around a bit, and tried walking with me. We moved back into the residential area and went into the first house I could find.

I put Ryan down on a couch in the living room and then moved quickly to block the doors the best I could. I had to create enough of a barricade to buy us some time. By the time I finished, Ryan had come to and had taken off his jacket and shirt. His right side was covered in blood that was still spilling out from a small, round hole in his ribs.

"Damn, man! Why were you shot?" I asked as I entered the room and moved to help him.

"They fucking shot me, and then sped off with them!"

"With who?"

"They took her, bro. Took Ashley, Chris and Charlie. Left me to fuckin' rot."

"Calm down, I have to try and stop this bleeding." I tore strips of cloth off his discarded shirt and began wrapping it around him. There was a similar wound on his back and I prayed that meant the bullet went clean through. Either that or he was shot twice. Trying to help him also distracted me from what he just told me. Someone had taken Ashley.

Ryan had lost a lot of blood and I didn't know if he was going to make it. After a few minutes of wrapping I had to stop and respond to a shatter in the next room. Alice led the way to where a zombie was trying to crawl through the window. I dispatched it, then took the dining room table and flipped it on end, pushing it up to the broken window. I went into the kitchen to check on the defenses there and get Ryan some water. Walking back into the living room, I saw Ryan trying to move.

"Don't do that," I said.

"You sound like Chris," he said, sending a slight smirk my way.

"He would tell you the same thing. Now lay still," I replied.

"We have to get out of here."

"We have a few minutes. Drink this." He took the water and downed it quickly. I went and poured him a second glass. When I came back I finally asked him what happened.

"We spent most of the day looking for you." He spoke in slow, ragged breaths. "As the storm rolled in we decided to call it a day and took shelter in an apartment over this deli. Ashley was a wreck, man. All she could think about was finding you."

"I never should have left."

He ignored me and continued, "Yeah, well...anyway... After dark we heard the vehicles approaching. They stopped just outside and began raiding everything. They way they were gunning zombies down I was convinced that they were enjoying it. Chris thought we should lay low, but we voted against it and went outside." He paused to catch his breath and drink more water.

"They were...they were fuckin' outlaws, bro. All of 'em. They started off alright, but got aggressive real quick. Said Ashley had to go with them to have some fun. A fight broke out, after we tried to stop them. Charlie went down and I drew my rifle to start shooting. Someone else shot first. I heard Chris say they'll go, just don't kill anyone. Then I blacked out."

I sat in silence hearing only the moan of the zombies outside. They were no longer my biggest concern. Somewhere the love of my life, the person I spent months trying to protect from the undead, was being held captive by men who chose to harm others in already dire times. I didn't let my mind consider the possibilities that could happen to Ashley.

"I'm sorry," Ryan said quietly. He knew what I was thinking.

"Not your fault. You did what you could."

"What are we going to do?" he asked.

"We?"

"I'm hurt, but you're not going alone."

I turned away from him. A few months ago I might have wished Ryan good luck and left him there. But after months of

171

fighting alongside another person you develop a sense of kinship with them that will not allow you to just leave them to die. No matter what you may have thought prior, when the moment comes, you can't leave a man behind.

"We'll get you a car. I want you to head..." I pulled out the paper the plane had dropped from my pocket, "...north of Charleston. We'll find a map. There's an evacuation point there. You can get help."

"No way! The military won't divert resources for only a few people in a hot zone like this."

"Ryan, what else can we do?" I asked. Then added, somewhat coldly, "You're no good to me in a fight."

"But you expect me to drive in this condition?" he countered.

"You're right. Still, I have to get you out of here." I thought for a moment and decided that finding a car would be the first step. "Can you move?"

"Barely."

"Good enough for me." I picked him off of the couch. It was easier now that he was able to assist more. He had lost a lot of blood and was pale. I hoped he wouldn't pass out before we found something useable. We went out the back door into the yard and looped back around the house.

The zombies were still gathered at the front. They turned toward us as we moved down the street. Ryan pointed a bit to the left and I saw a small sedan parked with two zombies inside. One was in the passenger seat in the back, the other in the driver's seat. Both had seatbelts on. The outside of the car was full of scratches and dents. I wondered how long the occupants had been trapped before starving to death and turning.

I leaned Ryan up against the trunk of the car while I disposed of the previous owners. There were no keys in the ignition. I checked the pockets on the corpse on the ground and found them. The car didn't turn over at first and I was afraid that it wouldn't start. After the third try it finally started. I got out and helped Ryan get in the passenger seat. Alice climbed in the back.

The rain was still falling and the clock in the car indicated it was about 1 am. Ryan was weak and needed rest. Ashley was taken from me by a gang of actual humans. It was shaping up to be a long day.

I put the car in gear and floored it in the direction the gang's vehicles had been heading.

Chapter Sixteen

I drove the car as fast as the environment would allow me. The gang had a good thirty-minute head start and undoubtedly knew the area considerably better than I did. Chances were good that they were already at their destination. If that were the case, then the odds were equally good that my friends, and my love, were in even more danger. I silently yelled at myself again for leaving Ashley without thinking.

"How are you feeling, Ryan?" I asked as I whipped the car around a curve. A zombie was standing too far out and the back end of the car fish-tailed into it. The walking corpse went flying backward about ten feet.

Ryan coughed as he spoke, "Hangin' in there, bro. Hurts like hell, though."

"Just hang tight. We'll find them and get Chris to patch you up right."

Outside the rain had finally lightened to a drizzle, but the roads were still soaked. I thanked my years as a reckless teenager driving with my friends for teaching me how to handle a car. When you spent most of your Friday nights as a kid learning to speed around curves and down roads without getting caught, fishtailing and doing donuts in an icy parking lot with friends, a wet road wasn't much of a challenge. The challenge was avoiding all the extra obstacles like abandoned cars and the walking dead. As the tires squealed when I avoided a car in the road and Ryan started to laugh.

"What's so funny?" I asked.

"Didn't think those 'heightened reflexes' would really do you any good." He laughed more, and then stopped when it turned to a cough that racked his body in pain.

"You think that has something to do with the way I'm driving?"

"Unless you doubled as a stunt driver while you taught high school kids the Civil War, then I'd say yes."

I hadn't considered it, but he had a point. Even though I spent a lot of time as a teenager goofing off behind the wheels of various cars, I didn't remember being this good. I glanced down at the speedometer. *Son-of-a-bitch.* I was going almost sixty in horrible conditions. At this rate I would either catch-up to my target, or get us completely lost. Or we would end up wrapped around a telephone pole.

Ryan coughed again, splattering flecks of blood across the windshield. I didn't think he was going to make it. Even if we got lucky and the gang was holed-up just around the corner at a hospital or something, he still lost a lot of blood and was already fading on me. It would be a small miracle if he made it through this.

Alice started barking and looking out the back left window as we passed an intersection. After she wouldn't let up I decided to spin the car around and head back.

The car nearly flipped as I spun the wheel all the way around. Ryan held on the best he could and yelled at me to warn him the next time I pulled a stunt like that. We made it back to the intersection. Alice was barking out the right window now. I looked past Ryan down the street. In the distance I could see a cluster of vehicles parked outside a large brick building. That had to be where the gang had gone.

The street in front of the building looked like something straight out of Hollywood. There were literally thousands of corpses in various states of decay. Blood mixed with rain and other fluids to create a swamp of rot. Tire tracks were visible in the bodies, through puddles of smashed organs and exposed bone. The smell was unbearable. I wondered if this was how the streets in Hell would look, paved with the remains of the dead. After another moment I started to wonder if I had died and this actually was a street in Hell...

Ryan threw up in the seat next to me. I couldn't stop myself from following suit, but I managed to turn around first. Even Alice looked sick from the smell. I wiped my mouth with the sleeve of my jacket and turned back to Ryan. His vomit was mixed with blood.

"This is unbelievable." It was all that I could think of to say.

"These guys definitely took care of business," Ryan said, wiping his mouth, "You'll need to be careful."

"Yeah, we'll have to be really careful."

"You're on your own, bro." He turned to look at me, "I ain't gonna make it..."

"What? Stop talking crazy. You'll be fine." I didn't want him to die without any hope. Even though I already knew it was true.

"Stop bullshitting me." He coughed and more blood came up. "Besides, I had a good run. Four months of fighting off the undead. Not too shabby. Wish I had gone down by one of them and not some trigger happy, crazy ex-con."

"Stop, Ryan."

"Promise me something?" He asked.

"Yeah, sure. Anything you want."

"After you save Ashley and get Chris out, keep an eye on him. I've been watching his ass since Iran. He needs it, believe me."

"Sure. I'll watch him."

177

"One other thing?" he asked.

"Yeah?"

"Find the mother fucker who shot me and feed him to the undead." He took out a handful of full ammo clips and gave them to me. "They should fit your pistol. Found'em just before they showed up."

"I'll find him. And I'll let you do the honor of feeding him."

"Good..." he coughed again, more blood, "...luck."

"You too." I opened the door and got out. Alice climbed over the seat, nuzzled Ryan, and then followed me. I closed the door after a moment and let Ryan die in peace. After a few minutes spent listening to the rain splash on the gore filled street I continued on toward the building.

The ground was soft underneath my feet. I looked down and saw I was standing on flesh surrounded by filthy water. Alice looked more uncomfortable then I was standing in the field of bodies. Of course, I was wearing boots. I couldn't imagine what it felt like to the touch, and I had no desire to find out.

The rain had lightened up, but I was not sure if that were a good thing or not. The rain would have suppressed some of the stench emanating from the bodies. At least, that's what I told myself. I took considerable care as I walked, not wanting to slip and find myself face down in the stomach of a corpse. And there was another danger.

Not all of the bodies were dead. Occasionally, I would pass a set of eyes that would follow me as I walked, or a jaw that still clattered even though the eyes had rotted away. I still couldn't believe how many bodies there were. It was like the entire population of the town was massacred in the street. I prayed that they were all zombies when they were killed and that they were not unfortunate victims of crossfire or random shooting from the building ahead.

As we moved closer to the brick building the body count rose and the mass became thicker. It was impossible to take a step without landing on a piece of rotting flesh. At some points my boot would sink a bit, and I was reminded of the feeling of walking on wet moss in a swamp. Even the sick popping sound of air and water being displaced was the same. Alice began whining a bit as we kept moving, not wanting to proceed further.

The building ahead was beginning to show some features. It was four stories high and took up the entire block. There were bars over all the windows and fence around the outside. The fence was mostly intact, although bent at some intervals. When I got closer I could read a small sign on the building: *Larshall County Prison.*

I was honestly surprised. I didn't think that ex-convicts would use a prison as a holdout. I suppose familiarity really does breed comfort. Of course, I was also assuming they were all ex-cons. They very well could have been a mix of innocent people who had a rougher edge than I was used too. Maybe there was a reason they shot Ryan and took the others against their will. Chris was a doctor. If they found that out, then maybe they wanted him to go with them.

I stopped and checked myself. Why was I making excuses for them? It was clear from what Ryan said that these people were savages. They were the lowest seed of society before the undead walked the Earth. Why would they be any different now? The resulting anarchy from the apocalypse simply allowed them to flourish.

Of course, an argument could be made that the only reason they were still alive was because of their rough style of living. Maybe their killer instincts were why they were able to destroy so many zombies. Maybe the swamp of corpses leading up to their stronghold was a testimony to what it took to survive in a world where the undead walked the Earth.

179

I slipped on a wet piece of exposed shoulder blade and had to put my hands out to stop my fall. My hand ended up in a pile of intestines spilling out of a festering corpse. My head was inches from a puddle of indescribable filth. I picked myself up and focused on the task at hand. Getting distracted would leave me face down in the waste again or possibly dead.

As we moved closer to the prison I started looking for a quiet way inside. It didn't look like I was going to find one. Prisons are generally as hard to get into as they are to get out. I had to give the convicts credit. It was a smart place to make a stand against the undead.

All of the vehicles were parked just outside what appeared to be the main entrance. There were several motorcycles, three SUVs and a truck – all damaged in some way. Bent fenders and ruined paint lay beneath bullet holes and broken windows. I decided to circle the building to see what I could find.

As I turned the corner to start down the side of the building I noticed a shadow on the roof. They had a guard. By now he had to have seen me. I decided that there was no way I was going to sneak in at this point.

"Hello?" I called up to the guard. "Hey! Can you help me?"

"Maybe! What's in it for me?" The voice was a bit raspy. I could hear laughter now. He wasn't the only one watching me from the roof.

"I'm looking for my friends," I called back.

"Well if they're from around here you're probably standing on them." More laughter.

I ignored it and continued. "A girl and two men. Someone told me you took them," I called up.

It was a quiet for a moment. "What's it to you?" It was as different voice and a new shadow appeared on the roof. The voice was deeper. Somehow it sounded familiar.

"Are they alive?" I was getting angry, but wouldn't give the bastard the gratitude of seeing that.

Two more shadows appeared on the roof. I wished it was light was out so I could make out some features.

"They're alive! Ashley's okay!" The voice sounded like Charlie. What was he doing up there? "You should get out of here! She'll be okay! Trust me," he called down.

"Charlie!" I started, "You should know me better than that by now! Let her go and I'll leave."

"Fat chance! Hot piece like that! She's staying here for a very long time!" said a voice I didn't recognize.

"Go away," the deep voice said again. I began to think this was the person in charge. "Now. And we won't shoot you."

"Listen to me! A plane passed over head yesterday. It dropped these flyers down," I pulled the sheet of paper from my pocket and began waving it around frantically, "There's an evacuation point not far from here. We can all go! We can get out of here!"

"Do you really think we'd make it?" the voice asked sarcastically. Other voices began to laugh at the remark. "Do you really think we *want* to go?"

I was floored at the thought. How could they want to stay here? We had a chance to get away from all of this, and they were going to refuse?

"We have everything we need here. We're safe, we're well supplied and we're free to do as we want," the deep voice reasoned.

"But it's not safe! Sooner or later, you are going to die!"

"So are you! But we'll die fighting. You'll die as a coward!" he yelled at me.

"You're out of your mind!" I yelled back.

A bullet pegged a corpse a few feet away, striking a piece of arm hanging from a pile of bodies.

"This conversation is over. Leave now."

181

"I'm not going anywhere without Ashley! Damn you, Charlie! Help me!" I screamed.

My reply was another gunshot, this one much closer than the last. The corpse right next to me suffered another wound. Alice backed up. I lowered my shoulders in defeat. There was nothing I could do right now. If I tried anything now, then I would just get myself killed.

As I walked away I heard Charlie call out to me that he wouldn't let anything happen to Ashley. He also said I should head for the evacuation point and get free of this madness. I wanted to believe him, to listen to him, but I no longer knew if I could trust him. I walked back through the swamp of corpses with Alice in close proximity.

Chapter Seventeen

The first thing I had to do was find a secure place to lay low while I stalked my prey. There was an apartment building several blocks from the prison. It was only a few stories high and had several entrances and exits. There were a few residents, but I dispatched them without any trouble. The concentration of zombies was definitely small, no doubt in thanks to the other type of scourge down the street.

After I found a suitable apartment on the second floor I secured the rest of the building. I broke into the superintendants office and I was able to get keys to the other units. I took an entire day gathering materials from the other apartments. There was enough food for Alice and me to last a few weeks. I also found a rifle and a full complement of ammo in one of the apartments on the third floor.

Once I was settled in I started planning how I would get Ashley back. After a few hours racking my brain I decided that I couldn't do anything without more information. Alice and I started making trips down the street. There was a small office building that was catty-corner to the prison, where one of the offices gave a pretty decent view of the prison. We found a way in through a back entrance so that the no one at the prison would know we were there. Crouched down from inside the window I could see a guard walking around the roof, automatic weapon in hand.

We left the office building and then went back at night under the cover of darkness. I spent the night hanging curtains in the windows so that I could move freely in the office without having to worry about being seen. I also brought along a pair of binoculars and left the rifle and rounds at my new perch. I decided that I would spend the days watching the prison and the nights back at the apartment. I hoped that it wouldn't take too long for me to figure out what I was going to do.

The longer it took for me to come up with a plan, the more of a chance that Ashley would be hurt, if she hadn't been already. I found myself wondering if she were better off trapped in the basement of her house when I found her months ago. At least if the zombies got to her she would only be killed. I couldn't imagine what types of torture she had to deal with in the prison. Charlie had better be keeping his word.

A week passed and any hope I had of making it to the evacuation point was crushed; another three days after the date on the paper passed. While I was observing the prison and making notes about guard changes and movements in the windows that I could see, I noticed that there were more people on the roof than usual.

They were doing something, but I couldn't see what. With the rifle and binoculars in hand I moved up the stairs looking for the way onto the roof of the office. I found the door, but if my orientation was correct, then it opened up toward the prison. Chances were good with the extra bodies on the roof that someone would see me. It wasn't a risk I was willing to take.

I went to the fourth floor and found a window that faced the prison. It was at an angle, so I couldn't see quite as well as I could from the corner view office I had on the third floor. It was also still too low a vantage point, and I could only make out the upper torsos of the convicts on the roof. From what I could tell the men on the roof were building something, but what they were constructing I couldn't tell. I decided to end my watch early and then come back after dark.

By now I knew the route back well enough to not worry. I also had never encountered a zombie on this street, or the adjacent one, with the exception of the handful I would run into while entering a building or in an alley. I had to wonder if they had learned to avoid this area. Or perhaps a red-eye was keeping them away from the obvious kill zone. If they could figure out where not to go on their own, then they were smarter than I had given them credit.

I knew they were out there, the red-eyes. Every now and then I would hear their distinctive scream off in the distance. From what I knew they only made that sound when they hunted, and that instantly put me on my guard. I wondered what they were hunting. Had a survivor in hiding revealed his or herself? Were there other people passing through town? Or did they hunt animals as well as humans? I had never seen a zombie directly attack Alice, but that didn't mean they wouldn't if that was the only option.

When we got back to the apartment I set out some food for Alice. Several of the apartments had dog food and she was eating like a queen. Definitely the best she had eaten since we fled the cabin. On the other hand, I was lacking in the nutritional department. Canned vegetables could only do so much. I had found a can of peanut butter, but despite its high protein I still felt weak. There was a frozen pizza, but I decided that I was going to save that for a good day.

What I really wanted was meat. If a cow happened to stumble into town and made it this far I would definitely kill it. I looked down as Alice hungrily devoured a bowl of dog chow, then I looked at the can of peas I had opened. At least one of us was enjoying a meal.

185

There were still a few hours of daylight left, so I decided a nap would be in order. I set the alarm for two hours; that would give me enough time to get ready as the sun was setting. I didn't want to miss anything at the prison.

* * * * *

When I woke up I was not in the same bed. And the alarm I set was not the sound that woke me. I heard a crow cawing loudly. There was a window open in the room I was in. I sat up and looked around. This was the room we stayed in at the cabin.

I climbed out of bed. Outside the window the crow was sitting on a tree branch nearby. There was no snow on the ground, but the trees were still bare. I turned around and examined the room. It was slightly different. There were no mirrors, for starters. There were also no decorations or supplies lying around like there had been when I was there. I could make out the sound of voices downstairs but hesitated to investigate.

Why was this constantly happening? What was my brain hiding from me? Why were these…illusions becoming more and more frequent? Was there a point to all of this? Was I supposed to learn something from these very real dreams? Or was I just going crazy? I prayed it was the former. If this was just a side-effect to whatever else was happening to me, then I was in a lot of trouble. But if I somehow knew something and my brain was just working it out…then there might be hope. Not having much of a choice, I left the room and headed downstairs to the source of the all too familiar voices.

"Good morning." Bill greeted me at the bottom of the steps and handed me a cup of coffee. The first thing I noticed was his eyes. They were coal black. Everyone else from the cabin was there too. Expect for Ashley, Mr. Craftford and Wes, all of their eyes were black. Mark and Samantha were also there again. And there were two other people. One kept his face hidden in the shadows, but the eyes were definitely red. Glowing, like in the movies. The other was...Keith. I hadn't seen him since the night this all started. It definitely surprised me to see he had worked his way into the mass confusion that was my memory.

Around the room the others were mostly silent. I made my way to the same empty chair that I usually sat in. Ashley sat across from me, her own red eyes fixed on my every move. Jenn stood sheepishly in a corner. Mr. Craftford sat in his chair, glancing and then waiting. Ryan and Chris whispered to each other. Elise sat on the couch watching Becca, who was playing with Alice on the floor. It was hard seeing Becca again. Even though her eyes were zombie black she seemed so innocent. I also noticed that Alice's eyes were red. That was a first. I hadn't seen any signs that animals could be affected. Of course, it was possible they couldn't and my mind was making it all up.

On the far side of the room stood Jesse and Charlie. Charlie refused to make eye contact with me. I took this as an affirmation that I didn't know where I stood with him anymore. I wouldn't until I could find out exactly what happened.

Bill stood near the mantle of the fireplace looking at the others. Keith was standing behind me near the entrance to the kitchen. After I was settled in the chair, the same chair I had sat in when I was introduced to everyone the first day at the cabin, Mark and Samantha moved to the staircase and sat down on the steps. The shadowy figure stood in the doorway to the porch. All of my exits were blocked. There was no escape.

"So what is it this time?" I asked. I was growing impatient with these events.

"You haven't thought about it much," Ashley said to me. I wondered if the reason it was always her that guided my thoughts was because of our relationship.

187

"I've been busy trying to save you." My impatience melted away as soon as I spoke to Ashley. Sometimes the affect she had on me was startling, even when it wasn't really her.

"I know you're worried about me."

"Are you okay?" I realized almost as soon as the words left my mouth that there was no way that she could answer that. If I didn't know the answer, then my hallucination wouldn't.

"What will you do if I'm not?"

"You know that answer."

"Will you try to save me, too?" Chris asked.

"If I can, yes. But I'm going after her first."

"What about Charlie?" Mr. Craftford asked.

"Depends on what's happening to Ashley."

"Would you kill him if she is hurt?" he asked.

"Yes," I said without hesitation.

"What if he did all he could to protect her?" Craftford asked.

"Then it depends on how convincing he is."

"Hmm...I wonder..." the red-eyed specter of my love trailed off. I decided not to ask what it was she was wondering about.

I looked down at the floor where Becca was playing with Alice. The little girl looked just like she used to, sans the eyes. She was so happy sitting on the floor and watching the adults talk. Alice's tail wagged lazily from side-to-side and she would lick Becca's face when it was close enough. I was surprised at how peaceful everything seemed despite everyone's new state of appearance. Everyone seemed to be at ease, except for the shadowy figure by the door.

"He's the one who took Ashley," Jesse said, bringing my focus back to the hallucination, which is ironic when you think about it. "He's the one from the roof."

188

"Why did you take them?" I asked the shadowy figure that stood near the door.

"There's no way I can answer questions that you don't know the answers to," He replied. Something about his voice seemed even more familiar in the quiet setting of my mind. Perhaps it was simply because it was not being shouted off of a roof top.

"Then why are you even here?" I asked.

"Should he not be?" Mark asked.

"I know nothing about him other than he took Ashley. He has no purpose here."

"Mark and I could be dead. You hadn't seen us in months before the apocalypse. The same argument could be made about us." Samantha looked at me with a sly smile. It was the same smile I used when I showed a debate student a flaw in a logic pattern, hoping they would catch it before I had to explain it to them.

"Yeah, you're arguing with yourself. That's sort of the point, Coach." Keith put his hand on my shoulder and chuckled.

"Arguing to come to a conclusion. Brilliant." I shook my head. Some of the other hallucinations were starting to make sense now. I talked it out with the figments of my imagination.

"Alright, let's go back. First time. Driving in the SUV with Mark, Sam and you." I pointed at Ashley, who watched me with a smile on her face. Before the apocalypse she always said she loved watching me work, watching me work out problems. "At first, you were all fine."

"And then?" Ashley prodded after I was silent a moment.

"Then you were not." I continued quickly to avoid interruption from anyone else. "Then in the second one you started out bad. This time it was me who was infected. Now here, everyone is, even my shadowy friend in the corner. Even Alice."

"So what does it mean?" Jesse asked.

189

"It means that there is no hope. We're all affected by what happened." I was confident, but it still felt like I was missing something. "No matter what anyone does, this problem cannot be ignored or hidden from."

"Certainly interesting, but that's a bit broad, don't you think?" Bill said. I was beginning to get annoyed with my own thoughts being filled in for me, but there wasn't much I could do about it. If this is what it took for my brain to figure stuff out, then I would just have to deal with it.

"Think about the details," Ashley said to me.

I thought for a moment. The eyes. That was the key. Everyone's eyes were different in that they were either red or black. Except for my own, which were sort of in-between brown and red. In each hallucination everyone had colored eyes. That meant more than everyone just being affected. That meant that everyone...

"Everyone is *infected*." Ryan said. "Doesn't make sense, does it?"

"If everyone is already infected, then why didn't we all turn into mindless walkers?"

"Reactions were different for everyone. Regardless of what that reaction turned out to be, it still resulted in everyone being infected to some degree," Chris finished.

"Alright, I can accept that. Then the question becomes, how did this happen and why do people still change if they're bitten?" I asked.

"You're not a biologist and there's no way you can know how. Both are irrelevant," Keith said.

"And while that's important in the long run, that's not what you're here to learn," Ashley said.

"So then what's the point?" I asked.

"Guess it will have to wait," she said.

"Why? Why can't we just work this out now? I hate this, you know."

"I know, but your alarm is going off." She smiled at me.

* * * * *

This time I woke up in the same bed I had fallen asleep in with the alarm going off near my head. I grabbed it and threw it angrily into the wall, startling Alice who had been asleep on the floor. It continued to wail and I was forced to get up to silence it, which I did with the heel of my boot. I was frustrated. It felt like I was so close to a real answer for once. I just wanted it to come already.

I took a deep breath. Then another. On the third I was finally able to force the confusion from my mind and focus on what needed to be done now. I fed Alice, ate a bit myself, and set out to find just what the convicts were up to.

Walking down the street was oddly serene. I was so used to the smell of the rot and muck that it did not bother me anymore. And I was able to walk down the street knowing I wouldn't encounter any walkers. I still wasn't sure how they knew to avoid the area, but I was definitely grateful that they did.

The sun had already set behind a nearby mountain, but the sky was still light enough to see without a flashlight. Street lamps, at least the ones that still worked, were beginning to turn on. The air was still crisp even though it was nearing the end of April. I was wearing a fresh outfit, substituting my white t-shirt for a black one and rubbing charcoal on my face to make me less visible. I still had the vest with various items and knives in the pockets, my pistol, the machete and my favorite gray, Irish wool cap. I also wore a light black coat with sleeves to cover my arms. The black leather driving gloves I wore had the fingers cut off – back at the cabin, I discovered it was harder to shoot when you couldn't properly feel the trigger.

Alice and I walked the same route as we always did. We walked onto the next block over, away from the street filled

191

with bodies, to the backside of the office building. We went in through the back entrance and walked up the steps to the third floor. On that floor was the outpost I used to observe the prison, but tonight I would be taking the binoculars and the rifle and heading to the roof on the fifth floor of the building.

As we moved past an abandoned Starbucks, Alice pinned her ears back and stopped. I drew the machete and looked around. Across the street near an overturned truck a shadow moved. As I watched a blur of motion jumped and landed in the middle of the street. It was a red-eye. I tensed, waiting for it to strike while looking out of my peripheral vision for others. They hunted in packs.

It was crouched in the street staring at me and hissing low, like a snake in a cage. The eyes focused on me. It was glaring, but there was something different. It was just watching me. I got the distinct impression it wasn't going to attack. It gave me the opportunity to look closely at one for the first time.

The eyes were not the only thing that made them different. Its muscles seemed to be over-developed, but not bulky. It moved more like an animal than a human, but it still looked like a man. It had scraps of clothing around its shoulder, but was nude everywhere else. In the past I might have laughed seeing this, but there was nothing funny about what I was now witnessing. It seemed hairier than a normal person, but I didn't know if that was from the infection or just a biological misfortune before the outbreak.

It continued to stare at me and after a few moments my grip loosened on the handle of the machete. Alice was still locked in an aggressive pose with her ears pinned back and her teeth barred, but she had stopped growling and was breathing steady. The creature continued to stare, but was moving from a low crouch to a standing position. It began making a guttural sound and cocked its head at me.

My eyes narrowed in confusion as it kept making the sound. Alice stood next to me and dropped the aggressive posture. She looked up at me like she was waiting for me to say something, but I had no idea what to do.

The red-eye spent a few minutes making the sounds, and then suddenly turned away and ran into the darkness. A second blur of motion also ran after it, darting from behind a car where it had been lurking. I knew there had been another one somewhere. I waited a few minutes to make sure they were gone before I dared to move again.

I still wasn't sure exactly what just happened, but I couldn't afford to waste anymore time investigating.

Ashley was waiting for me.

Chapter Eighteen

Alice and I made it to the office and went up to the outpost. Inside I used a small penlight to check the building. Even though I blocked the main doors, there were still some broken windows a zombie could have crawled into. After I made sure there were no unwanted visitors, Alice and I went to the floor with our gear and I grabbed what I would need for the roof.

I decided that I didn't want Alice on the roof with me. I would be able to remain still, but she had a tendency to wander. I set her up with some more food and water, and then told her to stay as I left the room. She did, but she definitely didn't like that I was going alone, whimpering as I left. I wasn't too thrilled either. It was always comforting knowing she was watching my back. When I was first separated from the others I never would have run into that trouble before I blacked out if Alice had been with me.

I took the gear and made my way to the roof. I took a deep breath when I got to the door. This was the part I was worried about. If someone was looking at the roof they would definitely see it open. If they were listening they might hear it open. I had a towel with me to keep it from closing behind me, and I readied it as I slowly put pressure on the door handle. With each breath I applied a little more, waiting for a shout from across the way to break the silence. When the shout never came I started to push outward. The door creaked open. Probably not as loud as I thought it was, but I still scolded myself for not thinking about bringing oil to lubricate the hinges first.

I got the door open enough to hear out onto the roof. I could hear laughter and voices from across the street, carried clearly on the still air of the evening. I put the towel on the ground and then started opening the door a bit more. The roof was lit by the activity from across the street, but no one noticed my shadowy figure slip through a door across the way. I lowered myself down into a crouch as soon as I had the door propped open and moved to the ledge of the roof.

I could see they had a built a bonfire on the roof. The prison rooftop was just a bit lower than my perch, and I could see everything from the knees up on those closest to the ledge. Two guards with rifles walked the outside edge, but both were more concerned with what was going on to be paying attention to watching the surroundings.

There were around thirty people up on the roof mulling around a bonfire and in the light I could see bottles in some hands. I wondered if I had needed to even bother with stealth. The convicts were loud, not paying attention and some, if not most, were probably drunk. After a few minutes of watching their behavior I thought I very well may have been able to walk onto the roof with a bullhorn and not be noticed. I moved to the corner of the roof closest to the prison and sat down to watch the activity through my binoculars.

The convicts were definitely celebrating something. Through the binoculars I could make out faces and hear some words. I could probably hear entire conversations if they were not surrounded by shouts and swearing. They were truly a vulgar lot.

I started looking at the faces carefully, hoping to find Ashley somewhere in the crowd. While I was looking I noticed the wooden structure constructed behind the bonfire. There was a cage on the bottom and a series of wooden beams and rope constructed above. Something was moving in the cage. It was…no…they wouldn't. I nearly threw-up when I realized what they had constructed.

It was a gallows. And the trap door led to a cage where two walkers were reaching out at passer-bys. The bastards were going to hang someone! And then watch as that person was eaten by the damn zombies below! I couldn't believe it. Part of me tried to deny what I was seeing, but there was no mistaking what the design was for. I wanted to grab the rifle and start picking the deranged pricks off, but I knew I had to wait. I couldn't risk putting Ashley in harm's way.

I found Charlie. He looked ragged. He was standing off from the main group whispering to someone else. As I watched, more people came out onto the roof. One group was a collection of people in chains, shackled together. Some of the people in chains wore guard uniforms. Some were women. Some were children. I scanned the faces through the binoculars. Ashley wasn't there. Neither was Chris. The group of prisoners were taken nearest to the gallows and forced to sit on the ground in a tight circle.

After a few moments another group of prisoners came out. They were both there, chained next to each other. Thankfully, Ashley didn't look hurt. Chris had a black eye. I let out a heavy sigh when I saw her eyes. Though distant, I could tell they still had strength in them. She was alive. And she still had hope. I watched her for a moment. Her hand was playing with the necklace again. She was nervous.

I found myself again reaching for the rifle. I wanted to shoot them all, but I definitely didn't have enough ammo. There were more than fifty people on the roof and there was nothing I could do to help them yet.

197

Several of the convicts were now on the gallows arranging ropes and checking bindings. I didn't see a formal noose, but it was possible that they didn't tie one. As one figure ascended the ladder of the gallows the others in the crowd began to quiet down. It was the leader for sure, the one I had shouted at two weeks ago, the one who condemned us to this hellhole and took Ashley from me. The shadowed figure from my own hallucinations.

My hand picked up the rifle. I put the binoculars down and watched the scene through the scope. No one was looking in my direction, so I moved to a position where I could see the gallows more clearly, right at the corner of the roof.

The crowd across the street was quiet. I could hear quite clearly now. The leader turned to face the group. Suddenly, the shadowy figure from my dream had a face. It wasn't the face of someone who spent a lot of time behind bars. This face was softer, yet still had a grim outlook. This was the face of someone who *took* the leadership of this group, not the face of someone who had *earned* it. Still, the way the rowdy crowd of convicts became silent told me they either respected or feared this man. Maybe both.

"Evening, boys!" he started. His voice carried well on the still of the night. In the sky the moon broke from behind the clouds. It was nearly full and added a ghostly pale to everyone in the firelight. The timing was incredible. "Nice night for an execution, isn't it?"

He was met by hearty cheers and shouts. He put his hand up and silenced the crowd.

"But who is it we're going to execute?" he asked loudly.

This time he was met mostly by confusion and awkward glances, except by a handful of the thugs. They probably knew what was going to happen already. Charlie and the two men next to him were in the group. I grew angry and tightened my grip on the rifle.

"Some of you have suggested the guards," he was interrupted by some light cheers, "Some of you have suggested the women who refuse us." Another round of cheers, I took hope knowing that Ashley wouldn't have fallen into the category of other women.

"Some of you have even suggested me." He laughed a bit, and many of the others did too, but there were some who took on a more serious tone of nervous laughter. Perhaps it had been tried once already.

"No, boys, we shouldn't kill any of them." He paused a moment. The crowd waited patiently, me included. "We need to kill only one man. A man who has betrayed us all. Among us is someone who has tried to usurp us all. He tried to steal from us. He tried to take from us what we have earned. He tried to organize against me! Me! The one who saved us all! And the worst part is he is trying to take our hospitality for granted and leave us, his brothers!

"Can you imagine it boys? He wants to leave us and take his chances out among the dead. Well, I say if that is what he wants, we show him his ultimate fate now. Let us feed him to the wretches. Let him see what 'freedom' truly means!"

The crowd was mostly silent. Some exchanged whispers and hard glances, trying to determine who the traitor among them was. One person had the courage to finally ask the leader who the traitor was.

"I know who he is," he replied calmly. "But we must be patient. We must decide what to do with this man before we condemn him. One option lies before you!"

"Kill him! Kill the traitor!" some called. These calls were taken up by many of the others. I was impressed by how this guy could move a crowd. He was going to feed one of their own to the zombies, and they were going to cheer as they watched him hang and be devoured. The leaders' ability to manipulate the crowd was impressive and I have a feeling it wasn't just the alcohol that allowed him to be so convincing.

"Is that what you want then? To feed the traitor to the undead?"

The question was met by a loud cheer of triumph.

"Bring forth the traitor!" he cried. He nodded into the crowd. I moved the sight of the rifle to where his gaze fell. Charlie was grabbed by the two men flanking him and was being dragged to the structure. He had a look of surprise and shock on his face. He fought against them, but they overpowered his large frame. The convicts around him began throwing objects at him as he moved past. I saw a bottle strike him in the side of the head and he stopped struggling.

I found Ashley's face. She was struggling at her chains. She and Chris were both screaming, but I could not make out what they were saying over the clamor that had risen up.

I knew I had to do something. If nothing else, I knew that Charlie was definitely no traitor to me if they were about to hang him and feed him to zombies for betraying their twisted leader. I had to do whatever I could to help him. I might be able to get off two rounds before I would have to deal with return fire. I flicked the safety off the rifle. Remembering some tips Ryan gave me, I started slowing my breath down. Not holding it, but making it as smooth and even as possible.

Charlie had been hauled onto the deck of the gallows. While he struggled, three men began binding his hands and feet with the ropes. Now I knew the true purpose of the device. They were not going to hang him! They were going to feed him alive by lowering him into the cage! The leader raised his hands and the crowd quieted. I could hear muffled cries of 'no' and sobs from some of the shackled hostages.

"This man has refused our hospitality! He has sown disorder and mistrust. He has tried to kill certain members of our hearty bunch. Now he will die. In this new world only those who follow order will survive. Only those who are loyal to each other will be saved. Those who stand against loyalty will meet their ultimate fate. Lower him in!"

The crowd was going nuts as Charlie was swung over the stage. Two of the men removed a section of the floor, opening it for him to be lowered in. His arms were bound and outstretched, his legs bound but left to dangle. One of the men removed his boots, but not before taking a kick to the head. The way he was being lowered in I knew he would feel a lot of pain before he finally died. The zombies would tear him apart piece by piece. The undead were standing beneath him now, arms outstretched toward his legs.

I had to choose a target. I could either shoot the leader or shoot Charlie and end his misery. Chances were no matter who I shot, Charlie was going to die. I took a deep breath. They began lowering him down slowly. He brought his legs up toward his chest, than dropped them quickly. He was trying to kick them away, but it would be useless soon. I made a decision. Centered the sight...

The shot rang out like thunder. Across the street a zombie's head exploded in the cage. I reloaded quickly, sighted the second one and fired again. The shot was slightly off and hit the second one in the shoulder. It fell out of sight behind the crowd that had gone silent. I reloaded another round and tried to find the leader. His face was a mass of confusion. I fired again just as he moved and the bullet struck a wooden post behind him. Now he knew he was under fire and began to shout and move.

I chambered another round. This time I scanned the ledges. The two guards still were not looking in my direction. They thought the gunfire was coming from somewhere in the crowd. I used the confusion to my advantage and shot the guard nearest to me. Now I could see arms rising in my direction. Several of the drunken fools finally recognized the muzzle flash. I reloaded again and shot another of the convicts, this one pointing at my location.

201

Concrete exploded a few feet from me. I was under fire. I ducked down behind the wall and began crawling for the door. The sound of weapon fire increased and the ledge of the building began to shower me with bits of concrete and dust. I crawled away and came up behind an air conditioner unit. The convicts were still shooting at where I was at a few minutes ago. I swung around the right side of the unit and sighted another target.

The body spun as it was struck and tumbled over the edge of the prison. A round pelted off the unit and I ducked back down and headed for the door. I ran inside and down the stairs. Alice was waiting excitedly. I went into the office and grabbed the box of rounds for the rifle. Two of the convicts were on the edges of the roof scanning the area. I waited a moment to see what they would do. I didn't have to wait long. The front doors of the prison flew open and several of them exited the building and began moving cautiously through the swamp of dead bodies in my direction.

"Alice, time to go!" I shouted. She went out ahead of me and down the stairs while I headed for the fire escape. When I reached the bottom she was waiting for me. I heard voices coming down the street and raised my rifle as I moved behind a garbage dumpster. The dumpster made a good level for the rifle.

"Find a way in! Check the back!" I heard someone call out. A shape turned the corner down the back side of the building in my direction. The shape was alone and stopped a few feet down when it saw Alice standing by the garbage, teeth barred and growling. The face searched the area, not noticing the dark figure with the rifle standing behind the garbage.

"Oh shit!" he said as his eyes finally met with mine. "Hey gu..."

His shout was ended as I squeezed the trigger and the round found its mark in his chest. His hands grasped the wound and his body convulsed as it hit the concrete. I reloaded and spun around. I lowered myself to one knee and waited. As I expected, a second convict came around the other side of the building. My first round found his leg. I ran to him and brought the stock of the rifle down on his head. Then I took his weapon (a crude looking submachine gun) and ran out into the street. I heard shouts behind me that were followed by more gunfire. A round whipped past my head as I ran down the street away from the prison. I was glad that they had been drinking.

I had no idea where I should go. After a few meters I turned and sighted the rifle on one of them that was chasing me. The shot missed, but they slowed down, opting to follow instead of chase. That worked for me. It bought me time to think. I kept moving, dodging between cover and hearing a shot or two fired almost every time. The further away from the prison we were, the more zombies there would be. I tried to think of how I could use that to my advantage. Then suddenly I felt a stinging pain in my foot that sent me sprawling.

As I tried to crawl to my feet I heard a voice behind me. "Yeah! Ain't so bad now, are you fucker?" I reached in my jacket and drew the pistol, then flipped onto my back. The source of the taunt turned around a car and I shot twice. The cocky prick went down, a look of surprise on his face.

I could hear more footsteps approaching, but I couldn't tell if they were human or zombie now. Probably both. I pulled myself toward the nearest building, hoping to find a place to hide. The pain in my foot was bad, but manageable. I reached down to pick up the rifle that I had dropped and instead found Alice lying on the ground nearby. She was bleeding and not moving.

I dropped to my knees next to her. The blood was coming from her back left leg, near the hip. She was breathing, but only in ragged breaths. I went to the dead convict and tore his shirt as others approached, threatening to shoot me if I moved.

I ignored their threats and moved back to Alice. I tried to stop the bleeding.

"I said, 'Get *up*, mother fucker!" a voice yelled from behind me.

"You shot my dog," I said softly.

"You shot my boys, asshole!" the voice replied.

"If she dies, then I'll kill you all," I said quietly. I was partially referring to Alice and partially to Ashley. I pulled myself up to my feet and turned to face the convicts. There were six of them around me. They all had a weapon pointed at me.

"Let's gat this fool," said a tall black man with a missing front tooth.

"No," said a bigger guy. This one stood with his arms crossed.

"What? He fuckin' shot Krieger. Kill the bitch!" a burly white guy said. He was covered with tattoos. They were similar to some of Charlie's. I had to wonder if it was an indication of some sort of gang prior to the apocalypse. That would explain why they didn't kill him at first.

"We're going to take him back with us and feed him to the fuckin' undead," the leader said to the others. Then he looked at me as he moved closer. "Think you'll like that, *hero?* Hanging upside down while we tease them with your body. It's going to be very slow, I promise you." He came up to me slowly and swung his arm around. I took the blow and fell into the building behind me, staggering but not going down. "Grab this asshole and let's get out of here."

My vision was blurred a bit from the blow, but I noticed that Alice wasn't where she had fallen. I hadn't heard her leave. I hoped that she was okay and hadn't just crawled away to die somewhere.

Two sets of arms grabbed me and began to pull me in the direction we came from. Another set began rifling through my clothes, taking the machete, Mr. Craftford's revolver and the pistol. I saw another grab the rifle off the ground. I still had a few knives in my pockets and I hoped that I would get a chance to use them.

I knew enough about the area to know that we were about four blocks from the prison. As I looked around I noticed zombies closing in around us.

"Hey fellas…" I said.

"Shut up." I felt another punch to the head. This one caused me to bite my tongue, adding a taste of iron to my mouth.

"Just…wondering if you noticed…" I gasped between coughs of blood.

"Man, we've killed more of these fucking creeps than anyone. It ain't a big deal." I couldn't see who said it.

After a few steps we stopped walking. The leader said something to one of the others that I couldn't make out. Up ahead I could see a mass of bodies blocking the way. We would have to find a different route back to the prison. My captors grudgingly went back the way we came, firing at the zombies who came too close for comfort.

We went farther down the street avoiding the larger groups of zombies that interrupted us. We went past where they shot Alice. A trail of blood led into an alleyway, and then disappeared suddenly. I had no idea what happened. We turned left to go around the block only to find our path obstructed again when we turned toward the prison at the next block.

It struck me as we were walking that these were not random groups of the undead. They appeared precisely where we needed to go, blocking our every route. I thought about the red-eyes ability to control them and began to panic.

We were being herded. I was terrified, but I kept my composure. I would rather face a horde of the undead than try to escape from the prison. I needed to wait and see what was happening.

I did not have to wait long. A few minutes later we were stuck in the middle of the street. Zombies were on all sides and moving closer. Cars and a downed telephone pole prevented our entry into the only doorway.

"Now what?" asked one of the convicts. I could sense that they were beginning to panic. They began firing at zombies randomly. Bodies began to pile up as they scored headshot after headshot. Even after drinking, these men were good, the result of having plenty of live targets to practice on. After a few minutes they organized themselves and set-up an impressive perimeter. The bodies of the undead began to get in the way of others. I began to think we would get out of this mess until their guns began to click empty.

"Shit! I'm out!" another called, the last of the group of five to run out of ammo.

"Let's go! This way!" The leader pushed through a small gap in the undead. I was pulled along by two of my captors. The fourth also made it through. A loud scream from behind told me that the gap had closed around the last man. My odds of escape only improved slightly. Within moments we were surrounded again.

"Hope you boys can fight better than you can shoot," I commented, though I was unsure why I kept egging them on.

"Shut up," the leader said.

"I could help you if you'd give me my machete back," I said calmly. The leader nodded and I felt a sharp blow to the back of my head again. I lurched forward and was allowed to fall to the hard ground. I tried to pick myself up and then a sharp, piercing scream filled the air. It was joined by at least three others. Adrenaline shot through me and I picked myself up all the way, the pain disseminating temporarily.

"Fuck, Mike! It's the other ones!" a tall one said to the leader.

"Son of a bitch!" he yelled. His face was clearly panicked now.

"Give me the blade," I whispered. Before they could respond six of the red-eyes entered the circle of zombies that had now stopped moving.

"Mike, give...me...the...machete," I said slowly. The convicts had stopped moving. They had obviously seen the red-eyes before and were paralyzed with fear. As the red-eyes spread out around us I saw the same one that I had encountered earlier. It made eye-contact with me. I didn't see madness in its eyes, but cool, calculating murder. We didn't stand a chance.

They circled us for a few minutes, grunting and snarling. They also made the guttural sound. I was convinced that they were communicating with each other. Did that mean the one from before was trying to communicate with me? If that was true, then it means that...

I took a sharp breath into my lungs, as the realization hit me like a blow to the chest. My head began to pound as I recalled everything that had happened in the past few months. When I blacked out in the cabin enthralled with pain I awoke and knew I was different. I healed faster than normal. I was stronger and faster and I barely tried.

The hallucinations came next. Everyone was infected somehow. Some turned to zombies. Some turned into red-eyes. Some went completely unharmed, but it still slumbered in their bodies. I still didn't know how it started, but it was there. Then, there was another type of result. A type that blurred the line between undead and human.

It explained everything. Why they tried to speak to me. Why I was left alive that night we first came to Larshall. The reason I could fight so well.

My vision blurred and the edges turned gray. As I tried to look at the red-eye who encountered me earlier the edges changed from gray to red. At first, I thought that blood was covering my vision. I let out a scream as I realized what was

207

happening. One of the convicts turned to look at me. He mouthed something, but I couldn't hear his words over the blood pounding in my head.

The other red-eyes had stopped circling. I looked at the one with the tattered clothes around its neck.

"Kill them," I said to it.

The red-eyes attacked.

It was a slaughter.

$\mathscr{P}_{art}$ *III*

It's funny when we look back before the apocalypse and think about all the things we took for granted. We were so concerned with money and objects and beauty that when the outbreak occurred no one knew how to survive. Millions were killed in the first weeks. Millions more over during the struggle for safety.

So much was lost that may never be recovered. Technology in particular. We were back in the mid-1900's again. People died of simple infections that had been curable with a pill at the turn of the century. No one was worried about cancer, but about a cold and the flu.

All of our satellite and space age technology had been rendered useless. Remember that fancy laptop? Useless. Cell phone? Useless. New car with the leather interior and built in GPS? Broken and busted down somewhere. Fancy wardrobe with three hundred dollar jeans? Definitely useless.

In our new world survival is top-priority. The war is essentially over, but the danger remains and is ever present. We must remain vigilante to that threat. Some oppose our efforts, calling them useless and mundane. They are the ones without hope.

Hope is what keeps us going. Hope is the element that makes us keep fighting. Hope is why we fled. Hope is why we fight to return.

Even in an undead world, hope survives.

Part III

Except from Ashley's Journal

I knew it was him as soon as the first zombie's head exploded beneath Charlie. No matter what anyone said I knew he wouldn't leave. Still, I kept my mouth shut. I let them have their rumors of zombies with guns or rogue cops out in the streets. It would only be a matter of time. Soon he would find a way in and get us out. Not just me, but all of the innocent people locked in these cages.

He would make it inside.

We would be free.

Chapter Nineteen

My world had changed.

After the slaughter of the convicts in the street I found myself alone and surrounded by red-eyes and zombies. The world looked different. Everything had a reddish tint to it. While the undead feasted the red-eyes watched me. They made that guttural sound, but I could not understand them. My own voice seemed raspy to my ears when I tried speaking to them. Soon after they lost interest in me and went about their way. With no other options and feeling exhaustion beginning to set in, I made my way back to the apartment I had taken residence in.

I limped as I walked. The gunshot wound had stopped bleeding and I suspected that it had already begun to heal, but it still hurt to put pressure on it. I walked slowly past zombies who took no interest in me. It was both comforting and disturbing to no longer be part of their menu. My biggest fear now was whether or not I too would want to experience the taste of human flesh.

I passed the spot where Alice was shot. The blood trail vanishing in the middle of the alley bothered me. I decided that I had enough strength for a cursory look around. I checked inside open doors and broken windows. I looked down the alley the trail led to and found nothing at all. My heart ached as I came to the conclusion that I might never see that dog again.

That feeling of emotion was a good thing. It told me that I was still, at least in part, a human. Feeling remorse is not something that I imagined the undead being capable of doing. I garnered from the composed look the red-eyes had before they attacked that they were also unable to feel remorse for the loss of a loved one.

I made it back to the apartment without incident. When I got inside I stripped my clothing off and fell to the bed.

* * * * *

I found myself standing alone in the middle of the cabin. I immediately knew it was another hallucination, or dream, or whatever it was. I waited for someone to show up, but after a few minutes I was still alone.

"Hello?"

No response. I waited a few more minutes, but still nothing happened. I walked towards the door and opened it. On the other side was another room exactly like the one I was in. Confused, I walked through the door anyway. And I was still alone in the room.

"What's going on?"

A growl filled the room, like the one a red-eye makes. I steadied myself and circled slowly, waiting for something to leap out and attack me. Ashley pulled herself up from behind a couch, red eyes fixed on me.

"Ashley, what's happening now?"

She opened her mouth, but only the guttural sound of the red-eyes came out. Her voice was lost.

"I don't understand you. What's going on?"

214

More of the same sounds, Ashley's face growing more desperate and frustrated.

"Please…please just tell me what is happening," I begged for release from this nightmare. I held my hand out and started walking toward her. She backed away quickly, like she was afraid of me.

"No, stop. Don't do that. I could never hurt you. Just tell me what is going on."

As I was about to touch her, the dream ended.

* * * * *

When I awoke I had no idea how much time had passed. I sat up and opened my eyes. Everything still had a red tint. The room appeared to be bright. I stood up and went to the window. Outside the sky was lit. It appeared to be a violet color instead of blue. The sun was high in the violet field. It was more orange instead of yellow.

I looked down into the street below. Somehow the world appeared to be in more detail. Was it because of the vision or was it because of some metaphysical new outlook on life? I looked closer and began to make out small movements that I had never noticed before. It struck me after a few moments that I was seeing small rodents scampering among the debris. Now I understood why the red-eyes were such good hunters.

I turned around to head for the bathroom and stopped when I felt soreness from my foot. I looked down to find the gunshot wound. It was already scabbed over. I sat back on the bed and pulled my leg closer. The bullet had gone in, but I couldn't find an exit wound. That meant it was still in my left foot. I had no choice. I would have to try and dig it out.

The pain was excruciating as I dug a knife into my skin. I thought I was going to pass out, but I had to keep going. I dug a bit deeper and finally felt the blade contact the metal fragment of the bullet. I grabbed a pair of tweezers off the bed stand and pulled the bullet out. After I did, the pain started to subside. I wrapped the freshly opened wound in bandages, even though I knew the bleeding would soon stop. Hopefully any infection I could get from the wound would be taken care of by the agent coursing through my veins.

I went into the bathroom and looked into the mirror. This was the first time I looked at myself in weeks, save for casual glances. My body was definitely different. Not big and muscular like other red-eyes, but more lean. My eyes were not quite what I expected. Only one appeared to be different. I closed my left eye. Nothing changed. Then I closed my right eye.

I became dizzy and disoriented as the field of red vanished and normal colors exploded in my head. The room became a lot brighter. It took a moment to adjust and looked back into the mirror. My body still looked the same, but my skin was back to its regular color. I looked at the open eye and saw it was unchanged. I opened my right eye slowly and the red tint returned to everything.

For a few minutes I tried to focus on looking out of my left eye only, but I was unsuccessful. I experimented with a few different ideas only to discover that my right eye retained dominance as long as it could see something. After taking a much needed shower I went back into the bedroom, letting the water drip off me slowly.

Dressing in jeans and a black t-shirt, I picked my boots up and pondered their usefulness of keeping my feet dry with a bullet hole in the top. I would have to look for another pair as I scavenged around. I went back to the bathroom to brush my teeth. Standing there looking at myself showed me that my hair was too long. Finding a pair of scissors I went into the bedroom to give myself a haircut, albeit a crude one. It didn't turn out too bad, considering.

I took a moment to consider why vanity had become important to me all of a sudden. In the months that have passed I took care of my hygiene, but I never fretted like this. Maybe it was because I was afraid of losing touch with humanity.

I went back into the bedroom and tore an old t-shirt into strips. Using the strips as a makeshift headband, I pulled it down over my right eye. After my vision returned to normal I put my hat and vest on, strapped my empty sheath to my belt and then went out to the kitchen.

I took out a jar of peanut butter and a spoon, but couldn't bring myself to eat more than a spoonful. I had no appetite. The taste was still the same, which boded well for me not wanting to eat humans, but I just wasn't hungry. Still, I forced myself to eat another spoonful and drink a glass of water.

I looked at the clock on the wall. It was almost two in the afternoon. At first I was concerned about losing daylight, but now that didn't really matter anymore. I had to reflect on what had happened last night. Did I save Charlie or prolong his torture? It was possible that I just created more of a problem. They would be on closer guard now, especially considering their own men would not be coming back. I wondered if keeping the ones who chased me alive would have turned out to be more beneficial.

That was assuming that I actually had some sort of control last night. Did the red-eyes really attack the convicts because I told them too? Or was it a mere coincidence of timing? The whole scene was somewhat blurry in my memory. If I did order their deaths, then it was conceivable that I also could have saved them from such a horrid end. I would have to find out whether or not I really had any power over the undead.

Regardless of what I did next I would need weapons. They should be lying a few blocks away and I would have to go and get them. I also wanted to look around where Alice had gone missing now that it was daylight. Hopefully, I would find out what happened to her. She couldn't have just disappeared. At the worst something ate her, and even then I should be able to find remains of some sort. After finishing my glass of water the search for my weapons, and some answers, would begin.

I went outside heading first for the spot where Alice disappeared. I found the blood trail on the sidewalk and followed it until it disappeared in the alleyway, crouching down and looking closer. There were some bits of fur stuck to the dried blood. She had been dragged to this spot, but by what? And where did they go? There were no signs of a fight and no extra blood. Being picked up would explain the blood trail disappearing, but where could she have been taken? And, more importantly, by who or what?

I decided to check the surrounding buildings, this time not discriminating doors that were closed. One door was locked, but all the others in the area revealed nothing. Halfway through my search I got the distinctive feeling that I was being watched. Except for some zombies who were not paying me any attention, there were no signs of anyone around. Some of them kept staring in my direction, and so I figured that was where the feeling must have been coming from. A while later I gave up on my search and went to find my weapons.

When I reached the sight of the slaughter I found a cluster of the undead. Unlike the night before they were no longer swarming. Like the others they were mostly just standing around. Some had the wherewithal to investigate the area, searching for something to eat, but not many.

Having time to watch them when they weren't attacking me made me reconsider my original ideas about them. First, they were definitely not all completely mindless. Some of them were clever enough to walk in open doors and climb in windows, even without the promise of food on the other side. I watched as two of them moved together over a pile of debris. They didn't really help each other in the traditional sense, but they realized they would only get past it if they moved at the same time, using each other to steady their movements. I had to wonder if they could be taught, perhaps by red-eyes.

The remains of the convicts spread over a wide area. There wasn't much left except for torn clothing and weapons strewn about the streets. Even some of the bones had been smashed open and the marrow sucked out. With this many zombies around I was surprised even that remained. I found my machete and pistol, and using some tattered cloth, I cleaned both off. Craftford's revolver – I still couldn't bring myself to call it mine – was almost unblemished. Then I began looking at the rest of the gear scattered around.

I found that two of the convicts were using the same caliber rounds that I was and helped myself to few scattered rounds that I found in their pockets. There was not much and all together, including what I had to begin with, I had seventeen rounds. Not much, but certainly better than nothing. Besides, apparently now it wasn't zombies I had to worry about.

Before I turned to leave I took one last look at the scene. How much of this was my doing? Did the red-eyes actually understand my command to kill my captors last night, or had the timing simply been a coincidence? If they had listened to me, then would they have also listened if I told them not to attack? I turned to leave and found a zombie blocking my path. Rather than just walk around him I decided to try an experiment.

The zombie was facing away from me. I decided to start small.

"Turn around."

The zombie turned slowly around the face me. So did all of the others that were around me. I couldn't believe it worked.

"Move."

It stood there staring at me blankly.

"Move," I said again. I raised my arm and pointed to the right.

It still just stood there. I knew it was too good to be true. I decided this wasn't worth my time and moved past the walker. As I did, I made a comment about its lack of intelligence. It turned around to look at me. I paused a moment, then went around the back of it again.

"I'm over here now."

Again it turned to face me. Damn. It wasn't taking orders at all. It was just following the sound of my voice. It probably thought I was food, and then when it saw me, it somehow recognized me as not being on the menu. I must have been producing some sort of pheromone or something that identified me as friendly. Or their black eyes saw me differently somehow. That was a good thing. However, unless they would die from getting dizzy, or there was a zombie disco around somewhere, then getting them to constantly turn around would be a useless talent. Frustrated, I started back toward the prison.

As I walked I realized that part of me was relieved by my inability to control the undead. First, it meant that I was not responsible for the brutal murder of the unfortunate remains that were scattered around. Second, it gave me another connection to humanity and one less toward the zombies. Controlling them could be useful, but I valued my humanity far more.

The office was my next destination. From there I could see if anything was different with the prison and plan my next move. Ashley was still inside and I wanted to get her out as quickly as possible. I was still afraid that my actions had actually made things much worse for her and Chris.

I turned a corner and almost instantly felt the sensation of being watched fall over me again. I was back on the block where Alice went missing. There was definitely something or someone there that wasn't a zombie. I hadn't realized that the feeling was gone until I came back here. Perhaps it was a red-eye stalking me from a distance. I went over to the spot where the trail disappeared and looked around. I started looking in windows of the buildings around me. There was a window on the fourth floor of a red brick building near where the blood trail disappeared. The window was open and the curtain was blowing in the breeze, but I couldn't see anything inside.

Now would be a good time to see if the red vision helped. I pulled the makeshift bandana up and let the field of red fill my vision. I looked back into the window. I couldn't see details, but I could make out a shadow moving among the rest of the darkness. Someone was up there for certain. It left me with two options: either find a way in or wait and see if I could learn anything else. Every minute I spent out here was another Ashley was in danger, but I couldn't ignore this. Alice could be up there. Or it could be a new threat.

I pulled the cloth back over my eye and looked up to find the entrance appeared to be the same door that was locked earlier. I should have figured as much. I decided to call out to the open window.

"Hello!" I called. "I know you're up there."

No response.

"I won't hurt you!"

Still nothing.

"I'm just looking for my dog!" I yelled.

I waited a few minutes but still there was no reply. It was possible that it was just a zombie in the window. But they were all over and I knew that feeling of being watched wasn't from them. And I didn't think a red-eye would be hiding. What need did they have to hide from me? No, there was definitely a human up there trying to avoid detection. Unsure of how best to approach the mysterious person, I decided to let old habits win out and settled on honestly being the best policy.

"Look, I'm going to find a way in, so you might as well come to the window and show yourself. I really don't have time for games." I waited a few minutes and then started for the door. A few feet from it I stopped as a bowling ball landed on the ground in front of me about three feet away. I looked back at the window in time to see a pair of arms duck back inside. The window shut soon after. Looks like whoever it was had intentions of making this difficult.

The door was solid and heavy and the windows on the bottom floor were too small to squeeze though. I walked around the back hoping to find another way in, but all I found was a fire door. They only open one way, and without a crowbar I had little hope of prying it open. Besides, if the place was secure I did not want to jeopardize that by breaking in forcefully.

The fire escape was raised too high for me to reach and after the third try I gave up. Whoever was up there found a pretty good spot to hide. It was definitely good enough to keep the undead out. But I was not undead…not yet.

I decided to keep my efforts simple. I began looking around for debris to stack up to reach the fire escape. After a few minutes of searching and stacking boxes and pallets I opened a door in a nearby building to find a 12-step ladder. "Problem solved," I said to myself, smiling.

I went back to the fire escape and with the ladder I was easily able to reach it and climb up the building. The window the bowling ball fell from was on the fourth floor, so I made my way up to the fifth before looking for a window to open.

I climbed in quietly. It was dark, so I removed the cloth from my eye again. The room brightened slightly and I was able to avoid any obstacles in my way. I wanted to get a jump on whoever threw the bowling ball at me. I wasn't out to hurt them, but I didn't want any more surprises. The apartment was definitely ransacked, presumably by the inhabitants below. I was able to move quietly into the hallway. Lights in the hall had been broken. I made my way down a staircase to the fourth floor. Beyond that the stairs were completely blocked by furniture. When I stepped into the hall I could hear muffled voices. I moved to the door and pressed my ear to it. There were two speakers. I could make a few words.

They were definitely arguing. The first voice, a female, accused the other, a male, of not being old enough to know any better, though both voices sounded young. After hearing the word "bowling" I had to assume that they were specifically discussing dropping the ball on me. From what I could understand the argument had to do with whether or not I was going to hurt them. I decided the best way to end their argument was to let them know I was here.

I knocked on the door. I kept it friendly, like I was a visiting neighbor. The voices inside went silent. After a few moments of nothing I knocked again.

"Hello?" I called. "I know you're in there. Please open the door."

"Go away!" the female voice called back. She was definitely younger, teenager at best.

"I heard you talking. I'm not going to hurt you."

"You're one of them! We saw you outside!"

"I'm not. Really. Please let me in."

"They don't bother you. That means you're infected."

I couldn't fault her logic. "Look, I just want to know where my dog is."

The other side was silent. Alice was in there. I waited, "I know she's hurt. I want to help her. She means a lot to me."

"She's in here. We're taking care of her," the female said.

"Thank you."

"Please go away now," she said.

"I won't," I replied calmly.

"Why not?" She was pleading. The girl was desperate to get rid of me. I felt bad that I scared her so much.

"I want to see her."

After a moment I heard the door locks unhinge. It opened as far as the chain lock would allow and the face of a young brunette teenager, no more than sixteen by the looks of her, appeared in the gap.

"If we let you see her will you go away?"

"Yes." I wasn't lying. I would leave, but I would definitely be back.

"No weapons," she said, eyeing the machete strapped to my side and the rifle slung around my shoulder.

"Alright." I began taking all of my gear off and tossing it aside where she could see. I even began taking knives out of my vest pockets. I wasn't afraid of going in unarmed. I also didn't want to give the girl another reason not to trust me.

"What's your name?" I asked as I continued pulling stuff out of my pockets.

"Carmen," she said after a moment of hesitation.

I gave her my name and asked her how old she was. As I expected she was young, only fifteen. Her brother, whose name was Jake, was thirteen. After I turned around twice to show her I had no other weapons on me, she closed the door to unlatch the chain.

When the door opened the two of them were standing there, armed. She had a large kitchen knife in her right hand. Jake held a baseball bat out in front of him. Carmen was slender and athletic with ragged hair grown past her shoulders. Jake was a bit smaller, but more rounded. I imagined he might have been larger before the outbreak. Months of not eating well would have significantly reduced his weight. I could picture him being the type to live off a computer before life was turned upside down. He certainly wasn't holding the bat right.

"The dog is in the other room. Walk slowly," she ordered. The children were scared. I had to wonder how they made it this long. They held the weapons out defensively as I passed them. I kept my hands visible and moved slowly across the apartment.

I walked into the other room and found Alice lying on a blanket. She was out, but I could see her chest rise and fall slowly. I felt relieved to see that she was still alive. As I bent down to inspect her wounds I thanked the two children for taking care of her.

"You've seen her. Now get out," the girl said fiercely.

"I'm not going until I clean her up a bit. Whoever dressed this wound did an okay job, but it needs cleaning."

"We'll do it," Jake said.

"I don't think so. Get me some water and some strips of cloth."

Neither one moved.

"Please?"

The boy looked at his sister. She never took her eyes off of me and never lowered the knife. After a moment he left the room and brought me the supplies I asked for.

I spent the next few minutes cleaning Alice's wounds. As I was wiping around the bullet wound I felt a lump indicating it was still inside of her. I could feel it just beneath the skin. I would have to try and dig it out like I did to myself.

"I need a knife," I said.

"Not a chance."

"If I don't remove the bullet, then it won't heal properly." I tried explaining.

Carmen simply stared back at me. .

"Smallest one should do the trick." I smiled as I said it. She continued to glare at me, untrusting. Again, the boy left without waiting for an invitation from his sister and came back with a small pocket knife. It wasn't from my collection and I assumed it was his.

After performing the crude surgery I cleaned and dressed the wounds. Without a word I stood up and went to the sink to wash my hands and the knife. Then I went out towards the door. Before I left I turned and handed the pocket knife back to Jake, then I told them that I would be back in a few hours.

"Why?" Carmen asked.

"I'll need to check on her. I plan on bringing a few things back. Is there anything that you need?" I asked.

"We're fine."

"Alright then, I'll see you later." I stepped out the door. It was slammed and locked behind me. I picked up my equipment and left.

Chapter Twenty

    My first stop after leaving the children's apartment was the office building that served as my outpost while I watched the prison. I went in to find the place completely torn apart; all of the windows had been smashed on every floor of the building and the blinds and curtains had been torn down. The few supplies I had left were gone, which didn't bother me too much since there was not much there. I kept myself away from the window, knowing the convicts would be keeping a close eye on the place.

    Back outside I headed toward the corner of the building hoping to peek around and look at the prison. I walked past the body of the convict I had shot in the alley and noticed it was partially eaten. Whatever was eating it had left. When I reached the corner I peered around slowly.

    I almost threw up. Hanging from the roof of the prison, about two floors up from the ground, a corpse hung from a thick rope. The clothing was covered in blood. An eye was missing. The left arm was gone. The right was charred black. The blood stain on the corpse's pants suggested genital mutilation. After a few minutes I realized it was what was left of Charlie. As a final insult and warning to me, what was left of the body was struggling. The bastards tortured him and then had him bitten.

I wanted to use the rifle I had recovered and end his misery, but I knew that would only cause more trouble. Right now they had no idea if I were alive or dead. I wouldn't do anything to spoil that small advantage until I was ready to move.

With only a few hours of daylight left I decided it was time to get some materials together and head back to the children's apartment. I wanted to bring Alice some food and whatever else I could scrounge up for the two kids. I don't know what they had in way of supplies, but if nothing else it would hopefully get the girl to trust me. As much as I wanted to rescue Ashley from the prison, my conscience would not allow me to leave the two children behind when it was time to flee Larshall. It would be easier if they came willingly. And Ashley would kill me herself if she ever found out I didn't help them.

I also wanted to ask them a few questions. First, how had they managed to stay alive and undetected for so long? Second, why were there no hordes of zombies clamoring for their flesh on the street below? They were far enough from the street of corpses, and there were zombies down on the streets below them. From what I had seen they became absolutely relentless when they discovered food in an area. So how had the two young kids managed to avoid that for so long?

I went back to my apartment and gathered what I needed. I also spent a few minutes re-bandaging my foot. The wound was healing rapidly. By morning bandages wouldn't be necessary. I took the rest of the bandages I had for Alice and went out. After a few minutes I made it to the building with the children inside. I walked around back to find the fire escape properly lowered. The kids were expecting me. That was a good sign.

It took two trips to the fifth floor to get all of the supplies up. I didn't have much, but the ladder prevented me from being able to do it all at once. I made a mental note to ask the kids how they got Alice upstairs. I doubted that either of them could have carried her up the ladder and there was no way they cleared the debris in the stairwell. I raised the fire escape after I was finished and went down to the entrance to their apartment. I knocked on the door. After a moment it opened, again stopping as the chain was pulled taught. Carmen's face appeared in the gap.

"Weapons," she said firmly. Her voice had lost its ferocity, but she was still cautious about me. I didn't really blame her.

I let out a sigh but proceeded to take off my gear as I did before. I put the bags of supplies near the door as I put the weapons against the back wall in the hallway. Once again I spun around the show her I was unarmed. Finally, she opened the door and I was able to go inside.

She still held the knife, but not as defensively as before. Her brother was sitting in a chair by the window. He glanced in my direction and kept his gaze on me as I entered the room. I had been gone just over an hour and a half, and in that time he seemed to have accepted that I was coming back.

"There is food in the large bag. Plenty for all of us," I said. I tried to keep my demeanor as friendly as possible.

"You can't bribe us. We have plenty of food," she said rather curtly.

"Oh. Alright then. I suppose I'll just enjoy it myself." I began unloading the best of the food supplies that I had brought with me. Mostly microwaveable goods and the frozen pizza that I had been saving. Jake's eyes lit up at the sight of the food and I knew they hadn't eaten well in quite some time.

"What's in the other bag?" Jake asked.

"Hmm? Oh, medical supplies and some food for Alice. I had this stuff at my place and brought it here." I explained.

229

I caught Carmen staring at the food I had pulled out of the bag and decided to put it back in. "I'm not too hungry though, so I guess I'll just go and check on Alice." I grabbed the bag and went into the other room. I closed the door behind me and waited. I could hear their muffled voices arguing again and smiled.

Alice was still unconscious, but she seemed to be breathing easier. From the bag I pulled out a water bottle and unscrewed the cap. I rested her head in my lap and poured the water slowly into her mouth. After I was satisfied that a decent amount made its way down her throat I gently placed her head back down on the blanket. Then I tended to her wounds. The fresh bandages from before were spoiled after my makeshift surgery. I removed the bloodied bandages slowly and applied fresh ones and antiseptics to prevent infection. When I was finished I went back to the other room.

Jake was standing near the table with my other bag on it yelling at his sister. He stopped when I entered.

"What's wrong?" I asked.

"Nothing that concerns you," Carmen said giving me a nasty look.

"Come on, Carmen! He brought food!" Jake was pleading with his sister.

"We can't trust him, Jake. We can't trust anyone. You know that!" She looked at him angrily as she spoke.

"But I'm hungry!"

"You're always hungry!"

"If I might interject," I started. After they were both looking at me I continued, "Your sister is right not to trust me, Jake. She doesn't know who I am. For all she knows I'm one of the guys from the prison, which I'm guessing you know all about." Carmen looked at me sternly. Jake looked disappointed that his sister was right.

"But, if you'll give me the opportunity, then I'll tell you about myself." I turned the last part of my words to Carmen directly. She looked at her brother, whose eyes continued to plead. The boy was hungry, that much was obvious.

"Fine. We'll listen," she finally relented. She put the knife on the counter and crossed her arms. Jake was all smiles.

"Excellent! We'll discuss everything over dinner. I'll do all the work and you two relax for once," I replied and ushered them away from the kitchen area before either one could say another word.

The meal actually turned out pretty well. I was able to come up with a nice spread. We had soda to drink, buttered microwaveable noodles and the featured dish, a deep-dish microwaveable pizza. For dessert I had brought along several cans of fruit and powdered sugar to pour on it. As the sun began to set in the west, I laid the food out onto the living room table and invited my hosts to join me for what I was calling a banquet.

As the kids sat down I decided that I should treat them as adults, even Jake, so that they would begin to trust me more. I raised my glass after they were seated. "I propose a toast," I started, then waited for them to follow suit with their own glasses. Jake raised his excitedly, while Carmen followed suit, but with less amusement. "To good food, finding new friends and, most importantly, our continued survival in a forsaken world." I clinked both of their glasses, then drank. They mimicked my actions.

"Please, dig in." I waved my hand invitingly over the food. Jake went right for the pizza. Carmen hesitated, but eventually gave in to her hunger and began eating. She started off slow, but her pace quickened as she tasted the food.

"You're not eating?" Carmen asked me. I had not yet reached for anything, content on letting them eat their fill first.

I decided to take her question as an invitation and helped myself to the noodles and a slice of the pizza. After a few minutes there was almost no food left. They were hungrier than I thought.

"It's really good. Thank you," Jake said with a forkful of noodles hanging out of his mouth.

"You are quite welcome. It was the least I could do since you were kind enough to rescue my dog." I raised my glass again.

"How long have you had her?" He asked.

"Well, let's see. It's around the beginning of May, so…about four months."

"She wasn't always yours, then," Carmen observed.

"No, she wasn't. In fact, I could probably say that she still isn't mine. We found each other right after the start of all this. Over the past few months we have survived by working as a team. When she was shot last night I was really afraid that she was dead. I went looking for her body to give her a proper burial, and when I couldn't find it I hoped she might still be alive. You really have no idea how thrilled I was to find you all here. Even if you did try to drop a bowling ball on me."

"So what happened after they caught you and dragged you off? We saw that part," Carmen said suspiciously.

I hesitated before answering. I wanted to spare them most of the details. "A series of events that eventually led to me being able to escape. Unfortunately, they were all killed."

"Why don't the monsters attack you?" Jake asked before either of us could say anything else. Carmen was silent.

Again I was cautious. I wanted to be honest, but I also did not want them to be afraid of me. Although I had doubts that I could prevent that from happening. "To be completely honest, Jake, I'm not entirely sure. But I will tell you what I do know. First, I am definitely somehow infected."

"I knew it!" Carmen spat and backed her chair from the table with a screech.

"But, I'm not completely turned, as you can plainly see," I rushed ahead before she could get ahead of herself, "Beneath this cloth here I have a red-eye that allows me to see more clearly, especially in the dark. I'm also a bit stronger and faster than a normal person. But not nearly as strong or fast as the real red-eyes. I heal well, also."

"Do you eat people?" Jake asked.

I laughed, trying to lessen the fear that had crept into his voice with the question. "No. I still only crave pizza and pasta, both of which are hard to come by. I don't know why they stopped trying to kill me, but I still have no quarrel killing them. Especially if they threaten my friends." I winked at him knowingly and he smiled back, the fear vanished.

As dinner ended and we moved on to dessert I continued to win the kids over with tales from my survival story. I embellished here and there for dramatic effect, but overall I never strayed far from what actually happened. I did leave out the worst bits such as Becca's death. I didn't think they'd care to hear that part.

Occasionally they would ask a question I couldn't fully answer, but as any skilled teacher could, I was easily able to redirect their prying curiosity. Soon they warmed up to me. Even Carmen stopped scowling and dared to break a smile at some parts. She particularly liked when I spoke of my plans to rescue Ashley from the convicts.

"So, how did you two manage to survive this long?" I finally asked as I spooned the last bit of fruit from my bowl.

"We stayed really quiet. All of the time." Jake emphasized the last part.

"Is that they secret then? Staying quiet?"

"Not quite that simple. Sometimes we didn't even eat. And we moved around a lot. We've only been here for a few weeks," Carmen added, "Sometimes we had help, adults who found us but eventually were killed or separated from us."

"We thought about going to the prison, but after watching them for a few days we decided that wasn't a good idea. Some of those guys are pretty scary."

I nodded in agreement and added solemnly. "Indeed they are."

"One time," she started, "they…" she couldn't finish what she was saying. Instead her eyes burst into tears and she began crying.

I got up and moved beside her. I slowly put my arm around her and whispered that it was okay.

"But they beat her!" She cried loudly, "She was only two years older than me and they tore her apart! They're worse than the zombies!" She broke down more into a series of "how could they" and "why." She had been holding this in for a long time. Whatever she saw was traumatic. I began to feel more anger at the bastards in the prison than I did before.

When it came down to what was worse, either the zombies or the convicts, the convicts won every time. They had proven to be absolute scum of the Earth. They were the lowest form of life I could imagine. Zombies acted on instinct. The convicts acted on choice.

"I think it's time we all got some rest," I said softly as she continued to sob. "You both go and lay down. Tonight you will be completely safe. Tonight I'll watch over you so you can rest easy."

Neither of them replied. Instead they silently went into the other room where Alice was resting. After a few minutes I checked in and found them fast asleep. I could only hope their dreams were pleasant.

I went out into the hallway and brought my weapons inside. I pulled a table and a chair over near the window and made myself comfortable. I opened the window and allowed the breeze to drift inside. Outside the air was cool and dry. It was pleasant, except for the constant scent of decay that I could still smell at first, but then quickly became used to.

The sun had set and a few streetlights were on. I was still grateful this place had power. I would be reluctant to leave. But after the horrors I had witnessed I knew I couldn't stay. Once I got Ashley safely out of the prison, we would leave Larshall for good. Probably head west, like the flyers from the plane had urged.

I spent some time cleaning my weapons. They were in pretty decent shape, considering. After I was satisfied with their appearance I rested my head back and began to fall asleep in the chair. The last thing I heard was a cricket chirping softly in the night. It went silent at the howl of a red-eye.

Chapter Twenty-One

I awoke just before dawn. It was going to be a clear day from the looks of it. By my account it was May 3rd, but that could have been off by a few days. Today would be an excellent day to start planning how I was going to get her out.

The kids were still asleep, but when I opened the door Alice opened her eyes. I petted her softly. She wagged her tail and licked my face. She tried to stand up, but fell over in pain almost instantly. I went into the bag I had brought and got her food and water. She ate hungrily. The sound of the two of us woke Carmen.

"Good morning," I whispered softly.

"What time is it?" She asked sleepily.

"Around 5:30am. You slept quite some time."

She got out of bed and came down to the floor. "Hey girl! You're awake." She reached out to pet Alice.

At first Alice tried to move away, unfamiliar with the girl. However, after she saw my reactions she stayed put and continued to wag her tail.

"She likes you," I said. "And she's definitely grateful for you saving her. So am I."

"You're welcome," she finally said. "But don't let her get shot again."

"Of course not." I bent down and whispered to Alice that I would be back later. Carmen heard me and stood up to follow me out to the other room.

"Where are you going?" She asked as she went for a glass of water.

"I'm going to get ready for my daring rescue." I smiled and put my arms on my hips as I said it. Carmen smiled at me in a "you're so corny but I like it" sort of way that only teenagers can pull off. If that was what it took to get the girl to trust me, then I would happily play the part.

"Oh, well be careful."

"I need to find a few working vehicles and get them ready. It would be nice to find some new weapons also. Those might not be enough." I gestured to the table. She went over and began looking at them. I was glad she didn't yell at me for bringing them inside.

"Did you try the hunting store?" She asked.

I stopped in my tracks. Her words were the answer to my prayers. "What hunting store?"

"I'm not sure where exactly, but we passed one when we first came here. It was tucked back in a small plaza."

"Any idea at all where?"

"Near the Wal-Mart, I think."

I closed my eyes as I thought about the last Wal-Mart I visited. The image of Jesse's face flashed in my head.

"I'll have to look for it. First, I need a ride though. And there's always a chance the convicts already hit it."

"They didn't," she said confidently.

"How do you know?"

"They only left once in the last month, and they went in the opposite direction that time." She had to be referring to the same time they took Ashley from me.

"I'll check it out." I started to pick up the machete. I was leaving everything else behind. I didn't think I would need it now. As an afterthought I tucked Mr. Craftford's revolver in my belt. More for luck than anything else.

"They haven't gone out since..." I meant it to be a thought, but the words found their way into my throat.

"No. Why?"

"Then they'll have to come out again." I left it at that and went out the door.

Outside it only took me a few minutes to find a working car. But it took almost two hours to navigate the streets. As I drove past, zombies turned to face me. Some in the distance would being to move toward me, but the closest ones just acknowledged my presence and moved on.

It was still odd not being attacked by them. I was able to actually watch them now, pick out details I would have missed when I was constantly on the move. I saw one that clearly had a rat tail hanging from its mouth; this answered one of the questions that I still had. It meant that nothing was safe from their ravenous hunger. That did not bode well for nature.

I found the plaza and was relieved to see that there was actually not a Wal-Mart nearby. There was a drug store off on the side, a tax adjuster, a pizza restaurant, some type of discount supply store, a few other useless places and my personal holy grail, a hunting and fishing supply store. A sign above the gated store read: *Eddie's Sporting Goods*. I knew I would need a larger vehicle.

Instead of heading right for Eddie's I went to the drugstore first. It was a national chain that carried a little bit of everything. I found the door locked. After I broke in I began raiding everything. They had those small hand baskets. I must have made a dozen trips, gathering everything from pantry items that were still okay to medical supplies and hair brushes.

The car was full of baskets and items just tossed in as an afterthought. Working alone I might spend all day in the

239

drugstore alone. I decided to head back and bring the kids along. The area was safe enough and any zombies in the area I could manage. Besides, they needed to get out.

When I got back I parked near the fire escape and went upstairs. Jake was awake now also. When I took them down and showed them the car their eyes went wide. Rather than haul each basket up and down the ladder, Carmen showed me the pulley system they made on the second floor. That was what they used to get Alice up the ladder. Despite the ease of the pulley, it still took nearly an hour to get the car unloaded.

"It's going to take awhile to organize this." Carmen said as we stared at the corner of the apartment where the baskets were piled.

"We'll do it later. There's still a lot more to get. And we haven't gone to the hunting store yet."

"What do you mean 'we'?" she asked.

"I'll be honest, there's a lot of stuff. I need help."

"That doesn't sound like a good idea."

"The area is quiet. I'll keep you safe from anything there," I promised.

She turned to Jake. "What do you think?"

Jake thought a moment then replied, "Can we eat first?"

I laughed. "Try not to fill up on junk food. No energy in that stuff."

Getting back to the plaza was considerably easier the second time around. This time we took a minivan that was near the apartment. I had two reasons for this: first, the van was bigger, and second, if I could get others out of the prison we would need more vehicles.

When we arrived I pulled the van right up to the door of the drugstore. The kids could climb in and out through the sliding door and zombies would not be able to get past into the store after them. I told them to get everything they thought was useful, and then I got out and went to Eddie's.

The zombies in the area reacted to the presence of the children and began making their way toward the van. I used my machete to kill the nearest ones before crossing the parking lot. It was considerably easier to kill them now that they were not attacking me directly. It was also odd. I actually felt morose after I slew the fourth one. Without their desire to attack me, they were essentially helpless.

As an experiment, I sheathed the machete and pushed a zombie into a nearby car. I pinned it to the car by the shoulders. It never took its eyes off of the van. I punched it twice in the head, but still it ignored me and moaned at the drug store. Somewhat frustrated that I couldn't draw its attention away from the kids, I snapped its neck and continued on. I used the machete to kill the ones between the sporting goods shop and the drugstore. There were not many.

Eddie's presented a new challenge; the store was locked and shuttered. I ran around the back of the plaza to find a fire door that was securely locked. Making my way back to the front, I began inspecting the security features for exploitable weaknesses.

The shutter was a roll down security gate. There were two small windows, but my arm would barely fit inside. The gate was somewhat pliable and probably wouldn't give all the way, so running a car into it didn't seem like a good option. I needed to apply some sort of leverage to the bottom of the gate and pull up. The problem was that I didn't have any solid tools.

At a loss with how to get in, I made my way back to the drug store to see how the kids were doing. A few zombies had made their way to the entrance and were banging into the van trying to get past. I dispatched them and then climbed through the van into the store. The van was beginning to fill up with the contents of the shelves. They were doing a good job.

"Hello?" I called out.

"Hey! We're back here!" I heard Carmen shout back.

I made my way through the store and found them in the small electronic section. They were taking batteries, flashlights and radios off of the shelves. I was glad they left the motley collection of mp3 players and computer peripherals behind. They definitely learned how to survive over the last few months.

"How's it coming?" I asked.

"Good. We're going to finish here and then go to the soap section and stuff," Carmen explained.

"Alright. I have to take a walk and find something to use to get me into Eddie's. It's locked tight. Will you two be okay for awhile?" I asked.

"As long as they can't get in we'll be fine."

"They can't." I assured her.

"Okay good." She reached into her basket and pulled a package out. "Take one of these." It was a portable two-way radio.

"That's excellent, Carmen! Great job." I bent down to help her open the package. We put batteries in, set-up a channel and were all set.

"Can we have cool nicknames?" Jake asked enthusiastically.

"Anything you want, buddy. Surprise me." I tussled his hair and then started walking away. I was glad the kid's imagination hadn't been completely destroyed. "You guys are doing great here. Keep it up."

I left the store and began searching the area for some way to break into Eddie's. After only walking a few hundred yards away, I heard the sound. It was a soft rumble in the distance. A few minutes later it became louder.

My heartbeat raced as I recognized the sound. The convicts were out! Were they coming here? If they were we would have to leave in a hurry. I radioed back to the kids and told them to get in the van and get ready to leave. Carmen wanted to know why, but I had no desire to scare her. I was certain she was more afraid of them than the undead.

I went down to the corner and looked in the direction I heard the sound. Several blocks away I saw the vehicles go through an intersection and continue heading away. It seems they were content with hitting houses and this time would have to venture farther. That also meant their search would take time.

I ran back to the drug store as fast as I could. I could see the kids in the van waiting, surrounded by several zombies. I killed the ones in my way and climbed into the driver's seat.

"What's wrong?" Carmen asked.

I ignored her question as I started the car and drove away from the plaza. I went faster than before. The faces of the kids snapped me out of my thoughts. I calmed down long enough to explain what I was thinking.

"Listen, the convicts left the prison. I saw them drive away from here. That means that there are less of them in the prison."

"So?" Carmen's voice was panicked.

"So, now I'm going in. It's the best opportunity I'll have to save Ashley."

"What?! You can't! You'll be killed!"

"Maybe, maybe not. Either way I have to try. I'll drop you off at the apartment, then I'm taking the car and going for it," I said.

"No! No, you can't!"

"Carmen, listen to me. I have to try. Look at it this way. Even if I'm captured or killed you'll still have plenty of supplies. You'll be okay."

"Please, don't do this. Please," she pleaded. Jake was quiet, but his eyes told me he felt the same way.

"Listen, both of you. I'm going to try and save Ashley. After I get her out, then we'll all leave this place. We'll find a quiet place without a lot of zombies. It'll be safe there. But I'm not going anywhere without her. You have to accept that even if you don't understand."

I knew they wouldn't understand, but there would be no stopping me on this one. It was too good of an opportunity to pass. Carmen turned her head away from me. The rest of the drive was silent as I drove the minivan as fast as I could. We made it back to the apartment in twenty minutes.

I went upstairs with them and grabbed my weapons. As I tucked knives into various pockets and strapped the Beretta on, Alice came limping out of the other room. She looked up at me and whimpered.

"Sorry, girl. I'll be going alone this time."

She whimpered more. I wanted to believe she knew what I was about to do, but I wasn't certain. She just saw me gearing up and getting ready. I knew she understood what that meant. I bent down to pet her. She licked my face. I whispered in her ear to watch the kids.

"Alright, time for me to go," I said to the kids.

"Good luck," Jake said.

"Thanks, bud. Do me a favor?"

"Yeah?" He asked excitedly.

"Keep an eye on your sister and Alice."

"I will."

"Carmen?"

"Yes?" She replied. She was definitely angry that I was leaving.

"I still have the radio. I'll keep you updated," I said.

"Sure. Okay."

"I will come back," I promised.

She nodded at me. I went out the door. I hoped that I would see them again.

Chapter Twenty-Two

I made my way swiftly down the streets to the prison. It was early afternoon and there was still plenty of daylight left. The swamp of bodies took on a more nefarious look in the daytime. All the corpses were easier to see, but everything was different now. This time the jaws were not clacking as I walked past. It was also drier and easier to maneuver among the filth. There hadn't been a drop of rain since the storm a few weeks ago and most of the fluids had since dried up. The only similarity was the pungent smell of decay in the air, and I had become somewhat used to that over the past few weeks.

As I walked I kept my eye on the roof. No one was walking the edge, at least as far as I could see. That worried me. What if the prison had been abandoned? Maybe the reason they left was to escape and not just to find supplies this time. If that were the case, then I might never find Ashley. They had too much of a head start and once the trail went cold I would have no way of picking it up again.

I shook the thought away. Either way, though, I would still be checking the prison. They didn't have enough space to take everyone in the vehicles that I saw, so that meant there were either survivors or bodies inside. Maybe both.

I reached the same corner of the prison that I had stalked from the office. As I darted through the intersection I finally noticed a figure on the roof. That meant there were more inside. I banished the demons from the previous moment and began devising a way in. The guard turned the opposite corner and I kept moving.

My options were very limited. The complex was entirely fenced in except for the main entryway. In some places the fence had buckled, but not enough to get through or climb over and avoid the razor wire at the top. The only way I was going to get in would be if someone opened the door for me. With nothing else to go on, I ran to the front entrance.

"Help me! Please help me!" I screamed as I frantically began pounding on the door. "They're going to get me! Please help!"

After a few minutes of screaming and pounding I heard a voice up above me.

"Who the fuck are you?"

"You have to help me! The bastards are going to kill me! Please let me in!"

"What's in it for us?" the guard asked.

"Just open the door!" I screamed. I put a touch of panic in my voice and looked around swiftly like I was planning on being attacked at any moment.

"No one gets in here without the boss' permission. And he ain't home right now!" The guard laughed as he watched my frantic behavior.

I needed to get inside, so I decided to offer them something that they wouldn't be able to refuse. "I know where he is!" I called up.

"The boss?"

"No! The guy who shot the others from here. The one who led them to die! I know where he hides out! Let me in and I'll tell you all I know!"

"How the fuck do you know about that?" He trained a weapon on me now.

"I met him! A few days ago. He bragged about it! He bragged about killing them!" I screamed wildly.

"Son of a..." The guard disappeared from the edge. I presumed he was on the way down. I reached beneath my jacket and into my vest pocket and took out one of my knives. I palmed it and waited. I also checked the cloth around my eye to make sure it was secure. After adjusting it and my hat I heard the door unlocking on the other side.

An arm reached out and hauled me inside the door. There were three people including the same one from the roof. They stood aggressively and were well armed, but none of them had a weapon pointed directly at me. I readied the knife to strike.

"Get him some water," the tallest one said. "Then he can tell us what he knows."

I took the glass and forced myself to drink even though I wasn't thirsty. By acting complacent my captors would let their guard down more.

"Alright, fool. You're inside now. Tell us where he is and what he did to the others," the guard from the roof said.

"I don't know much about him. I just know where he is."

He grabbed the shoulders of my jacket and shoved me into the door I just came through. "Where the fuck is he?"

I smiled as I brought my right hand up and slashed the knife I had tucked away across his throat.

Before the other two could react I switched the knife to my left hand and drew the machete. I dodged left around the falling body of the first convict and then straight at the tallest one. He tried to move but the swing of my machete clipped his shoulder, slicing deep and sending him sprawling.

The third one had swung a submachine gun out in my direction, but never had the chance to pull the trigger. My knife found his side as he raised the gun. Before he could scream, a second strike from the machete split his skull open.

I moved to the tall one who was recovering from his slashed shoulder. I sheathed the machete and spun him around. Then I pinned him to the ground with my right hand pushing into his wound. He screamed at first, but at the sight of the knife I was holding in my left hand he quieted down quickly.

"Where is the girl?" I demanded, although calmly.

"What girl?" He asked.

"The girl that was brought here the same night that Charlie was. Where is she?"

"She should be in her cell, I guess." He was panicky, but cooperative.

"Where is the cell?"

"Through those doors, up the steps. Down the right hallway. That's where all the bit...I mean, women are." He corrected himself, realizing that insulting Ashley wasn't a good idea.

"Where would I find the keys to that cell?" I asked.

"Mason keeps them when the boss is out. They're on the third floor playing cards in the guards' lounge."

"How many are there?"

"I don't know. Three or four maybe. Ah! Christ this hurts!"

His cooperation was definitely unexpected. I removed my hand from his wound as I contemplated the odds that he was setting me up. Regardless, I had no choice but to trust him. And after he cooperated I couldn't just kill him.

"I'll be coming through this way again once I find her. I don't expect to see you in the way," I warned.

"Take me with you!" He begged. I was shocked. I hadn't expected that reaction from any of them.

"Why would I do that?"

"I'm dead either way. Better to take my chances with you then with Rico."

"Rico?" I asked.

"The boss," he clarified.

"If you're still alive when I come back, then you can leave with us." I left it at that and went through the door that he indicated would lead me to the stairway. I went as fast as I could, clearing two floors in under a few seconds. I didn't know how much time I would have until the others came back.

Opening the door cautiously, I saw that the hallway beyond was empty. I could smell food and cigarette smoke in the air and could make out the sound of laughter a little ways down the hall. Drawing the pistol, I moved as quickly as I could. The door to a lounge was open and I could hear the voices of those inside. There were four people in the room, three men and one female.

"Alright, Mason. This time we're doubling in."

"If you want to lose twice as much then go ahead." the female responded. I was surprised to hear that it was a female was the one who held the keys.

I entered the room with the gun raised and centered my first target. I shot the man and the one next to him, left of Mason, before they knew what hit them. I swung the gun over to the third man and pulled the trigger twice. He fell backwards out of the chair with a look of shock on his face. I brought the gun to Mason and held it there.

"Don't move," I ordered. "If you do, then you die."

She had a paralyzed look of shock and fear on her face. My sudden, merciless assault left her without any choice but to do as she was told.

"What do you want?" She managed to ask after a moment.

"You have the keys to the cells on the second floor. On that floor is the girl who was brought here the same night Charlie was. You're going to take me there," I said.

"Bubble girl? Why the hell do you want her?" Mason asked with an incredulous look on her face. At the moment I didn't care to ask about the nickname.

"Now. Let's go." I ordered and motioned with the gun.

She stood up slowly. I moved toward her and removed a pistol from her hip. It was similar to mine and I decided to keep it. I tucked it in my belt and then moved her to the door. One of the guards on the ground had a shotgun near him. I holstered the pistol and picked up the more menacing weapon.

I pushed my captive through the doors and back down the steps. We exited the second floor and moved through the corridor past various cells. Most of the cells had prisoners in most of them. Some of them held zombies. Whoever ordered that zombies be kept near prisoners was seriously deranged.

"We put her in solitary with the doctor while they try to find a cure," she said while we walked.

"The cure to what?" I asked.

"Whatever is killing her."

My heart was in my throat. I prayed that Ashley was still able to be moved. We came to a door at the end of the line and moved through it. Inside were two other doors, one on each side. The one door had a plastic cover over the only opening. That was the door Mason moved toward.

She removed a set of keys from her waist. I prodded her to hurry it up. After the door began to open I hit her with the butt of the shotgun. She went down, knocked unconscious from the blow.

I opened the door and pushed past a second plastic drape. I stopped suddenly when I saw Ashley. She was lying on a bed with several pieces of equipment hooked up to her. Her hands grasped the anchor charm still hanging from her neck. The distinct pulse of heart monitor filled the room. She turned her head toward me. He eyes lit up as she recognized me and she let her hands drop. Chris, seated next to her, was already out of his seat.

"Holy shit! It was you!" he said.

I ignored him and went to the bed. Ashley began to sit up. I told her to lie back down, but she was already tearing cords off of her body.

"What are you doing?!" I asked. I was afraid she would hurt herself and tried to stop her.

"Relax, I'm fine," Ashley started. "Kiss me."

Without hesitation, I kissed her hard and wrapped my arm around her. I held her for a few minutes, ignoring everything around us. I couldn't believe that I made it this far. I kissed her again then took a small step back, looking at Chris. He stuck his hand out to me. I shook it and embraced him.

"What's all this?" I asked as he moved to help her unhook the equipment.

"Can you think of a better way to keep them from touching me?" Ashley asked.

I smiled. The idea was genius. "Whose?" I asked.

"Chris'."

"Thanks, man. You have no idea how…"

"Save it. It was the least I could do," he said.

At that moment the radio in my pocket began to beep and Carmen's voice sounded from it. "They're coming! Get out of there!"

"Who's that?" Ashley asked.

"I'll explain later. Let's get out of here." I put the radio to my mouth. "We're coming back."

"Hurry, I can hear the engines," Carmen replied frantically. I hadn't asked her to act as a look-out, but was definitely glad she took the initiative.

"What about the others?" Chris asked. He moved to the wall and picked up two large duffel bags as he spoke. I didn't waste time asking him what was in them. I trusted he knew what was important.

"No time. We'll be back," I said as I handed him the pistol that had belonged to Mason. Ashley grabbed several notebooks off of a table near the bed and we left the room. I led the way

251

down the corridor back to the stairs. A few of the prisoners began begging for our help, but there was no time to save them. I had to hope that my promises of coming back for them would be enough to keep their spirits up.

We went downstairs quickly. In the entrance lobby was the convict that I had slashed earlier. His arm was covered in blood stemming from a makeshift bandage, but he seemed to be okay. He was holding all of the guns from his dead comrades. Chris raised his weapon at the sight of the man, but lowered it when I kept moving.

"What's your name?" I asked.

"Thallwood. Eric Thallwood." He began opening the door. "Charlie was a very good friend of mine." Now I understood why he was being so helpful. I nodded to him and we went outside.

"Head straight for the alley behind the office building on the right. We'll hide there until they stop. Just follow me and you'll be fine," I told the group.

"Zombies?" Chris asked, checking the pistol as we moved.

"Not an issue," I said as we cleared the perimeter of the fence.

The rumble was growing louder as we sprinted across the street. Not once did I let go of Ashley's hand. If I could, I would have held it forever. We made it across the street and down the alley as the sound of the engines turned the corner. As we made our way down the alley away from the prison, the engines were silenced one by one. It was close.

I couldn't believe it. We were safe.

After a few minutes we began walking, still sticking to shadows as we made our way back to the apartment of Carmen and Jake. No one spoke, but everyone was smiling. We heard a loud scream and several gunshots from the direction of the prison.

Everyone's smile but mine disappeared. I had what I wanted.

Except from Ashley's Journal

Thanks to some quick thinking by Charlie, Chris and I are being relatively left alone. We're still subject to the daily routine and harassment of the guards. Still forced to watch the sick games that the prisoner's here are forced to play. But because they think there's some value in Chris' work and because Chris convinced them I was essential to that work, we're being kept together and mostly left alone.

Chris wasn't entirely lying when he said there was value in his work. There's a medical wing here and it has some supplies he had been putting to use testing the living, the dead and even the undead. It's disturbing what he's found out. After running a whole bunch of tests that I don't understand, he told me thinks this whole thing started as some type of "super cure." A promise to end all of humanities problems that has gone horribly awry.

But while we were talking about it, an even worse thought entered my mind. What if it wasn't a mistake, but sabotage? Think about it. How many billions of dollars a year are spent on medicine and medical treatments? How many billions would be lost if all of a sudden no one was sick anymore? I think it's entirely possible that the apocalypse is the result of war being fought behind closed doors, where decisions are made based on money. Maybe the "super cure" was tampered with and now we have zombies to deal with. Probably not what the party responsible wanted, but at least they'll still be in business when and if this nightmare ever ends.

Chris thinks I'm crazy. I think he's impossibly naïve. Probably one of the reasons a handsome, thirty-five year old doctor never married.

Chapter Twenty-Three

When we were safely in the building introductions were made. Carmen actually bonded with Ashley right off the bat, which was definitely a good thing. She was still mistrustful of the others, but I couldn't blame her. Jake seemed fairly intimidated by everyone, but was still not as hostile as his older sister.

We were all gathered in the living room. Chris was in the process of stitching Eric's arm from where my machete had slashed him. Carmen and Jake had begun organizing supplies; they had moved most of the stuff into the apartment across the hall and brought it back here to sort. I was in the kitchen preparing food for everyone.

Ashley sat on the couch with Alice in her lap, trying to get her cleaned up before Chris took a look at her hip injury. While I watched them, I couldn't help but reflect back on the first time Alice had seen her. Alice had growled and instantly moved to protect me after only a few minutes of knowing me. Now here they both were, not even five months later, sitting on the couch together nursing each other's wounds and easing each other's suffering.

I was still elated to have my love back with me. The last few weeks had been a nightmare not knowing whether or not

Ashley was okay. Now I had her safe, at least safer than she had been previously. I had blown the element of surprise, and it would be a hard fight saving the other prisoners.

The conversation so far had been light and cheerful. Despite the anger we know we would soon face from the convicts, our own mood was one of celebration. We hung thick blankets on all of the windows so that we could have lights on without an issue. We hadn't moved on to any really serious topics, so I hadn't yet explained or shown them my eye, which remained covered. Chris asked about the covering, but I had diverted the question with an, "I'll explain later."

I was in the best mood that I had been in for quite some while. As we sat around laughing and talking, life somehow felt normal. If there were any beer around, then my day probably would have been as close to perfect as it could get.

During the conversation with Eric I learned a bit about him and more about Charlie. Eric knew him before the outbreak; they were in a biker gang together. At first, they stayed out of trouble; however, over time some of the shadier members had gotten a bad rap and began giving them their tougher edge. Towards the apocalypse, they had begun working with a Mexican gang in human trafficking and drug trade. Things had certainly gone downhill quickly for the group.

As Eric explained many of the members were inadvertently caught up in everything and then couldn't leave, the price of betrayal being death. When the apocalypse occurred, it had been a chance for many of the members to escape. Charlie took that opportunity and eventually met up with us.

Eric was in prison on a marijuana possession and trafficking bust with a few others when the dead stopped dying. The gang had shown up a few months later and, finding some of their own people inside, took over the building. According to Eric, before the others had shown up life for them was pretty much the same. The guards took relatively good care of them and kept them as informed as they could as to what was happening.

"So who's this Rico, then?" I asked as I moved around the stove. I was making pasta and trying to make my own sauce out of some things we had found.

"Not really sure," Eric explained. "He showed up at the beginning and somehow took over. His big philosophy is that the world is lost and only by sticking together and showing no mercy toward others can we survive. Something about how mercy and decency died early. He's in the habit of preaching. The problem is that most people listen, because what he says makes sense in a twisted sort of way."

I turned around to study Eric and inadvertently met with Ashley's eyes across the room. Her stare locked into mine.

"What?" I asked her.

"I spoke to Rico early when he kidnapped us."

"And?"

"Do you remember the night in the truck after you saved me?" She asked.

I thought back to those first nights. So much had happened it was difficult to remember specific days now. I was distracted a bit as I found that interesting. So many things had happened that I thought I would never forget, but now they were sort of blurred together like normal memories. I took a deep breath to focus. It hit me like a train.

Rico. The guy who was trapped in Bryantsville. He begged for our help. We had refused because he was too far away for us to reach.

"*Impossible,*" was the only word I could think of.

"It's him," Ashley confirmed. "He told me his story. He was trapped with a radio. We weren't the only ones who refused to help him, but he blames everyone who did for what happened. For 'abandoning decency and human kindness.'" She made quotes in the air as she spoke.

257

"You didn't tell him?" I asked suddenly. If he knew who we were then...

"No!" Ashley said before I could finish the thought. "He definitely would have killed me and would have hunted you."

I nodded at Ashley and smiled, then turned back to the stove. The smile vanished once I was no longer looking at her. The implications of this piece of information were far reaching. If Rico blamed the people who didn't help him, then part of that blame goes to me. Was it possible that he was only this deranged because of my actions? If that were the case, then in no way would I be able to consciously take any revenge out on him. I would feel like it was all somehow my fault that he acted the way he did in the first place. I wouldn't take responsibility for his actions, but I could certainly accept blame for creating the monster. I was pulled away from my thoughts by the boiling water on the stove.

"What was it like inside?" Carmen asked.

Chris and my love exchanged a few glances, but neither one was willing to answer the girl's question.

"It's better out here." Eric said after he realized the other two weren't going to say anything. "I was thrilled when I realized what was happening earlier when he killed Rupe and Chomolski. I was either going to die or escape, either way I was finished with the place. Don't ask for more than that, hon. Anything you've seen out here is nothing in comparison."

"Which is why we have to go back," Chris said. "There are a lot of innocent people still trapped inside. Who knows what they're going through since we were able to get out. We can't just leave them to be tortured."

"Jake, would you take Alice somewhere she can do her business?" Ashley asked from the couch.

Jake nodded and led Alice out the door. Apparently whatever she was going to say was not the best conversation for an eleven year old.

"Carmen, you can stay if you want, but it's pretty horrible." Ashley gave Carmen a moment to leave, but when the girl didn't make a move she continued. "Inside that hell people are dying in the worst ways. Women *and* men are both being brutally raped. People are kept in cells next to zombies for torture and amusement. Zombies are being used for sport. And the children...Jesus Christ...they are forced to watch things that no one should ever have to see."

I took it all in and then released a long, slow breath. I didn't want to think about that right now. Right now, life was okay. I didn't want my peace to end so soon. But if Ashley was unhappy, then the decision was already made for me.

"Then I suppose we have no choice but to try and help them." I said as I stirred the noodles. "But not tonight. Tonight we're free." The noodles were done and I moved the pot off of the stove. "Carmen, get your brother back and we'll all sit down and eat."

Chris finished cleaning up Eric and they both went to wash up. Ashley moved to help me in the kitchen. Before she could reach for the plates I grabbed her and pulled her closer to me. I whispered in her ear that I loved her as I embraced her. She looked at me and smiled before kissing me. I was lost in those sparkling blue eyes that I had missed terribly. We were interrupted when Chris came back and made a joke about us getting a room.

He asked about Ryan as we sat down to eat. I hadn't yet told him about Ryan's death. I explained everything that had happened. He was upset, but accepting of Ryan's fate.

"I want to find that car. Make sure he didn't turn." Chris said.

"Of course. I remember where it is. We can go tonight if you'd like." I offered.

"That would be good." After a few minutes of silence he finally asked about my eye again.

"You didn't tell them?" Carmen asked, looking at me with a confused look on her face.

I sighed. This time there would be no avoiding the question.

"Not yet. But I guess I have to now," I replied. Putting the fork down and removing my hat, I began to unwrap the cloth around my head. I kept my eye closed as the wrapping came off. I opened the eye slowly, letting the increasingly familiar red wash flood my vision. Then I looked around the table at each person. I stopped when I reached her gaze, sitting next to me.

Ashley didn't say anything at first. I waited as she took it in. Finally, she smiled and began laughing. That was definitely not the reaction that I was expecting.

"What's so funny?" Eric asked, looking uncomfortable. He began chuckling nervously, not sure if he should be.

"I'm sorry," she tried to regain her composure, "It's just that your hair is bloody mess." She continued to laugh out loud.

I began laughing with her. I remembered the haircut I gave myself and wondered if it was really that bad. After a few minutes the whole table was caught up in the raucous laughter. A scream outside the window indicated that a red-eye had heard us, but the laughter only increased after Chris went to the window and told the beast where to stick it.

The laughter was refreshing. I couldn't remember the last time that I had laughed so hard. Here I was, nervous about how she would react to my eye, and instead she was making fun of my hair. Even at the cabin we hadn't laughed this hard. Now here we were, laughing and carrying on like nothing had ever happened. I thought about that beer again. It would taste really good right about now. My side was hurting by the time I stopped laughing enough to get back on topic.

Chapter Twenty-Three

"Really though, it doesn't freak you out even a little bit?" I asked.

"Do you want to eat me?" Ashley asked.

I began laughing again. Her face turned red as she realized what she said and everyone began laughing more. The joke was probably lost on Jake, but he laughed along with us anyway. It took another moment to refocus again.

"Ahem...Let me rephrase that," Ashley began. "Do you want to eat...people?"

"Only you," I responded. I couldn't resist. It was like old times again as another round of laughter consumed the group. This time she obliged me with a smack to the head and I continued. "Seriously, though. No. I see differently when the eye is exposed. Definitely better in the dark, but I don't want to kill or eat anyone."

"Then there's no problem," she said. "It actually looks kind of cool." She winked at me.

"What's it like?" Chris asked. "The vision?"

I thought for a moment about the best way to describe it. "It's like taking a piece of cellophane and putting it over your eyes. Or those old, 3-D movie glasses, but with no blue lens."

He thought for a moment then sat back in the chair.

"They don't attack me anymore," I said.

The room was quiet as the three newcomers processed that piece of information.

"So, red-eyes too?" Ashley asked.

I nodded in response. "I'm pretty sure they have tried to communicate with me."

She returned the nod. "That's definitely interesting."

"Quite," Eric chimed in with a look of suspicion in his eyes. Chris glanced at Eric then back at me. I could see the gears in his head working through everything I had told him. He stayed quiet.

The conversation trailed off awkwardly and we finished our meal. After dinner was cleaned up Chris asked if I would take him to see Ryan. Of course I agreed, even though I really did not want to leave Ashley again. But this time I knew she would be safe.

Chapter Twenty-Four

"Grab that pistol and a blade," I said as I picked up the rifle and strapped on the machete. My own pistol was still slung over my shoulder. I rarely took it off these days.

"I thought you said they don't attack," Chris said cautiously.

"I said they don't attack me. You're still food. And it's not zombies I'm particularly worried about anyway." *Never thought I would say that.*

He armed himself and we left the apartment. After we reached the alleyway where the two vehicles were parked, I removed the cloth from my eye again. It was dark and we had flashlights, but Chris was comfortable with the idea of me guiding us. We checked to make sure the blankets were keeping the lights in the apartment. After we found they were, we began making our way to the street the prison was on.

"So," he started as we walked, "any other reactions you're not telling Ashley?"

"Nope. Everything is as I said."

"Good."

"Did she lie to me?" I asked.

"About what?"

"What happened to her at the prison?"

"No. At least, not that I know of. She spent very little time away from me, and we came up with that ploy two days after we got there. With Charlie's help. He was a good guy. Definitely wish he was still alive."

"I wish I could have done more. When I saw his tortured body hanging from the prison, I had to wonder if I made the right call to shoot," I said.

"You did. I would have done the same," He assured me.

"Thanks."

"No problem."

"No, I mean for everything. Looking after her and all. You'd better survive this whole thing," I said.

"Not that I was planning otherwise, but can I ask why?"

"I'll need a best man at my wedding. No one else could do it after this," I said.

"It will be my pleasure."

We continued down the dark street. Chris truly was a good friend. I thought about the promise I made to Ryan about watching his back. I swore that even though Ashley would always come first, I would never leave Chris behind. He was someone I could count on, and that was a rare quality even before the apocalypse.

"Medically though, nothing bothering you?" he asked again.

"I was shot in the foot about a week ago. That mostly healed already."

"Just checking," he said, trailing off.

"What? What's wrong?"

"I had the opportunity to run some tests while I was inside. Took a few days to convince Rico that it would be worth the effort for me to do some research, but he eventually caved. When I did start testing, I learned some things."

"Such as?" I prodded after Chris went silent again.

"It's rather complicated."

"Best you can then, doc," I said. If he knew something about what was happening, then I wanted to know regardless of the consequences.

Chris took a deep breath. "What is causing this is definitely a biological agent."

"A weapon?"

'No, not necessarily. In fact, I don't think that's the case at all. I meant biological strictly in the sense that it's sort of a living organism. And completely dependent on a host."

"Like a virus?"

"Exactly. It doesn't fit the exact parameters, but I can't think of a better word to describe it."

I immediately began thinking of all the media portrayals of zombies before the apocalypse. All the movies, books and games that ended up getting it right.

"But as disturbing as it is, that isn't the strangest part." Chris said. "It actually cures the host of any internal ailments. And I mean *any*."

"How'd you figure that out?" I asked while giving him a skeptical look. "Wait...hold that thought."

Something was moving up ahead. We crouched behind a bench and waited. It was a zombie crawling along the ground. We avoided it and continued on.

"Anyway," Chris continued once we were alone again. "One of the hostages said she had lung cancer. Later on she was infected – don't ask how. After she was put down for good I opened her up. No cancer. Not a single trace of the stuff."

I gave him a long look. "You're sure she had cancer to begin with?"

Chris nodded vigorously. "Absolutely. Granted I didn't have an MRI to use, but all the external signs were there, her blood tests were beyond positive and listening to her lungs I just knew she wasn't lying. Before she was infected she had to be in stage four, no question. There should have been tumors the size of golf balls in her lungs."

"So I began to look closer," he said before I could get a word in. "I took blood samples from everyone. No one, and I mean no one, has any trace of virus, bacteria, anything in them anymore. No harmful substance at all in the blood."

"So it's not just me? Everyone can heal?" I was confused. "How many zombies had we seen with wounds? Why didn't they heal? Why had little Becca contracted the flu all those months ago?"

"No, not everyone can heal. Maybe that is what it's supposed to do. Maybe that is what it was designed to do. There was another inmate who seemed to recover from his wounds faster, but not like you do. But I do know that no one can get sick anymore. At least, not from conventional methods. I came up with a theory."

"I'm listening," I said, trying to divide my attention between our surroundings and the conversation. The conversation was winning.

"I believe that this was all an accident. Somewhere, someone thought they were doing something good. Imagine it…curing all disease. But it backfired. It didn't do what it did in the lab. Outside a lab there are an endless number of variables we cannot control. Someone thought they had it right, and they were wrong."

I stayed silent. What could I say?

"Of course, it's just a theory," Chris said, sensing my tension. "I could be totally wrong. Maybe this *is* what was supposed to happen. Maybe aliens did it. Maybe God just got pissed off at us. Who the hell knows?"

He made no effort to hide the frustration in his voice. Aside from surviving the only thing any of us really wanted was an answer for what happened. Before the apocalypse the world was literally at our fingertips. There was nothing you couldn't find out from a cell phone or laptop. To be completely cut off from all sources of information was blinding. Still, I envied Chris. He had at least had an opportunity to search for answers. But it was like a trying to see clearly after accidently staring into the sun.

Still, if Chris was right and this was intentional, then that means that all of this could have been prevented. *Everyone is infected.*

The words from the hallucination filled my head. I had to tell Chris. "Ever since we fled the cabin I've been having these intense...visions, or hallucinations or whatever. Like my brain already figured something out and was just trying to find a way to tell me. The last one I had somehow brought me to that same conclusion." I explained as best as I could.

"Hmm...interesting," Chris said.

"That's it? Just interesting?" I knew he wasn't saying what he really thought.

"What else am I supposed to say?"

"I don't know. Explain to me how I knew that already," I said.

"Well, I've read things like that before, so that's nothing new. I suppose that you might be able to somehow detect the infection in people, even if you don't know it," He explained.

"Alright, I guess that makes sense. But now why isn't everyone a walking ghoul or a red-eye...or like me?" I asked. I thought back to what Ashley had said in the hallucination again.

"Different levels of exposure. Different DNA reactions. Varying degrees of reactions based on height and weight. There are an endless number of variables that could affect whatever this is," he explained.

"Some of those notebooks from our cell have my notes in them. I'm going to look over everything again and see if I missed something," he said.

"So all of those notebooks weren't hers then?" I asked.

"No. Only two of them. Why?"

"Just curious. Ashley's been writing from the beginning. Very protective of them and won't let anyone read them. Not even me."

"Yeah, she told me. I asked her about what she was writing and she said it was just general impressions about day-to-day events. I wouldn't worry about it. If that's how she copes, then that's how she copes," he advised. Then he changed the subject back to me. "When we get back, I want to run some tests on your blood."

"How?" I asked.

"The bags I grabbed from the prison. Some basic laboratory supplies I managed to get together, including a microscope. It won't tell me much, but it might shed some light on your condition."

"Fine," I said. "You know, you might know more about whatever this is than anyone else on the planet."

He was silent. "That's a chilling thought. I hadn't considered that."

It was quiet the rest of the walk to the car. From a distance I could make out the silhouette of Ryan's body in the shadows created by the streetlamps. The corpse was moving inside the car. I had hoped that maybe he wouldn't turn, but of course he did. Without saying anything Chris walked towards the car and opened the door. Ryan, or at least what used to be Ryan, made an immediate lunge at him, but Chris already had his pistol drawn and ended his friend's suffering without hesitation. I left Chris to pay his respects and stared down the street toward the prison.

From this distance it was an indistinguishable building as it had been so many weeks ago. The street had changed too. The tire tracks were a bit more defined. The mass of bodies seemed smaller, probably do to the effects of decomposition. But if this thing killed ailments, couldn't it postpone decomposition too? It didn't make any sense to me so I stopped thinking about it. Leave the science to the scientists. I just wanted to keep her alive.

There were no flies in the area. No scavengers of any kind. The bodies did not teem with maggots like the one from that house. The only thing I could figure was that if this thing was concentrated enough, then the usual agents of decomposition did not affect the corpses. The bodies would last considerably longer with only the elements working to destroy them.

After a few moments Chris moved up beside me. I looked at him. There were tears in his eyes, as I expected.

"You okay?" I asked.

"I've known him for a long time, since we fought together in Iran. He was close to me. He was my brother."

I put my arm on his shoulder as he continued.

"He was the hero of our unit in Iran. Personally rescued me. He deserved better than this. He deserved better than to be shot by a damn coward."

"I know, Chris."

"I'm going to kill him. I hope you know that. When we go back, I'm the one who will kill Rico. First Ryan. Then Charlie. It's too many of my friends killed by one man."

I was silent. I wasn't quite sure how to respond or even if I should.

"Promise me something?" He asked.

"Anything."

"Rico is mine."

Chapter Twenty-Five

His voice was cold and hard. The tears had been replaced by an angry look in his eyes. Chris' desire for revenge went deep.

"He's yours," I said quickly. I wouldn't deny him his vengeance. If it wasn't for the guilt I now felt about making Rico what he was, then I would have wanted it myself. Then we might have had a problem. But we didn't. I didn't want revenge. Chris would have his.

"Let's head for the prison before we go back," Chris said as we began walking.

"Why?"

"Just want to see what's going on." His voice was grim. I had a bad feeling about what he was thinking. If he thought he would get retribution tonight, then that would be a problem.

"You won't get your revenge by rushing in and dying," I cautioned.

"I know. I just have to see it."

I nodded and led him down the street toward the prison. We went up a block and approached in the same way I used to get to my office outpost. As we made our way up the steps to the office something felt different, but I didn't know what.

271

We went to the office and looked out the window at the prison. It was dark save for a few lights in the windows. I had no trouble seeing the building, even some of the occupants as they walked by open windows thanks to the effects of the red-eye vision, but I wished the moon was brighter so that Chris could see better. I watched him as we stood there, trying to read his emotions. I was looking at a man who was staring down his enemy.

"Let's go. The others will be worried," I said after a few minutes.

He nodded and we headed out. I led the way down the steps and out the back door.

"Nobody move!" A voice called after the door closed. Chris and I froze.

"Turn around."

I instantly recognized Mason's voice. We turned slowly to find four convicts with weapons trained on us.

"How's the head?" I asked Mason.

She glared at me. "You're predictable. We knew you'd come here tonight."

"Am I supposed to be impressed that you got lucky?" I asked. Chris put his hand on my arm and I backed off. I hadn't realized that my hands had balled into fists. Another few minutes of taunting and I may have attacked. With four armed men trained on me, the odds of survival were considerably slim.

"Come away with us, Mason," Chris said calmly.

"Can't do that," she replied.

"Why not? You're out now. Rico isn't here."

"He saved me. He saved us all. Even you," She countered.

"No, he didn't. He took us, unwillingly, and shot my best friend," Chris argued.

"I'm not here to argue with you again," She said.

"Then why are you here?" I asked.

"Message from Rico. The girl. Bring her back. He knows she'll die out here without the medical equipment. He doesn't want that to happen." The look on her face said otherwise. Rico wasn't interested in saving her – that much I knew.

"She's fine," I said. Again Chris' hand was on my arm. Again my hands had clamped up.

"Tell Rico we'll bring her back on a few conditions," Chris started. "First, him and all of his men put their weapons outside. We don't need anyone accidently getting shot. Second, Charlie's body. Cut it down and bury it properly. Finally, everyone inside who is locked up gets free. Then we'll bring Ashley back."

I looked at Chris somewhat surprised. Even though I knew to trust him, I did not like hearing that my love was being used as a bargaining chip. I hoped that he had a good plan in mind.

"I'm sorry, Doc, did you think this was a negotiation?" Mason nodded to her men and they began moving forward with weapons raised. I moved my hand up a bit and tensed my muscles. If I was fast enough I could at least get one and roll away, but that would mean Chris would get shot. I couldn't risk it. How were we going to get out of this one?

The scream of a red-eye answered my question. I smiled at Mason in the faint light of the alleyway. The convicts began looking around frantically. The one closest to me shined a flashlight at my face.

"Hey," I said to him slowly with a hint of menace in my voice. "You should be very careful."

Another scream filled the air. It actually sounded very distant, but I used it anyway. I stepped into the light and flashed my eyes at the nearest convict. His face went pale as he recognized that one was red.

"You see…they're friends of mine," I let my lips curl into a sinister smile.

The convict I was looking at threw his weapon down and ran. As the others turned to watch him flee I drew my pistol.

Chris followed suit. He shot the nearest one in the leg. The last one and Mason turned to us. Mason had no weapon drawn. The red dot of my sight was aimed at her forehead.

I smiled and spoke after a moment of tense silence. "We're leaving now. But tell Rico we'll definitely be back. I hear there are children inside. Can't have that now, can we? Put your weapons down and get out of here. And pick up your friend before you go," I ordered.

They dropped their guns, picked up the wounded convict and left. We gathered their weapons and left once they were out of sight. After we turned the corner Chris turned to me.

"What the hell was that?" He asked.

"What do you mean?"

"The red-eye screaming." He looked angry at me.

"Hmm...coincidence. I just used it to my advantage."

"You didn't, like, call them or anything?" he asked skeptically.

"Look, Chris, whatever happened to me may not put me on the food chain anymore, but believe me. I have no plan of ever communicating with them. I was glad I couldn't control the walkers. If I could, then I'm not sure that I would want to, unless it was to have them walk straight into hell. I don't want them anywhere near me, let alone people who are still considered food."

"Alright, relax. I was just making sure. Talk about defensive." He laughed.

* * * * *

We walked back the rest of the way without incident. When we went inside we explained our delay to the others. Ashley wasn't thrilled we were almost captured, but there wasn't much I could do about that. Before we separated for the night, Chris drew several vials of blood from each of us, including Alice.

With other apartments available there were plenty of places to sleep. Chris stayed with the kids and Alice. Eric set himself up in the apartment adjacent to them. My love and I made our way to the fifth floor, away from the others.

Neither of us could sleep. We had been apart for so long that it wasn't an option. It wasn't until the early morning sun crept into the sky that we realized that we hadn't even closed our eyes.

I silently cursed the sun. It had moved too quickly though the night. I wanted to spend more time with just her. In the comfort of Ashley's presence I could forget about all of it. But with each sunrise I knew I would have to face another challenge in the world of the undead.

* * * * *

The next morning we went downstairs and found Chris already awake. He was pouring cereal into a bowl and when we walked in he took down two more bowls for us.

"No milk," he said.

"Never is," I commented. We took the bowls and some water to the couch and began eating.

"You're up early," I said.

"I never went to sleep."

I looked at him again and could see the shadows under his eyes. I guessed that he had been running his tests all night. "Learn anything?"

"I think so, but I'd rather wait for everyone else to get here," Chris didn't make eye contact with me and instead turned his gaze back to a notebook he was holding.

I continued to busy myself getting some food together for myself and Ashley. Alice's bowl was filled with some scrounged dog food and she had already started to happily

275

chomp on it. Ashley and I ate, and when it became apparent that the other three weren't getting up anytime soon, decided to go and wake them. Eric was a bit grumpy, but Jake and Carmine were excited. I guessed that their previous companions didn't treat them like members of the group.

Chris had moved into the kitchen and so that is where we all gathered. The kids and Eric chewed silently on some food as we waited. I sat on a barstool next to Ashley, Alice panting softly at our feet.

"I've had some more time to look over my notes from the prison and I have come to three conclusions," Chris started, flipping the pages as he spoke.

"First, the agent that caused this is in everyone and everything. We all have it in us, as does Alice."

"Then why didn't we all turn?" Eric asked, repeating my question from earlier in the streets.

"I'll get to that in a minute," Chris said. "Secondly, that same agent was not designed for this. Given what I saw happen in the prison and what I saw looking at all of your blood, I can definitely say that this agent was created in order to eliminate disease. All disease."

I raised my hand slightly before speaking. "Then why did Becca get sick in the woods?"

Ashley threw her elbow into me. "Let him finish."

"Sorry. Go on, Chris."

"Yes, thank you. Third, the reason that everyone seems to be reacting differently definitely has at least something to do with blood type. Everyone here is a type negative blood. Eric, Ashley and Carmine and Jake are all O negative. And I know from when we served together that Ryan was O negative also. I am A negative," he turned to me. "You're AB negative, extremely rare."

"So what happened to the positives?" Eric asked.

276

"As far as I can tell, they turned. Maybe not all of them, depending on level of exposure, but the majority." Chris said solemnly. "The agent reacted differently to the rhesus factor, which determines positive or negative blood types."

The room was silent a moment as everyone digested that information. Jake had the most confused look on his face, and Chris took a moment to explain blood types and how they work to him. I spoke up when he was finished. "Is that why I am the way I am?"

"It seems to be the primary factor, yes."

"So what about the red-eyes?"

"I have no actual data, so I have to go on what I was told. Ashley, when I asked you in the prison you told me your mother was AB positive, right?"

"Yeah," she replied. "At least I'm pretty sure she was."

He waved his hand at the room. "There you are then. The red-eyes are the result of people who had AB positive blood. What scares me about them besides the intelligence is the drastic way they have been changing over the past few months. They are changing somehow, becoming more beast-like. I can't explain that type of rapid mutation without more information about them or about the agent." No one spoke for a few minutes and he added, "Again, this is all speculative, but it's the best we have right now."

"It's better than nothing," Ashley said. "Go back to Becca, though. If this is some 'super cure' then why did she come down with the flu back at the cabin?"

"The agent is airborne and spreads rapidly," Chris said. "But, because we were so secluded it is possible that she didn't have enough of it in her at the time. Remember that was, what, two months into the chaos. Or it simply reacted differently to her given her age and body type."

"All those are still factors?" I asked.

"Those are always factors."

"Good," I said. I had a hard time accepting that everyone who had a positive blood type was now a zombie. That was a lot of people who didn't stand a chance if that was the case. "So does this mean there might be more people out there like me?"

"Possibly, yes." He looked down at the notebook and flipped to another page. "I wanted to ask you something about your encounter with that one the other day, when you said it tried to communicate with you."

"Tried, but I couldn't understand anything."

"How was it behaving? Was it just standing there like you and I are?"

I thought back to the strange encounter before speaking. I wanted to make sure I gave Chris accurate information. "No, it was more, I don't know, animal-like. It was hunched over, cautious."

"What was it doing with its head?"

"Besides making those noises, it was up, in the air. Kind of like it was... I don't know..."

"Smelling you?" Chris finished my thought.

"Yeah, sure. Smelling me."

"That's what I was afraid of," he looked back down at his notebook. "I've been thinking about them a lot. We know they can communicate with each other, display a level of intelligence that is scary, and can control the undead. I think they do that with a type of pheromone. And I don't think it was trying to communicate with you that day."

I realized what he was getting at. "It was trying to control me?" I asked.

"Yes, and it was gauging your reaction to its attempts."

I was quiet while the others asked Chris a few questions. If it was trying to control me, then it saw me as one of the undead, which made sense since the rest of the zombies seemed to do the same thing. And though I never told Chris or

Ashley what happened to the convicts who had run me from the prison after I attacked, it made sense now why the red-eyes didn't kill me. They thought I may have been one of them.

"Wait, I'm confused. If this was a cure then what happened? Why are there zombies everywhere?" Carmine asked.

"There are two theories about that. Mine is that whoever released the agent did so before they were really ready to do so. They didn't run all the proper tests and controls. They didn't test all the variables. They found or created something amazing and rushed to get it to the world. And the result of that sloppiness is a world of chaos." He waved to Ashley. "On the other hand…"

She sat forward on the stool and placed her head in her hands. "On the other hand it could have been sabotaged. The medical industry would have collapsed without sick people. A trillion dollar industry, nearly wiped out overnight. Greed is a powerful thing."

I reached forward and took her hand in mine. Ashley's dark view of the situation bothered me, but I couldn't help but wonder what if she was right. I couldn't imagine what kind of depraved person would actually plan for this all to occur, but I couldn't doubt that it was possible.

Regardless, this was a side of Ashley that I did not see often. She didn't even seem sad about the conclusion, just very matter-of-fact. I thought about asking her to let me read her journals, to see what it was she was going through since she very rarely let me in. It was frustrating really. I depended on her to get by, even when she wasn't around I was still thinking about her. She didn't seem to need me for that same reason.

The conversation died down after a few minutes of Chris clarifying what he had come up with. He took a deep breath before finishing. "Look, I know this is a lot to absorb and a lot of it might not make sense, but quite frankly I'm encouraged. It gives me a starting point to try and identify the agent further, maybe even find a cure."

I looked at Ashley, who stared at me with the same skeptical look. We were both thinking the same thing. It was great that Chris was able to figure some of this out, but already making the leap to try and cure it was pretty far out. No one said anything, though, for which I was glad. We all needed something to cling to in order to keep from cracking under the constant pressure of this new world. Ashley had her notebooks. I had Ashley. Now Chris had his puzzle.

"So what do we do now?" Eric asked after it became apparent no one was going to comment on Chris' remark about finding a cure.

"Whatever we have to do to keep surviving," Ashley said quietly.

Chapter Twenty-Six

After some conversation we decided that the best option we had was to go back to the shopping plaza and stock up on whatever we could. I knew that the pharmacy still had a lot of useful things in it, including food and I didn't want to leave it for the convicts if they decided to come outside again soon.

"So we go in, split off into two groups and get everything we can?" Eric asked.

"Right. The van fits against the door of the pharmacy perfectly. The kids can work freely in there. With the radios we can stay in contact. We'll get another vehicle from the lot and you three will find a way in the hunting store and get as much as possible."

"And what will you be doing?" Ashley asked.

"Zombies are no longer a threat to me, but they'll still go after you. I'll act as crowd control and let you know when it becomes a little too much for me to handle," I explained.

She nodded. Her eyes told me that she wasn't convinced zombies wouldn't attack me. She was in for quite a surprise.

We had enough small arms now that the adults were all able to have a weapon with some ammo to go around. In comparison, we had more now than when we fled the cabin, so I was definitely comfortable. I was armed with my usual complement: machete, pistol, Mr. Craftford's revolver, and various small blades.

The kids found the radios in the piles of unsorted equipment and handed them out. They were also armed. Carmen took a club and Jake, his favorite baseball bat. I made a mental note to teach them how to shoot.

I had planned to leave Alice behind. She bit my pants leg as we were leaving, though. I told her to stay, but she refused. Her wound was freshly stitched and she was still limping heavily. I wasn't thrilled with the idea of her going, but it became obvious I would have little choice. Using the pulley, the kids showed us how they got her up the fire escape and we lowered her down.

We piled in the minivan and headed for our destination. I was able to get the trip down to just fifteen minutes now that I was more familiar with the route. We arrived at the plaza and found it just as we left it. After pulling the van up to the doors of the pharmacy we got to work.

Eric looked at the scattering of bodies around the lot. He looked at me and I nodded, taking responsibility for the bodies as we moved to the hunting store. Eric and Chris spent a few minutes analyzing it, and then turned to me.

"Back door?" Chris asked.

"Fire door. Secure." I said.

"Roof?" He asked.

"Didn't have time to look, but I doubt it. These plazas usually don't have roof access from each unit."

"Good point. Why don't we just drive a car through it?" He asked.

"Won't work," Eric said.

"Why not?" I asked.

"Brick base comes to about here, if I'm reading it right." He moved his hand to about waist high as he looked at the building. "You can tell by the separating walls between stores and the different size bricks," he explained further.

"So then we have to break through this damn security gate somehow," I said.

"Did anyone think to look for a key?" Ashley asked, standing behind us.

We all sort of stopped and looked at each other for a moment. I turned around to face her. She was standing there with a smug look on her face.

"And where, pray tell, do you suggest we look for a key?" I asked.

"These places usually have a manager's office with master keys to all the stores. For emergency situations," she answered, smiling.

I turned back to the other two guys. They looked at me. Eric spoke first.

"You never looked for..."

I shook my head no.

"Nice," Chris snickered.

We went down the plaza to look for a manager's office. A single door was at the end of the complex with a sign with the word "Office" on it. I looked at Ashley. Her face was even more smug now.

Breaking into the office was easy once Eric shot the door handle out with the shotgun. We went in and found a small room with a computer and several filing cabinets. Along the wall were various pictures and notes taped up, as well as a lockbox bolted to the wall. The box had a padlock on it. Alice turned back toward the entrance and began growling.

Outside a handful of zombies had taken notice and were moving toward us. I walked past my companions and out the door casually. I spared a glance backward to find the others staring at me from the doorway, weapons raised at the approaching ghouls. I gestured for them to put their weapons away. "Check the desk. Might be a spare key," I said. "I'll be right back."

Now it was my turn to be smug. I began whistling the song that the dwarves sang in *Snow White* as I brought my machete to bear on the zombies. Even Alice looked a bit surprised with how they completely ignored me. I wiped the blade nonchalantly on one's tattered shirt and went back to the office.

"No one checked the desk yet? Do I have to do everything?" I let the smugness soak in as I walked past Ashley and began searching the desk. She shook her head and smiled at me.

A search of the desk turned up no keys at first. We were about to give up when she mentioned the possibility of it being taped underneath. It wasn't, but it was taped to the side of a drawer facing the wall the desk was up against. We then opened the lockbox and found the keys to every store neatly labeled. We took the keys to Eddie's and also ones to a store called Discount Supply. It was the only store in the plaza that didn't have a description and so we weren't sure what was inside.

As we were walking back to Eddie's, I began scanning the parking lot for a decent vehicle. Over the last few months I had learned how to identify a good option. An ideal vehicle in an undead world was tough to come by. It had to be practical and it had to have an occupant, preferably in the driver's seat. Otherwise there would be a tough time finding the keys. Not seeing any viable options in the nearby area, I knew we would have to go looking before we raided the store. I talked it over with the others and we decided to get the kids and go looking in the van for another vehicle before we started working.

Thanks to the radios, the kids were already waiting for us. They had already piled up the back seat with supplies, so it was a little tight. After hearing their report we decided not to go back to the pharmacy for the day. There apparently wasn't too much left that we would be able to use.

We drove around for a few minutes before finally finding a suitable vehicle. It was a white, flat-panel van – almost perfect except for the simple fact that there was no driver around. The doors were open, though, and in the back a corpse began banging into the sides as we approached. We killed it and searched the body, but there were no keys. Defeated, we left to find another solution.

Our salvation came at a used car dealership. There were two large vans and pick-up on the lot. A debate about which to take ended when we considered the people we had to rescue. We would need as many vehicles as we could find. We broke into the trailer that served as an office and took the keys for the pick-up and one of the vans. Eric took the van. Chris drove our first van with the kids and I drove the pick-up with Ashley and Alice. It felt like old times again, when we were running from house to house trying to stay alive.

It was almost noon when we made it back to the plaza. We pulled the empty van up to the hunting store and then used the other two vehicles to block up the area. It formed a sort of triangle that would keep the undead back should they start to gather in greater numbers. More and more were beginning to wander into the region, attracted by the noise we made and the moans of others. I wasn't immediately concerned with them, though.

My big fear was attracting the red-eyes. I knew there were a lot of them out there. I hadn't seen them since they helped me escape from the convicts and I didn't know how they would react if they saw me still killing zombies. It was possible they wouldn't care about what I did, but I couldn't be sure. I wasn't interested in taking the chance with Ashley around. I drew my blade and urged the others to go as fast as possible. Alice ducked underneath the pickup and followed me out into the parking lot.

Despite her injury and the simple fact that the zombies weren't going after me, it was comforting to have Alice fighting at my side again. She was a soothing presence in combat. As we moved toward the zombies that were making their way into the lot she began to move a bit faster. She was determined to keep pace with me regardless of her injury. I admired her spirit.

I kept my movements conservative. Instead of flourishing the blade I systematically killed one zombie after another with the same three movements: sidestep and move behind, chop downward, spin around to find the next. We moved around the parking lot as more zombies arrived.

The radio beeped and Ashley's voice came over it. "Hey – question."

"Go ahead," I said after I pulled the radio off my belt.

"How do you feel about explosives?"

I paused making sure I heard her right. "Say that again."

"Basement of this place is full of illegal weapons. Trap-door behind the register. Very… Tarentino-ish."

I smiled. "Explosives would be useful, I guess."

"And fully-automatic weapons. Those are okay too?" Chris piped in. I could hear the giddiness in his voice.

"God Bless America!" I said. "Ryan would have been thrilled."

"Goddamn right he would have!" Chris laughed, but with a hint of sadness in his voice.

For just a moment I thought about how people in other countries were faring against the undead. Countries with strict gun control laws. How were the people in those places surviving? How the hell were the British dealing with the undead walking when the police didn't carry firearms? What were the tribes in Africa or the impoverished in South America doing? It was then I realized that no matter how bad things were, I was still glad to be trying to survive in the U.S. and not somewhere else.

I laughed into the radio and then asked how long they needed. Chris said only a few minutes. We couldn't get everything, so he decided only to get what would be useful in attacking the prison. I advised him to lock up when he was done and began to make my way back the other direction. I still wanted to know what was in the Discount Supply store. I took the keys and found the store two units down.

When I raised the security gate I started laughing almost uncontrollably. I was greeted by a giant sign that read: Eddie's Army & Navy Discount Supply Store. I found myself wishing this guy Eddie was around so I could thank him. Whatever neo-military gun-toting rebel whacko he was in the past, he was a savior to us now.

I went back to the gun shop with a large grin on my face. When I made it back they had the second van full of weapons and ammo of all sorts. To me, it looked like they had looted the entire store. Chris and Eric came out carrying a box labeled: Danger! Explosives!

"What's in there?" I asked.

"Anti-personnel fragmentation grenades," Chris said, smiling. "And dynamite."

"Well load it up and get the others. This next place just adds to the flavor," I said to him.

We moved the vehicles into the same defensive perimeter outside the Discount Supply store. I raised the gate again and watched their responses. Chris just started laughing. Jake let out a cry of, "Oh cool!"

"Let's go shopping!" I said as I unlocked the front door. Before us were racks of clothing, boots and gear for all types of weather and situations. We had tents, entrenching gear, rope, medical kits and even survival and military manuals to aid us. The display cases on the walls held night vision equipment and even a thermal read-out gauge. One of the best finds in the store though was the cases of freeze-dried meals. I lowered the gate behind us and we went to work in relative peace.

Chris was in his glory. He ran between all of us and told us what we'd need and what we wouldn't. He rambled on about camouflage benefits, how to pack a rucksack and the advantages and disadvantages of different style footwear, all of which he would interject with references of Ryan and how he had learned so much from him in Iran.

We left the plaza with more gear than we really needed. We were now well-equipped for at least a few weeks, assuming we weren't killed trying to save everyone from the prison. That was our next big task, to find a way in and figure out how to save as many people as possible.

Excerpt from Ashley's Journal

While we were gathering supplies at Eddie's I had a chance to talk to Chris again. Ever since we escaped I haven't really had a chance. But I wanted to run an idea by Chris that I know he wouldn't want to hear. My love has enough on his mind right now.

When we were talking about how this "super cure" might have been created and sabotaged, I thought popped in my head. What if the saboteur knew what would happen? What if zombies weren't a new phenomenon?

Before the apocalypse, how many different versions of zombie movies and stories were there? Hundreds, at least. But all of them built on the same recurring ideas. And all of those ideas had to originate somewhere. What if the reason it was so accurate was that because someone, somewhere had seen them before?

Chris, again, thinks I'm nuts. But I can't shake the feeling that it's no coincidence that the movies got it right. Someone has seen the undead before. Someone knew what they were capable of. And instead of doing the right thing and warning everyone, they made a fucking movie.

If I ever find out who that someone is, I'll make sure they see the results of their practice in person.

Perseverance

Chapter Twenty-Seven

It took the rest of the day to get the gear inside the apartment. We then had to rearrange how the vehicles were parked, since there were now five at our disposal. We used one of the vans to block the opposite end of the alley where our entrance was and then arranged the other four in a manner that allowed us to take any of them in a hurry. We also decided to make their arrangement as random as possible, in case the convicts came out looking for us.

Everything was kept in the first apartment on the fourth floor. We used thicker tarps to cover the windows on both the fourth and fifth floors so that we could work with all of the lights on. Then we cleaned up all of the apartments so we could work better.

Before we moved anything Ashley decided to inventory items as we worked. We came up with a simple chart and everyone was responsible for writing down everything they touched. The inventory eventually had five categories: food, equipment, hygiene, weapons/ammo and miscellaneous. It was very useful once we had everything put together. Ashley and Carmen worked tirelessly to combine all of our lists together into a single cohesive list.

It took all of the next day to finish organizing everything. All the while we began discussing how we would assault the prison. The bottom line was that no matter what we came up with, we would be outnumbered. Only a carefully laid plan would have the slightest chance of success. From what Eric told us, there were at least fifteen of the convicts left inside, with around thirty-five prisoners. They were still well-armed and were definitely in the fortified position.

We numbered seven, including Alice. Only four of us could shoot, but I was still certain I could teach Carmen well enough before we were ready. Jake might be able to learn, but I would not trust his accuracy. Not that it really mattered, because I refused to put either of them in a dangerous situation. Carmen was satisfied when I told her she could drive the van. I was glad that she finally trusted me.

The next morning at breakfast I decided it was time to teach the kids how to shoot. Ashley and I took the kids back to the plaza area. Alice was limping a bit worse than the day before, so I forced her to stay behind so that she could rest. We brought along our least powerful rifle and handguns for the kids to practice and learn. While we were out, Chris and Eric had plans to scout around the prison to see if there was an entrance or something that we missed. If we were lucky they would at least find a place that they could see inside and try and figure out what was going on.

"So, what did you do, you know, before all this?" Carmen asked me while we were driving in the van. It was the first time she ever talked about life before the apocalypse.

"I was a social studies teacher," I replied. "Loved my job."

"Wow," She commented.

"What?"

"Just…not what I expected."

"What did you expect?"

"Well, I guess I expected you to say soldier or cop or something. You don't really seem like the teacher type," she said. "Except for the hat, I guess." Jake and Ashley chuckled.

"I guess I'm not anymore." I knew that she didn't mean anything by it, but somehow Carmen's words struck a chord. Months of fighting and hard living had completely erased my previous life. That and whatever it was that had infected me. There would never be any going back.

In many ways, it was like a completely fresh start. Everyone that was still alive when this was over would have a chance to recreate themselves. If you could survive the apocalypse, then you could probably do anything. It would be up to each individual to choose to make the decisions that would benefit them and those around them the most. Individualism itself was no longer important.

That's what made the convicts so utterly terrifying. When the world collapsed the convicts did nothing to help. They caused more harm than good. Sure, they killed zombies – a lot of zombies, but they also committed horrific crimes that even zombies were incapable of doing. Zombies acted on instinct. The convicts chose to do evil.

We arrived at the plaza and drove to the far end near a bank and a tobacco store. There were only a few zombies roaming around. We took the guns out and began showing the kids the mechanics of the weapons. Ashley taught them the rifle while I worked with the handguns.

My other job while we were there was to finish off any of the undead that came too close. I adapted it to showing them some hand-to-hand techniques that I had picked up over the last few months. At first they were nervous about getting close to a zombie willingly, so I had to restrain the undead. Jake had the fortune of not having to kill one throughout the apocalypse, up until this point. His first kill visibly shook him. I felt bad, but it was necessary to get that out of the way now while the situation could be controlled.

Before the end of the day both of the kids received as much experience as they could in so short a time. I still would never intentionally put them in a dangerous situation, yet it felt good to know that they could defend themselves a bit better when they next had to deal with the walking dead on their own.

The van ride back to the apartment was oddly serene. Music was playing over the CD player and the kids both had their eyes closed. My mind flashed to another life, with a family coming home from a fun day at the park instead of a day spent learning to kill. It was a much more pleasant thought. I knew I would probably never get to experience it in my life, even if the zombies all up and died...again. I reached my arm across the seat and took Ashley's hand in mine. She smiled at me. I hoped she was thinking the same thing.

The tranquility of my thoughts was broken as I was forced to slam on the breaks of the van. The sudden stop jarred the kids awake with calls of "What's wrong?" I simply stared straight ahead. A red-eye had jumped out in-front of the van and now stood staring and snarling at us. I recognized the tattered clothes hanging from its neck instantly.

It howled and four more came out and surrounded the van. The kids were panicking now and Ashley was asking them to load the weapons in the back.

"Everyone quiet down," I said. They stopped what they were doing and looked at me. I began unhooking my seat belt.

"You're not going out there!" Ashley yelled.

"Relax. They aren't after me." I took the seat belt off and began unwrapping the cloth around my head. The field of red flooded my vision. "I'm going to just try and scare them off."

"Can't we outrun them?" Jake asked. He was nervous.

"They're strong enough to flip the entire van over if they want too. I'd rather not take the chance. Let me see what I can do." I turned my attention back to Ashley and leaned across the seat. Even in the red-covered vision she looked beautiful to me. "I love you," I whispered.

"Be careful," She whispered back.

"If anything happens…"

"Then I'll kill them all," she finished, recalling my words from months ago. "I love you."

I opened the door slowly and stepped out. One was immediately next to the van and was staring inside the tinted windows. I turned to see who it was looking at and was surprised to see that I could not see past the tint at all. That was a serious drawback to the vision, but it also meant they might not have seen the kids in the backseat.

Once I closed the door I drew the revolver and flicked the safety off. Mr. Craftford's weapon definitely packed biggest punch and made the loudest noise. I was glad to have ammo for it once again. I aimed the weapon right at the one with the tattered clothes around its engorged neck.

"Hi, Tatters," I said, deciding to name the red-eye that had been stalking me for the past few weeks.

It hissed at the sight of the weapon and took a step back. It knew weapons and it knew caution. That meant they were learning. That also meant they knew fear.

"We're just passing through," I said to it.

It grunted in its guttural language and two more of the red-eyes appeared. These ones focused solely on me. There were now seven of the red-eyes surrounding us. My heartbeat quickened. I knew this would not end pleasantly. In the van Ashley moved slowly over to the driver's seat.

The red-eye, Tatters, continued staring at me and making the same noises. It had to be trying to communicate with me somehow, but I still had no clue what it was saying. I decided to just start talking. Maybe it could understand me better than I could understand it.

"What are you saying?" I asked.

It made the noise, slightly different in pitch. A second one on the right chimed in with a sound. I lowered the revolver a bit, hoping it would be able to acknowledge my effort to be civil.

"I do not understand you." I spoke slowly and deliberately pronounced each syllable.

It howled and slammed its fist into the ground, reminding me of a giant ape. I raised the revolver back-up. It howled and motioned to its partners. The two on the sides smashed the windows on the van and began reaching in.

I fired at Tatters, who jumped away the moment the others struck. I then turned back to the van. One was grabbing at Ashley, another trying to climb in through the passenger's side window. A third was in the back ripping at the trunk, but I could see through the front window that Jake had a rifle trained on it. I raised the gun to fire at the one reaching in the driver's side but was knocked away before I could fire.

A red-eye grabbed me and spun me onto the ground. I took the fall on the shoulder and was able to roll away before a second one pounced on me. I swung the revolver up and shot at the first one, catching it in the shoulder and sending it spinning away. The second reached me and kicked me in the side, sending me to the ground.

I heard gunfire as I fell to the pavement. A howl and another gunshot told me that one of our foes was dead. Before I could move, another of them jumped on top of me and grabbed my head. It began pulling at my hair and ears. I screamed at the pain while I grabbed its arms, trying to relinquish its grasp. It slammed my head into the concrete. The pain was incredible but I kept fighting. With no other options, I reached up and grabbed its throat.

I squeezed as hard as my strength would let me. I could feel its grip loosen as it began to struggle. It slammed me down again. I kept squeezing. It let go of me and tried to pull away, but I held onto it. It grabbed my arms and tried to pry me off, and I responded by squeezing harder. I held it up above me and screamed as I tightened my grip even more. Finally, I felt its body go limp and watched its head fall forward. I threw my foe's body aside and jumped up.

The second one ran toward me again, but I was able to dodge right and trip it up. It fell into a car and was stunned. I picked up the fallen revolver and shot it before it could move again. The thunderous blast exploded in its back, sending bits of flesh out into the street. I turned back toward the van and saw Ashley being pulled through the window. There was an eighth monster on the roof of the vehicle smashing at the top.

I could make out dark liquid running down Ashley's face. Probably blood. My own blood began to pulse in anger as I saw her fighting to free herself.

The rage that ignited inside of me pulsed to my very core. I felt like I was about to lose control. Foolishly, I threw the revolver down and lunged across the gap and tackled the red-eye at the waist. The impact forced it to let go of Ashley. I stood above the creature and kicked it in the side, screamed and fell upon it, pummeling it over and over again.

I remembered the escape from the cabin when I blacked out. Ashley said when I attacked that one I had done the same thing and it took both Charlie and Wes to get me off of it. I hadn't remembered the fight after I went into a rage. Now I could see exactly what I was doing, though I still felt like I wasn't in control.

I forced myself to breath, but all the while my fists continued to smash into the monster. Its arms were still trying to fend me off, but it was fighting a losing battle. I could see the blood pouring from its mouth. Its eyes no longer looked ferocious. It was scared. Again I forced myself to breath. I felt my pulse begin to level out. My fist fell into it again.

After another moment I was finally able to stop myself from hitting the creature. I stood up and backed away. The creature tried to stand and run, but fell on wobbly legs. I began to feel a bit of remorse for what I did as I watched its slow death, but that feeling evaporated instantly when I felt a sharp pain in my back.

The monster on top of the van had come down and struck me from behind. I fell forward in the direction of the dropped revolver, but it was still just out of reach. I rolled over and drew my machete just as it jumped on me. It landed clean on the blade, its body falling down to the hilt. I threw it aside with the blade and moved to pick up the gun.

Five of the red-eyes were now dead. Two were wounded and ran away. Only Tatters was left. I checked the immediate area, but could find no sign of the beast. Deciding it was safe enough to let my guard down, I ran back to the van.

Ashley wasn't too bad, considering. The blood was coming from a scratch on the face, and her foot might have been sprained. She was still conscious, even if she was disoriented. The kids were panicked, but safe. A red-eye lay dead near the trunk, shot by Jake. Blood pasted the passenger's side window where another had been shot.

I went over to the passenger's side and helped Ashley move back into the seat. She was already recovering. I was glad that she was not more seriously injured. I radioed ahead to Chris and warned him that she was wounded, and then drove us back to the apartment. As we pulled away I heard a howl from down the street. The red-eyes were still out there.

Chapter Twenty-Eight

Back at the apartment, Chris helped Ashley clean up the scratch while I tried to calm the kids down. They were freaking out over the ordeal. Occasionally, we would hear a scream from outside. I had the distinct feeling that we were now being taunted by them.

"So what do we do about it?" Eric asked as he helped me in the kitchen.

"They sound pissed," Chris said. "Might not be a good idea to wait."

"I'll get a shotgun!" Eric said and began moving away.

"No!" I yelled at him, "Not yet. Don't give them the benefit of rattling us. We eat first, then I'm going hunting."

"*We're* going hunting," he said.

"I can handle it. No sense putting you in danger," I was glad Ashley was in the other room and couldn't hear the conversation.

"Bullshit. You're not going alone," he replied.

"I said I can handle it."

"Goddamn it! When are you going to drop the loner-hero bullshit! There's no point in going alone! You wanna lead this outfit, that's great! But that doesn't mean you have to do everything by yourself, damn it!" he slammed freezer-burnt sausages onto the counter.

I turned slowly to face Eric, "I never asked to be a leader."

"Well guess what? You are."

I turned away. Mr. Craftford's voice entered my head.

The best leaders are the ones who do the job when no one else is willing. A leader earns it, either intentionally or not.

But what if I don't want to lead? I just want to project her.

Real leaders don't ask for responsibility.

Instead of arguing with Eric or Mr. Craftford's voice, I threw my hat into a wall and stormed out of the apartment. I went upstairs and sat on a chair that faced out the windows. The sun had fallen behind a building next door, but the sky was still bright. I took a deep, calming breath and tried to collect my thoughts. A red-eye screamed again. It was farther away now. Hopefully, they had given up on tormenting us and wouldn't come back.

Why was I so angry of the idea of leadership? I've led before. I've been acting as a leader since the cabin. So why did I get mad at Eric for calling me what I was? I wrestled with my thoughts. All the while I was so distracted I did not hear Ashley enter the room. When she put her hands on my shoulder, I jumped.

"Sorry," she apologized. "I didn't mean to scare you."

"It's okay."

"So?"

"So what?"

"Are you really going to make me ask?" she asked.

"No," I shook my head. "I just can't figure out why it bothers me."

She moved around and sat on my lap. She draped her arms around me and kissed me on the cheek. I knew this ploy. Ashley was going to make me talk it out. I wasn't particularly in the mood, but I suppose no one is when they are forced to face something they've been avoiding.

"It all started with Craftford," I began. "In the truck on the way to Canick."

"The day Jesse died," she said.

I nodded. "Yeah, well, on the way there I asked him why he didn't step up and command us then. He told me it was someone else's turn."

She started laughing.

"What's so funny?" I asked.

"You really were the only one who didn't see it," Ashley said, still chuckling. She kissed my forehead. "My poor baby."

"See what?" I asked, annoyance showing in my voice.

"He was training you to do it! We all saw it. Those late night conversations the two of you would have. The stories he told you and no one else. It was all deliberate."

I thought back to our days at the cabin. Was it true? Was the reason that I was in charge now because he started me on the path? Was I blind to all of this?

"But why me? Why not Ryan or Chris? They at least have this kind of experience," I argued. It didn't make sense to train me.

"Ryan is dead because he made a bad call and threatened people willing to kill anyone. You wouldn't have done that. You would have recognized the danger and waited to make your move."

"I'm not perfect. I rushed head-first to save you! That wasn't exactly smart," I said. "And I did it twice! So I don't learn my lesson."

"No, it wasn't smart. And that's why he knew you would be a good leader." She said.

Now I was completely lost. I waited for her to continue. After a moment Ashley took the hint and explained her point.

"You don't do things 'by the book.' You're impulsive and reckless. But that's what kept us alive. That's how you saved me...twice. Ryan and Chris are ex-military and 'by-the-book.' If Ryan was alive and in charge, then you would have left with the evacuation, or at the most Chris and I would still be inside."

"You make decisions based on what's *right*. You make decisions based on what's best for everyone." Ashley stood up and grabbed a bottle of water, leaving me in the chair to ponder.

"I make decisions based on keeping us alive. You and I. No one else," I said quietly.

"And that's why you're having trouble accepting that you're in charge. You need to start thinking about saving as many people as possible, not just me. One day you might not have me to worry about."

"Don't talk like that!" I yelled sharply. "Besides...if something happened to you, then I would stop fighting."

She charged forward and the next thing I knew my face was stinging from where she slapped me. "Don't you ever say that again!" She was furious. "That is the stupidest fucking thing I have EVER heard you say!" Her arm came up and hit me again. "People are going to look to you. People are going to need you. And you'll help them, because you're that kind of person! You always have been...that's why people look up to you. That's why I love you."

Ashley wheeled and stormed out of the room, slamming the door behind her. I stood silently a moment and then went into the bedroom. I stopped in front of the mirror and stared at my own reflection.

Why was this so hard for me? Was I afraid of the responsibility? It was certainly easier to say that I only cared about her. It made it easier when someone died. I never once felt sad that Bill and Elise had died. I never questioned Wes just up and leaving the group. I just accepted it as life in this new world. Yeah, it wasn't easy, but I didn't dwell on it as being a result of my own actions.

It all came back to Ashley. I was afraid of losing her. I was using that as my excuse to ignore the burden I had unwillingly taken on. As long as I was only worried about her I could ignore everything else. I had convinced myself that I could keep Ashley alive no matter what. As long as she was, then I would be okay.

But I had to acknowledge her point. What if she does die? What if she had been killed in the prison? Would I have let myself be killed or would I have just run away, completely forgetting about the kids and the others trapped inside?

I looked at myself in the mirror. The cloth was still around my head and I looked much the same as I had months ago. Except for my hat, which was downstairs, I was pretty much wearing the same clothing. I stared at the cloth. Beneath it was the proof that I was not the same person anymore.

That was the problem. There it was, plain as day. I was simply afraid to admit the change. I talked about it, watched it happen, but was guilty of trying to avoid it myself. I tried to hide it and cover it up with normal clothes and cloth patches. I was afraid of having changed physically and it helped me ignore that I had changed mentally as well.

I stripped the t-shirt and jeans off. Then I stared at myself in the mirror. I ran my hand over the scars I had acquired over the past few months. The screwdriver from Canick, the gunshot to the foot, the cuts and scrapes from various encounters with the undead. The more recent ones from a few hours ago, already clearing up. I was glad the scars didn't disappear. They were good reminders that everything was different.

After a few minutes contemplating my wounds, I decided to take a shower. It was cold, but strangely refreshing. For months I had feared the responsibility of others, but that fear seemed to wash away now that I was forced to acknowledge the change. I closed my eyes and let the water wash over me.

* * * * *

Almost in an instant I was back in the cabin, seated in the same chair I was in before. Outside the windows was a brightly lit scene of summer, the air smelling sweet even from where I was sitting. Inside I was alone, holding a cup of coffee and waiting for something.

"So, you figured it out then?" it was Ashley's voice from behind me, but I made no effort to turn and face her. I felt her place her hands on my shoulders and the light touch of her hair on my back as she bent over to kiss the top of my head.

"I think so," I said relieved that I could understand her this time.

"You couldn't understand me before because you couldn't understand yourself." She was reading my thoughts again as was becoming common in these dreams.

"So what now?"

Mr. Craftford appeared in his chair across from me. "Now you fight, damn it! You know yourself now, and that was the first step. Now you have to get those people out of that godforsaken prison."

"And then?"

"Survive."

Chris walked into the room from the kitchen holding a notebook. "And hopefully find the cause to all of this. Maybe even a cure."

I pondered it for a minute. "I don't think there is one, Chris. I think you're just a manifestation of a hope that I had."

Almost as soon as I said the words Chris faded away. I was right, it was just a hope I had. If there was a cure to this "super cure," I held no fantasy of our ragtag group actually discovering it. Our job was simply to survive.

"You know that he'll keep looking, right?" Craftford asked, his eyes never leaving mine.

"I know. And I'll let him, but only as far as it doesn't interfere with keeping us alive." I was referring to Ashley and myself when I said us. My subconscious knew that.

Ashley moved to stand in front of the chair, blocking my view of Mr. Craftford. She reached her hand down toward me. "Let's get up then. It's time to go, love."

I took her hand and stood up. We walked outside where a warm spring rain was falling gently among the trees. I turned to Ashley and bent down to kiss her.

* * * * *

The hallucination ended. There was no rain, of course, just the shower water pouring over me. Still, I smiled. I felt more confident with myself. More certain of what I had to do. I got out of the shower and went to the closet. Inside was combat gear that I had taken from Eddie's. I changed into black fatigues and combat boots. Above a black t-shirt I wore a utility belt with various small pouches and a black military style vest instead of my civilian one. I put my gloves on and then gathered up my old clothing. I took everything downstairs with me and went into our make-shift armory. Eric was there, taking stock of our supplies.

"Do we have lighter fluid?" I asked.

He looked up at me quizzically.

"Seriously," I said.

"Umm…yeah…over there." He pointed to a corner and went to grab me a bottle. He also grabbed matches and gave them to me.

"I'm sorry about before," I said as he handed the stuff to me.

"Hey, no problem." His grin reminded me of Charlie's. I was glad that I didn't kill him in the prison.

"No, I'm serious. I was blinded by a false-reality and afraid to face the truth. It made me angry when you shut that

305

reality down on me. I acted stupid and immature. I really am sorry." I continued my apology, not so much for him but for myself.

He just nodded his head. I shifted stuff around in my arms so that I could shake his hand. He pumped it twice and smiled. I turned and went into the other room.

The others were eating and they stared at me silently as I walked in.

"Jake, do you have your baseball bat?" I asked.

"Yeah, it's over here." He got up and grabbed it for me from the corner of the couch. I took it from him and turned to head out. Before I left I made eye-contact with Ashley. Someone moved my hat to the counter and I grabbed it on my way out.

"I'll be on the roof."

I went up the stairs and put the baseball bat in the doorway to keep it open. Then I threw all of my old clothes and even the boots in small pile. My hat I tucked into my pants at the hip. It would be the only relic I would keep, a reminder of days gone by. It's good to remember the past, even when it's time to move on. I took the bottle of lighter fluid and doused my old clothing. The bottle was empty by the time I was finished.

I was about to light it when the door opened and the others came out to see what I was up too. I gave them each a nod and warned them to stand back. I looked at Ashley and thanked her. She had a curious look on her face. I lit the match and threw it into the pile.

Anyone watching from the prison certainly would have seen the blinding flash in the fading evening light. But the flames came down quickly and only the charred remains of my old self remained. As a final step I removed the cloth from my eye. I adjusted to the field of red and tossed the cloth into the fire. It went up slower, but after a few minutes it was indistinguishable from the rest of the pile.

Chapter Twenty-Eight

I turned and faced the five people standing behind me. Ashley was smiling.

"The red-eyes are gone for now. Everyone rest easy. Tomorrow we begin getting ready to free the others."

"And then?" Chris asked.

"Then we're leaving Larshall behind."

"To go where?"

"West."

Chapter Twenty-Nine

Three days of preparation led up to this moment.

I was standing on the corner of the street right next to the prison, waiting for someone to see me. As soon as they did the plan would go into action. There was no sun today. The sky was overcast gray, but to me it appeared dark red. As I stood waiting I could feel drops of rain begin to hit my skin. I had hoped it wouldn't rain, but it seemed like I was finally out of luck. This fight was going to be hard enough without the weather.

Alice was sitting on her hind legs next to me. She could run, but was still limping. From the way she was healing I had to wonder if she was infected in the same way that I was. Maybe that was why we were so connected. It didn't matter now. What mattered was that she was there beside me.

The only thing I had with me was a radio. When they saw me I would radio the others who were waiting for the signal. Then the countdown would begin. I saw a shadow on the roof and knew I wouldn't have to wait long now. The shadow disappeared. Several moments later the front door opened and no less than ten of the convicts came out. They had guns trained on me. I held the radio to my mouth, told the others waiting on the other end to go, and threw the radio away.

Mason led the group as they surrounded me. "Throw your weapons over."

"I don't have any." I really didn't have anything else with me.

"Bullshit," she spat.

"Search me if you want."

Mason nodded to two of the men and they began patting me down. Alice stood beside me, not moving, but growling low. One of the convicts had a gun trained on her. They were nervous. Undoubtedly they were expecting a trap.

"Where are the others?" she asked.

"I'll only talk to Rico," I said.

"Why?"

"Because I said so. Let me talk to him directly and I'll tell him everything."

"Fine. Take him inside," she ordered the others.

"Wait." I stopped the two men from grabbing my arms.

"What?"

"The dog comes too," I stared at Mason who shifted uncomfortably beneath the gaze of my red eye. She nodded and we all went inside.

Three more of the convicts were inside the lobby. The one in the center I recognized as Rico.

"Well, well, well…" he said as I was shoved through the door, "Look at who we have here. If it isn't the goddamn hero."

"I'm no hero, Rico. I'm a survivor. Same as you," I said.

"So what's your grand plan here? You can't possibly kill us all," he said. I could see him swallow hard. He was trying to be tough, but was afraid of whatever was going on. His caution was good.

"I'll tell you everything you need to know. On one condition."

My head exploded and I fell forward, held from the ground by the two men who had my arms.

"You filthy fucking rat! You're at our mercy now! Talk!" Mason was screaming at me. She was probably thrilled she had the opportunity to hit me back.

I shook my head to clear the clouds that had formed. As soon as I tried to raise it the butt of the gun struck me again. Alice barked and leapt at Mason, not willing to see me hit twice. Mason side-stepped Alice and I was able to call out "No!" to Alice before a guard brought his gun muzzle to bear on her. With my call came fleck's of blood and an iron taste filled my mouth. It seemed that every time I got into a fight I had that taste in my mouth. At least I didn't like it more each time. That would have been a bad sign.

"Don't hurt her!" I yelled. "Alice, Down!" she stared at me defiantly at first, then stopped. She kept her teeth barred and stayed in a low crouch.

"The dog dies if she tries that again," Rico warned.

"She won't," I promised.

"Good. Now tell me where the others are."

"I will. I'll tell you everything. But not here."

He stared at me.

"Let's go upstairs," I said. Being in the lobby would be bad in about five minutes.

"Why?" he asked.

"Because I want to."

"Just kill this bitch, Rico!" a convict called out. "And the damn dog!"

Before I could even turn to find the speaker a shot rang out and the body of one of the convicts fell backward. Rico stood holding a gun in his hand aimed at the body. It was obvious how he maintained order. That was also good. I could definitely use that to my advantage.

Rico nodded and led the way to the stairs. I was pulled along. After a minute I found myself in the area in front of the cells. Prisoners heard the commotion and many were watching the scene that was being carried out. Zombies in some of the cells moaned in our direction. Three minutes…

"Now talk," he said. The two men holding me shoved me to the center of the circle that had formed.

"I'm sorry, Rico," I started.

"For what?"

"For not helping you. I'm sorry I never even tried," I said.

"What the fuck are you talking about?" he asked.

"It was selfish for me to not even try. If I could go back, then I would have at least told you that. Instead I acted like a coward, and told you I was sorry. That led you down this path. That led you to become a man, who, when the world needed good people, decided to go in the opposite direction all together. I suppose that, in part, a lot of this is my fault." I turned my head and looked at the convicts. They all had confused looks on their faces. Rico's was the most confused, that much was obvious. Two minutes…

"What the …? Are you insane?" Mason asked.

I smiled and turned to her. I began making eye-contact with all of them as I continued.

"Whatever you were in the past, whatever you are now, you have a chance to change that. I hid for months about what I had become. Let me promise you the weight feels good after your shrug it off. This is your chance to cast it all off. I urge you. It may be the last time you have such an opportunity." I gave the warning with a menacing look. In some of their eyes I could begin to recognize understanding. Even Mason was thinking about what I was saying. I turned back to Rico. One minute…

I am sorry, Rico," I dropped to my knees. "And I beg for your forgiveness." Alice moved closer to me and I put my hand on her.

"Sorry for what?" He said coldly. I think he knew, but needed me to say it. Forty-five seconds...

"I'm sorry for abandoning you." I slid my hand to Alice's stomach, where a small set of three throwing knives were taped and hidden under her fur. I removed the sheath of knives just like we practiced. Rico never took his eyes off of mine.

"Say it!" He yelled as he raised the gun to me. "Say who the fuck you are!" Twenty seconds...

"It's me Rico." I paused to burn ten more seconds. Timing was going to be everything. "I'm the one who never tried. I'm the one who abandoned you in Bryantsville. I'm the voice on the other end."

The building rocked with the sound of an explosion. As it happened I rolled right in time to avoid a bullet from Rico's gun. I brought one of the knives up and threw it at him, striking him in the arm, the blade traveling deep. I spun from the throw and struck the nearest convict in the throat with my fist. He went down instantly, gasping for air. I saw two more of them drop their weapons and flee.

I moved left and side-stepped around the muzzle of a machine gun bearing down on me. I grabbed the arm and spun it around me. The convict was now an unfortunate human shield. I raised my blade to his neck and waited. Mason and seven others were standing with guns bared on me, the initial shock of the attack finally wearing off. Rico and two convicts had fled out the back.

"Let him go!" Mason ordered.

"Forget it! It's over Mason! If you kill me it no longer matters. If I die, then the others are still coming. If you kill us all, then you still have to deal with the zombies," I warned.

"Zombies don't come around here, dumbass," one of the men said.

"They didn't. Now that the front of this place has been turned to rubble by a van packed with explosives, they are going to be more inclined to start visiting again," I said. A few of them turned their heads to regard Mason.

"Bullshit! Don't listen to him! They're afraid of us. Just like Rico said they would be. You all know that. He doesn't know a damn thing." Mason stared at me while she yelled at the others.

I smiled at her and winked my red-eye. "Oh, I know."

Several of the convicts were now clearly rattled. The door into the block opened and in came three figures dressed in all black and carrying menacing looking automatic weapons. Their faces were hidden beneath masks, but I could make out the figures of Chris, Eric and Ashley.

Chris moved his hand to a radio on his shoulder. "Contact, Bravo! Seven plus two."

Over the radio came Carmen's voice. "Copy, Alpha! Identify and engage!"

I smiled. Part of the plan was to make them believe that there were more of us then they could deal with. I let go of my hostage and shoved him forward. "Make your choice."

The next few seconds were the most intense of the entire ordeal. If anyone fired, then the scene would explode into a firefight. A lot of people would die that didn't have to. Definitely me. Even Alice froze, waiting for someone to make a move. I stared straight at Mason. It would be hardest on her.

She looked around slowly at the faces of the men around her. Their eyes kept darting around between her and the three figures at the door with weapons trained on them. It was clear they had no quarrel with surrender. I was surprised they were loyal enough to wait for the word, though.

"Put 'em down," Mason said quietly.

I allowed myself to breathe a sigh of relief as I heard weapons fall to the floor. I nodded at Chris. He and Eric stepped forward with hand ties. We decided before the attack that we would need to secure them even if they surrendered.

Until we could sort everything out and it was all over, we would take no chances. Rico was still somewhere in the building, so it wasn't over yet.

"Thank you, Mason," I said to her.

"The keys to the cells are in my back pocket. Cell number 34. There's a guard in there named John. He's their leader." She said with her hands in the air. Eric moved his arm down and extracted the keys. I took them and with Alice and Ashley with me, went to find the cell.

John was already waiting. He watched most of the ordeal from his cell above us. We reached the cell and he started to thank me. I cut him off as he asked where the rest of my men were.

"There are no others," I said.

"What?" He asked incredulously.

"It was a ploy," She said.

"But the radio?" He motioned to Chris down below.

"Fifteen-year-old girl on the other end of the line," I said.

"Wow," He was clearly amazed.

"Listen. We have to find Rico."

"Yeah, alright! Let's get him!" He said enthusiastically.

"Not so fast," I started. "You're not going. I need you to stay here, free everyone and get things ready to leave. Send someone to the roof and cut down Charlie's body. If it's still moving, put a round in the head first."

He nodded.

"John, I'm trusting you to treat the prisoners with dignity. Whatever they may have done, no one will stoop to that level. Eric will be here to make sure of that. Are we clear?"

He nodded and snapped into a military style salute. "Sir, yes, sir!"

I let him believe I was military; at least that way I knew he would obey my commands. At least order would be maintained. I called over the balcony to Chris. He turned and met us below at the door where Rico went. Alice was sharp on

315

our heels. As we reached the bottom of the steps Carmen came in the room and crossed the gap. She handed me my equipment. I thanked her and told her to get her brother inside and help out. Chris and Ashley removed their masks.

I drew my pistol and nodded to Chris. He opened the door and I swung inside. I checked left and right, but could find no evidence or Rico. Alice moved past me and began sniffing around. After a moment she picked up the scent and dashed down the hallway. We followed close behind.

Rico would not escape.

Chapter Thirty

We ran down the hall and a set of stairs that led to an emergency exit. Alice stopped and barked at the door while she waited for us. Without hesitation I ran through the door and outside. I was greeted by a flurry of gunfire and had to pull back inside.

Chris came up and removed a cylinder shaped grenade from his belt. "Flash bang."

I nodded and opened the door as he threw it around the side. We heard the pop and threw the door open. The convict shooting at us had been stunned from the grenade's effects. Still, he swung the barrel around and fired blindly. Chris downed him with a short burst from his gun as the convicts rounds struck the wall well to our left.

We moved outside and looked around. Rain fell lightly on the ground. I barely caught sight of someone running around a corner and knew it was our prey. I took off running with Alice beside me. Chris and Ashley did their best to keep up, but I was soon far ahead of them.

I paused when I reached the corner and waited for the others to catch up. Chris moved up and we swept around the corner. We slowed down and systematically began tracking

317

them. If it weren't for the zombies, then he would have gotten away.

The undead were simple. They would turn and chase after a meal even after it was long gone. So whenever we turned a corner we first looked for zombies, and then headed in the direction that they were facing before they turned to face us. Using this method we were able to keep tracking Rico for twenty minutes through the streets of Larshall.

We caught up with Rico and the other convict when they were completely off-guard. They had stopped to rest, thinking that they were safe, when we came around the corner. Guns on both sides began to fire wildly. I took cover behind a car as round after round punched through the rain. Chris popped from around a doorway and fired in short bursts. When there was a moments rest, Ashley ran through the gaps and found her way next to me.

"I'll cover you. You two go left and around," she said to Alice and I.

I nodded and kissed her quickly before getting ready to run. "I love you."

"I love you more," she said.

"I love you best," I smiled at her. Another throwback to simpler times.

Ashley rose up from behind the car and opened up on the convicts' position. Chris followed suit. While their attention was drawn, Alice and I flanked left. A man came into view. It wasn't Rico. I raised my pistol and shot three times. The second round found its mark and he went down.

Chris moved up. As he did, Rico shot another burst. Seeing he was definitely out-gunned, he threw down his weapon and ran.

"Alice," was all I had to say. We both took off. I threw my weapons down. Rico was unarmed. Alice caught up to him first and bit his leg as he ran. He screamed and fell forward. In the next moment I was on top of him, my knee finding his side. I spun him around and punched him in the face. I then pulled him up to his feet.

Chris came forward with a pistol drawn. Rico recovered and pulled himself up straight.

"You won't do it, doc. You're not the type," he taunted.

"You have no idea what type I am you son-of-a-bitch! You killed my best friend! You raped people who needed your help! You used people who were only looking for refuge! You deserve to fuckin' rot, you prick!" he yelled.

I took a small step back. I had never seen Chris like this. He was really holding back when he said he wanted revenge. I was glad Ashley hadn't caught up yet to see this side of our friend. Hopefully, it would be over before she did.

"Go ahead and do it then," Rico goaded as he wiped blood from his mouth.

Chris lowered the gun and pulled the trigger twice. The rounds found their way into Rico's legs. He fell to the ground screaming in agony.

"I had planned to kill you. I thought about it every day since I watched you shoot Ryan. But not anymore. I can't kill you," Chris said coldly. "That would be too easy."

I stood silently and watched Rico groan in pain. He would surely be set on by zombies. His death would be slow.

I turned and looked at Chris. He met my gaze and nodded. I returned the nod. Chris had his revenge. I then turned to find Ashley. She wasn't nearby. I froze. Alice perked her ears up.

"Where is…" was all Chris was able to say.

* * * * *

I took off running in the direction we had come from. I leapt over the bullet-ridden car and felt my heart enter my throat. Ashley was lying with her back against the car

319

breathing hard. Blood was pooling on the road beneath her. I fell to my knees. *This can't be happening.*

I reached my hand out and touched her gently. She raised her head.

"Hey," Ashley smiled and started coughing. I felt blood strike my cheek.

"Where?" It was all that I could manage.

"A few places." She coughed again. "That last burst from Rico."

Chris caught up and instantly began checking her out. She reached up and put her hand on him.

"Don't bother," she whispered.

"No! Damn it, Chris! Help her!" I screamed at him.

"It's useless. I can already feel it. Please, don't be angry," Ashley said calmly.

"No! No you have to live! You can't die! You can't die now!"

"I love you."

"No! No! No! No! No!"

"Please...kiss me again."

This was impossible! We had come so far! We had fought through so much! She couldn't die now. I...I didn't know what to do.

The rain fell harder as she reached her arm up and rested her hand on my cheek. I felt my eyes burst into tears at her touch. Ashley was everything to me. She couldn't die. I followed her arm down to her face and kissed her softly. I could taste blood on her lips and could feel her pulse getting weaker.

"I don't know what I'm going to do," I whispered.

"You're going to do what you said you would."

"What?" I could hardly speak. I could barely see with the tears that blinded me.

"You're going to keep going. You're going to survive."

"I can't do that without you. I don't know how."
"Yes you do." She reached her head up for another kiss. I leaned my head down and put my lips on hers. She was weaker. She pulled her necklace off and placed it in my hand. I couldn't bear what was happening.

"Please don't go," I cried softly.

"I love you."

"I love you, too."

Her head slouched forward. I caught her body and pulled it to mine. I cried into her hair for what seemed like hours. Rain pounded the pavement as the sky continued to darken. Chris stood silently by. Alice laid down next to Ashley and licked her hand. I didn't want to let go. I didn't want to believe she was dead even though I was holding her body in my arms. I didn't want to admit I would never see her sparkling blue eyes looking up at me again.

Ashley was gone. My world was dead.

The apocalypse was complete.

$Epilogue$

Ashley was buried in the forests outside of Larshall. Eric and Chris helped me dig her grave in a small clearing about a quarter mile off of the road. Before we placed her in the grave I took my Irish wool cap off and placed it neatly in her hands across her chest. She had given me her anchor charm, so it only felt right to give her something of mine. Something to take with her.

The grave was marked with several large stones and one of the survivors carved her name into a tree nearby. It turned out to be the closest thing we had to a funeral since the beginning of the apocalypse, though it was, of course, cut short by the arrival of several zombies.

But as I stood there, alone, overlooking her grave, I knew that I would come back to this spot someday. When the world was a more peaceful place I would make a pilgrimage here. Despite the horrors that we experienced in Larshall, despite the struggle and loss, despite Ashley's death, I hoped to make my home here someday. This was where she would always be.

Until that day, I had a job to do. I had to help get these people somewhere safe. Especially Jake and Carmine. I knew after what we had all gone through here, I could never cut

323

those kids loose. Ashley would have killed me if I even thought about it. I had to go on. I had to keep fighting.

The plan was to head west, across the plains and towards the Rockies, like the flyer dropped from the plane had advised. Hopefully, somewhere out there was a place where mankind made a stand against the tide of the undead. Maybe there was even a place where zombies never walked.

The pace will be slow. We will only be able to move as fast as our weakest member. Unlike before, I no longer harbored thoughts of abandoning anyone to save anyone else. Not unless it became absolutely necessary, like back at the cabin in the woods. Ashley had shown me that I couldn't do that anymore. I cared too much. Not only for myself, but for everyone around me who looked to me for guidance.

And there would still be zombies around us everywhere we go, or worse, the red-eyes. Whatever they had become, they were still our biggest threat. A large enough group of them working together could decimate us, of that I had no doubt. I hoped as we traveled that we would never find out. Maybe with so many of us, they would leave us alone. Either way, death will surround us every step of the way. But we will keep moving.

The only other choice is to sit back and wait for death to come to us. Or undeath.

And that is not a choice any of us are going to make.

www.ingramcontent.com/pod-product-compliance
Lightning Source LLC
Chambersburg PA
CBHW072055020726
47501CB00003B/605